LIES LOVERS TELL

"My, my, my, my, you sure look good tonight."

"Thank you," Maya responded. She started to walk around him, believing if she didn't she might not be responsible for her actions. The man looked good enough to eat right there!

"Uh, could I get this dance?" he said, stepping in front of her once more and placing a hand gently on her arm.

The hand could have been an iron, that's how hot it made Maya. Now she really needed something cold, like a shower. "I was on my way to the bar," Maya said.

"Then allow me to join you for a drink."

Maya looked up into eyes the color of dark chocolate, framed by long, thick lashes. Her mouth watered. Remembering the "lonely single" thoughts she'd had only hours ago, Maya decided to try and relax, enjoy herself.

"My name is Sean," he said, after he'd placed his order. "And what is yours . . . besides lovely."

Maya sipped her drink to delay an answer. What if this man worked in the Brennan Building or knew any of her associates? Maya fiercely guarded her privacy, always mindful of her professional reputation. But she didn't want to think about work tonight, she wanted to have fun, and forget about Martha. *That's it. I'll adopt another persona, just for tonight.*

"It's, uh, Macy," she said, when Sean turned back to her, the name coming to her because she'd listened to Macy Gray.

Lies Lovers Tell

Zuri Day

Dafina
BOOKS

Kensington Publishing Corp.

http://www.kensingtonbooks.com

DAFINA BOOKS are published by

Kensington Publishing Corp.
850 Third Avenue
New York, NY 10022

All Kensington Titles, Imprints, and Distributed Lines are available at special quantity discounts for bulk purchases for sales promotions, premiums, fund-raising, and educational or institutional use. Special book excerpts or customized printings can also be created to fit specific needs. For details, write or phone the office of the Kensington special sales manager: Kensington Publishing Corp., 850 Third Avenue, New York, NY 10022, attn: Special Sales Department, Phone: 1-800-221-2647.

Dafina and the Dafina logo Reg. U.S. Pat. & TM Off.

ISBN-13: 978-0-7582-2881-9
ISBN-10: 0-7582-2881-3

First hardcover printing: October 2008

10 9 8 7 6 5 4 3 2 1

Printed in the United States of America

*To readers of romance everywhere and
the women (and men) who write them . . .*

Acknowledgments

To Selena James for this opportunity, Natasha Kern for her constructive critiques, my sister Marcella Hinton for her invaluable spirit, Realtor Rolanda Lang for helping me navigate the real estate industry, and Spirit, with whom I co-create.

1

Maya fumed, the steady tapping of her foot an outward sign of her annoyance. The man standing five feet in front of her was taking forever at the ATM. On another, less harried day she might have welcomed the sight. He was tall, she guessed about six-two, broad-shouldered, with long, thick legs encased in jeans that emphasized nicely rounded, tight buns. She'd wondered what his face looked like until his transaction had taken longer than the sixty seconds she thought appropriate, considering the hurry she was in. As if Monday mornings weren't busy enough, her assistant had phoned to inform her that Mr. Brennan was waiting on her in his office. Zeke rarely came into the office before 10:00 a.m. on Mondays; she couldn't imagine the urgent matter that had changed his normally predictable schedule.

The stranger at the ATM looked at a receipt he'd retrieved from the machine, and began another transaction. Maya looked at her watch and sighed audibly, hoping the man would get the message. *Will you hurry up? Jeez!* She no longer cared about his attractive backside; he was making her late.

"Excuse me, but could you hurry? There's a line," Maya said in a firm, authoritative voice. The fact that she was the only one in line was beside the point.

The stranger stopped punching in information, looked up from the ATM screen, and slowly turned around. Maya breathed in quickly, and almost forgot to breathe out. The man was platinum fine; at least what she could see of him. He wore a Dodgers baseball cap and sunglasses, so she couldn't really see his face. What she could see was mouthwatering: a strong, firm chin with perfectly groomed day-old stubble, a strong aristocratic-looking nose that tapered over the most delectable lips she'd ever seen in her life. A small cleft in his chin gave him a roguish air.

The stranger's mouth turned up in a slightly amused grin. Maya realized she was staring at the man's lips and tried to regain her composure. She slowly exhaled, set her shoulders back, tilted her head slightly, and continued in her best authoritative tone. "Are you finished?"

The smile deepened in the stranger's face. "Are you?"

His teeth were straight and white and lit up Maya's heart like a fluorescent lightbulb. She looked briefly at his chest, slightly exposed by two open buttons, revealing a light layer of curly black hair. Maya blinked her eyes, tried to get her mind to work. She couldn't figure out what was wrong with her, what about this man had her so flustered. She figured it must be the phone call making her nervous, the phone call that said her boss was upstairs, waiting.

That thought shook Maya from inactivity. "Look, I'm in a hurry. Are you done?"

Maya watched the smile fade from the stranger's face and she could tell his eyes were intense, even hidden as they were behind dark glasses. He shrugged, turned to the machine, canceled his transaction, retrieved his card, and stepped away from the machine.

"It's all yours," he said, unsmiling.

Maya hurriedly conducted a transfer and retrieved two hundred dollars from the ATM, all the while aware that she was being watched. She tried to forget about the stranger as she stuffed the bills into her purse, retrieved her card, and headed toward the elevator. She'd glimpsed the stranger step back up to the ATM after she walked away and couldn't help but consider what he'd done chivalrous. She also found herself wondering what was hidden behind the ball cap and dark shades.

There was little time to ponder that though; duty called. She phoned her brother to tell him she had transferred money into his account, and that it was the last time she was going to rescue him from his irresponsible actions. He was her beloved twin brother and all the family she had left in the world. The night before her mother died, Maya had promised to watch after him. All of eight minutes older than Stretch, she'd always been the sensible one, he the rebel. But she couldn't continue to clean up the messes he made. It was time for somebody to man up.

As soon as the elevator doors opened onto the penthouse floor of Brennan & Associates, thirty-three stories above the hustle and bustle of downtown Los Angeles, Maya was all corporate business. She bypassed the luxurious break room and her roomy corner office, not even stopping to put down her purse or briefcase. She'd been summoned by Zeke Brennan. And when Zeke called, people came running—quickly.

"Good morning, Zeke," Maya said. She'd called

him "Mr. Brennan" the first three years of her employment. But last year, when she was promoted from first assistant to executive assistant, working directly with Mr. Brennan on a daily basis, he had told her it was okay to call him Zeke. She only did so when they were alone, however. Whenever clients or other staff was around, he was still "Mr. Brennan."

"Maya," Zeke replied simply, shuffling through papers on his desk.

"You're here early," Maya said. She sat down in a chair opposite him, set down her purse, and opened her briefcase to retrieve a pen and notepad. Sensing Zeke was in no mood for chitchat, she remained quiet, waiting. She casually scanned the immaculate office: an exquisite blend of African mahogany and stainless steel. The floor-to-ceiling windows covered the east wall, giving Zeke an uninterrupted view of not only downtown, but miles beyond, into Orange County. Unlike the rest of the carpeted offices, the CEO office's floors were a rain-forest-brown marble, imported from India. Matching maroon suede area rugs under his massive desk and the large conference table on the office's opposite side warmed both the floor and the room, as did the freshly cut bouquet of bird-of-paradise, yellow callas, reddish orange amaryllis, and vibrant blue mokaras, set in Tiffany crystal, and adorning the middle of the stately table for ten. Maya had been a key player in the office's redesign; and the weekly delivery of freshly cut exotic flowers created especially for the executive office was her idea. She noted that the cleaning team had done an exceptional job, as she demanded. There was not a speck of dust, or a paper out of place. She was pleased.

Zeke opened a folder and took out another

document. He handed it to Maya. "Ever heard of this company?"

Maya's attention immediately returned to business. She took the paper from him, scanning it quickly. It provided scant details of an investment company, S.W.I., International, from London, England. Their holdings were listed at an impressive twenty billion, with properties on all seven continents. Several personnel were listed, one of them highlighted, a Mr. Sam Walters.

Maya shook her head, handing the paper back to Zeke. "No, I haven't. But it seems as if I should have, they're impressive."

"I thought the same thing," Zeke said, rising from his chair and walking over to look out the window. "How did a company of this size and with this reach elude my radar? Unless . . ." Zeke turned to Maya and continued. "Unless this is a new company being developed under an old, established investment company, created to keep the competition in the dark about who's actually buying what."

Maya knew this was a definite possibility. Investors weren't known for shouting their transactions from proverbial rooftops. Research was one of Maya's fortes, and what had led to a bachelor's degree with honors. And she loved a challenge. "You want me to find out more about them?" she asked, already making of list of various resources she could tap for information.

"Actually, I want you to find out more about *him,*" Zeke said, this time handing Maya a photo with a name highlighted at the bottom. "Sam Walters."

"Me?" Maya knew Zeke employed men and women from various occupations, geographical areas, communications and background check companies

etc., to research competitors and others' histories.
What could she possibly do that a professional background check company couldn't?

Zeke smiled for the first time that morning. He sat
down in the chair next to Maya instead of behind his
desk. "I know what you're thinking, and you're right.
I've done the background checks, reviewed the buzz on
this guy, and he comes up legit, a land developer who
made billions redeveloping for the rich in Africa. Sold
his company and is now looking to expand his land
ownership portfolio, primarily in the large metropolises
of the United States."

"So what do you think I can find out that your
people couldn't?" The guy sounded legit to Maya
too, so much so that if not for her professionalism,
she'd ask if he was married.

"I don't know," Zeke responded. "It's just a feeling
I have, a gut instinct, that all's not how it looks with
Mr. Walters. He comes out of nowhere, no one knows
about him over here . . ."

"Did you ask Mr. Trump?" Zeke and Donald Trump
were golfing buddies, and had also participated in several joint real estate ventures.

"He doesn't know him either. Knows about the
parent company, though, the one we think is serving
as an umbrella for S.W.I."

"So how can I help?"

Zeke leaned forward, choosing his words carefully. "I need someone to get on the inside of this
company, to get close to Sam Walters, someone who
has the smarts to obtain confidential information and
the savvy to pull off the duality this job will require.
In short, I want to find out if this Sam Walters is
really who he says he is."

Maya frowned. "I don't understand. Do you think

this man isn't the *real* Sam Walters, or do you think there is no Sam Walters at all?"

"I'm not sure what I think," Zeke answered. "But what I know is that my gut instincts have guided me accurately for over forty years, and something . . ." he paused to look at Sam's photo, "is wrong with this picture."

Maya studied the photo again. "So you want me to try and get a job at"—she looked again at the paper— "S.W.I. Company?"

"Not exactly."

Maya was still confused. Was Zeke asking her to try and date this Mr. Walters? That had actually been the first thing that came to mind when Zeke mentioned "getting close."

"Ahem, how do you suggest I get close to Mr. Walters?" Maya was usually very comfortable talking with Zeke, even when discussing multimillion- and billion-dollar business deals. Now, however, was not one of those times.

"Well, I'm certainly not going to ask you to sleep with him," Zeke said, once again reading her thoughts.

"Was I that obvious?" Maya asked, relaxing.

"No, I'm that smart," Zeke countered lightly, before turning serious. "I do want you to become a part of his household, though, and I've got it all prepared, all worked out."

"How do you propose I do that?" Maya asked, confused once more.

Zeke hesitated and then answered, "As his maid."

2

Sean Wynn sat back in a plush leather chair and pondered his new identity as Samuel K. Walters. As one of the most sought-after private investigators in the world, he was used to assuming identities. Few, however, had been trickier than this one.

He'd had to study for two straight months just to get up to speed on all the real estate and investment lingo that would have to roll off his tongue naturally in the myriad of meetings he had scheduled for the upcoming week. Even though he'd invested heavily in real estate, and was a silent partner in a company that acquired premium properties, he hadn't become well-versed in the market's lingo until now. He'd had to research Canaccord Adams, the financial services company under which he'd assumed identity, and memorize their many global investment opportunities, which thankfully included real estate. His clients had set this cover up for him, obviously having some pretty extensive connections with them to be able to do so. They'd done an excellent job; he'd been given the name of one of the partner's uncles, and all subsequent information, with the exception of birth date photos, which obviously had to be of him, had been transferred from a white, obscure, and anonymous South African businessman. That their initials were the same was a lucky coincidence.

For the physical transformation from Sean Wynn to Sam Walters, Sean had chosen a conservative, human hair, black Afro wig lightly sprinkled with gray. He'd also purchased a mustache and beard, having learned from a top makeup artist years before how to apply such disguises professionally. He'd gotten so good at using the faux fuzz that his own mother had once mistaken it as real. Finally, Sam had adopted a spot-on perfect British accent.

Looking over at the couch, he frowned slightly at the midsection paunch he'd purchased from a Hollywood costume shop. It wasn't the most comfortable thing to wear, but it did give him a convincingly sloppy-looking midsection, one he'd cover at all times with an ill-fitting designer suit coat. His plan was to give the appearance of a rich, yet bumbling businessman, ripe for the pickings of his smooth-talking, more debonair American counterparts.

Sean rose from the chair, stretched his lithe frame, and walked into his large, stainless steel kitchen. Upon hearing his assignment was in California, he'd informed his assistant to immediately begin looking at beachfront properties. After living in London the past two years, he knew he wanted to be near the ocean. His assistant had done a fine job of obtaining just what he'd requested: an impressive yet unobtrusive ocean-front property with a stretch of private beach, pool, Jacuzzi, and space between the houses. His was a corner property, with only one close neighbor on the east side. The west side and back of his home was surrounded by ocean—the front, a gated, private drive.

The furnishings were simple, yet elegant, perfect for the bachelor status Mr. Walters claimed. Sean claimed that status as well, but here, for all intents and purposes, he was strictly Sam Walters. All matters that didn't have to do with the task at hand, especially matters of the personal kind, like thinking of his bachelor state, would have to wait.

Sean walked into the kitchen, poured himself a large orange juice, and returned to the living room. He reached for a folder lying on the table next to the leather chair and took it and the juice outside to the patio. It was a beautiful summer California evening, with a cool breeze coming in off the ocean. A few sailboats drifted lazily on the water, children splashed in the waves closer to shore, and a couple of fishermen sat perched on a rock at the end of the marina. Sean stared out at the picturesque scenes for a moment before reclining on a chaise lounge. He thought of the irony in the contrast: how to those on the outside, his appeared to be a serene, lazy life of leisure while in reality, it was a life filled with suspense, mystery, intrigue, and, occasionally, danger. The mystery and intrigue thrilled Sean; the danger, he could do without.

Finishing the orange juice, he set the glass down and opened the folder. An eight-by-ten photo of a distinguished-looking gentleman was taped to the left side. He wasn't attractive as much as he was commanding: angular facial features, a thick head of wavy salt-and-pepper hair worn combed back from his face, clean shaven, piercing green eyes. His suit was immaculate, with smart matching shirt and tie. A large gem sat in the signet ring worn on his left pinky, displayed prominently as his chin rested between the forefinger and thumb. Beneath the photo, a name: Zeke Brennan.

Sean rubbed his chin as he reread the report he'd studied for weeks now. He'd basically memorized everything there was to be found on Brennan & Associates, or B&A as it was known in like circles, their projects and acquisitions of the past several years, primary competitors, and key personnel. Flipping through the pages, he pulled out another one with several photographs lined up on the left, descriptions on the right. His eyes rested on the information regarding Zeke's executive assistant, Maya Jamison. Sean studied the attractive yet serious face, brown eyes partially covered by blunt-cut bangs, high cheekbones, medium-sized lips, and smooth mocha skin. Her hair was pulled back in a conservative ponytail, her suit an equally subdued navy blue with high neckline. She wore little if any makeup. He shook his head. *Definitely not my type.* He had started to go to the next page of key staff descriptions when a thought came to him and he looked at the picture of Maya again. Was this the rude woman who'd snapped at him earlier today? He tried to remember the woman who had demanded he finish his transaction and move out of her way. He had purposely gone to the Brennan Building to scope out the place before his meeting with Zeke Brennan two days from now. But where there was fire emitting from the woman he'd encountered earlier, the woman in the picture looked as cold as ice. *She's probably a bitter workaholic with a cat for company,* Sean thought, before tossing the paper aside and finishing his study of the company, and more specifically the man he'd been hired to bring down.

3

"Can you believe it? Can you believe he actually formed his mouth to suggest I be a flipping house-keeper?" Maya, who'd maintained a calm demeanor in Zeke's presence, was now releasing her anger. Her black Persian cat, Lucky, might have been sympathetic but as is often the case with cats, one never knew. He raised a paw, licked it, stared at Maya for a moment, and then pranced out of the room with his tail high in the air.

"Great, just great," Maya said to the now empty room. "The one person I can talk to, which is actually a cat, just walked out on me. Lucky, I was talking to you!" Maya pulled back her comforter cover and plopped down on the bed. Her head was reeling from the early morning meeting with Zeke. The rest of the day had passed in a fog as she quickly brought Jade, the first assistant under Maya, up to speed on various projects and details she was handling for him. There had been another quick meeting in which Zeke had in-formed key staff members that Maya would be mostly working out of the office for the next several weeks, and that Jade would be the one to report to on all matters for Mr. Brennan. There were a few questioning glances sent Maya's way, but everyone knew better than to question Mr. Brennan about anything. Maya was definitely not offering any information. Her coworkers would just have to wonder.

The worst part about the whole clandestine affair was that Maya had been sworn to secrecy, prevented from discussing what she was doing with anyone except Zeke. Maya desperately wanted to talk to her best friend about it; she and Trish usually shared everything. As if summoned, her phone rang. Trish.

"Hey, girl."

"Ooh, what's wrong with you? Was it a stormy Monday?"

"Yes, and Tuesday will be just as bad," Maya responded, quoting the popular blues tune.

"What happened? Zeke lose his mind with the workload?"

"Something like that."

Trish waited for the details she knew would follow; except they didn't. "So . . . what's he got you doing now?" Trish almost felt she worked for Brennan sometimes; that's how much she'd discussed the company goings-on with Maya. Trish had even dabbled with the thought of going into real estate. "Maya, you there?"

"Oh, I'm sorry, guess I'm preoccupied."

"Obviously," Trish said, a smile in her voice. And then, "Ooh, girl, I met a fine honey today, name's Tony."

"Really?" Maya wasn't in the mood to talk but hoped Trish's chattering about her love life would take Maya's mind off her own.

"Yes, and I think this one could be a keeper." Trish went into detail about how Tony looked, what they'd talked about, and the fact that they were going out Saturday night.

"That's great," was all Maya said in response to Trish's long rambling.

"Girl, you are not paying me any attention. Why don't we hook up tomorrow? I just got an assignment that will have me downtown for the next two weeks. Let's do lunch." In between Trish's quest to become the next Angela Bassett, she supplemented her income with temp jobs.

"Uh, no, I won't be in tomorrow. I'm, uh, working from home."

"What?" Trish asked with a hint of incredulity. Maya hadn't missed a day of work in three years, except for the day when her brother, Stretch, was sentenced to prison. "Maya, what is going on?"

"It's no big deal, really. I'm just working on a personal project for Zeke, and I have to do a lot of research on the Internet. He thought I would have fewer interruptions at home."

"Oh, okay. What about Wednesday?"

Maya took a deep breath. Keeping this maid mess away from Trish was going to be harder than actually being a maid! "This is a pretty big project. I might be working from home all week."

Trish tried to read through what Maya said and find what she meant. But she knew Maya could shut up tighter than a paint-closed window. She decided to drop it, for now.

"All right, then, girl, let me know when you want to hook up."

"Okay, I'll call you."

Maya hung up, glad to be off the phone. She and Trish could talk for hours and often did; this was definitely a change of events. Maya rubbed her shoulders, tense from the pressure of dealing with a situation that was only hours old. How would she hold up acting like somebody else? And just how long was she expected to? Maya got up from the bed and began pacing. She'd never even thought to ask Zeke about that. How long was this charade supposed to go on?

That thought made Maya revisit just what this charade entailed. She was to act as one of Sam Walters's housekeepers. Just what that meant, she'd find out tomorrow, when she met with the woman who until now had been cleaning the home. Maya could only guess what kind of favors Zeke had called in to get this whole thing to work. She knew that because of his many real estate holdings, Zeke had access to most of the major cleaning companies in the city. But how he worked it out to find which one cleaned the house that Sam Walters was renting was anyone's guess. Zeke seemed to know everything. It was one of the reasons he was where he was . . . on top. But where would this "assignment" put Maya? She'd get that answer soon enough, but tonight it put her in a frenzy, tossing and turning, alternately dreaming about a man with a bushy beard and mustache, and another one with lickable lips, a cleft chin, and dark glasses.

The next day, following Zeke's instructions, Maya telephoned the cleaning company and introduced herself as the Martha Jones who'd been referred to them for the Walters home. She spoke with Maria Hernandez, the friendly and efficient office manager. Maria went over the basic assignment, and included a list of Maya's duties: dusting, mopping, washing, changing bed linens, and washing any dishes left by the client, Mr. Walters. Maria informed her that she could fill out the required paperwork when she arrived at the house the next morning, and told her a

woman named Cecilia would be there to help her
get started. Maya, who was practically stunned into
silence, said little.

"Any questions, senorita?" Maria asked. "You
seem worried. Well . . . don't be, I think you'll do
very well."

Maya managed to find her voice, and a little friend-
liness. After all, Maria was simply doing her job. It
wasn't Maria's fault that a corporate executive was
trading her designer duds for dishwashing gloves.
Inside, Maya cringed. *This is not what I signed up for
when I joined Brennan & Associates' elite staff. What
in the world am I doing?*

She was still asking that question when a half hour
later she found herself in the aisle of a Goodwill
thrift shop. Maria had suggested she wear sturdy,
comfortable clothes and tennis shoes. Maya couldn't
think of anything in her closet that would suffice for
cleaning. She usually wore cutoffs and an old T-shirt
when tackling her abode. But since she thought it
best to somewhat hide what she really looked like,
she needed something frumpy, plain and big. The less
attention she drew to herself, the better. Remembering the plot of an old movie, she also decided to buy
a wig and scooped up a pair of old, thick prescription
glasses. How she wished she could discuss this with
Trish. Her friend was the actress, after all.

Several hours later, Maya was back home, her purchases spread across the bed. Looking at the motley
ensemble stirred her anger again. Here she was, an
honors graduate from the University of Southern California with a bachelor's in business administration,
getting ready to mop a floor for money? It didn't
make sense. None of this made sense. *Just do your
job Maya*, she reasoned, while holding a large, wrin-

kled dress up to her fit, curvy frame. *You'll get your payday sooner or later. I owe Zeke now. Maybe after this, he'll owe me.*

Maya owed Zeke, literally. He'd loaned her over a hundred thousand dollars, money that had paid for the high-powered defense attorneys who'd kept her brother out of federal prison and a twenty-five year sentence. Zeke had alluded to ways she could work off the loan, one being of the horizontal nature. Maya wasn't trying to be anybody's mistress. She'd opted to pay back cash with cash, and through bonuses had already lowered the bill to just over seventy-five thousand. When she left B&A and formed her own company, she wanted to leave with her self-respect. She wanted to stand on her own two feet, not spread them for Zeke Brennan.

With renewed resolve, Maya reached for another outfit, this one a big pair of sweat bottoms and a large T-shirt. She picked up the wig and glasses and headed to the bathroom to do a dress rehearsal. In just a few hours, it would be showtime.

4

Sean, now dressed as Sam Walters, eyed himself critically in the mirror. His fro, though looking a little dated, looked like his real hair. The beard and mustache were perfect for lessening the impact of his Cupid lips and hiding the cleft in his chin. The gray highlights added years to his age, as did the paunch he wore under a large sports shirt. His khaki pants were just a tad too short, revealing white crew socks that he wore with sandals. One thing was for sure, Sam Walters would never win any *GQ* awards. But he wouldn't unduly stand out in a crowd either, and that was just as he wanted.

Sean left his bedroom and walked into the kitchen. The clock on the wall told him it was about time for the maid to arrive. He was a bit irked that the first one had left so abruptly. She'd been quiet, quick, and efficient, just like he liked his help. She'd also seemed to be the kind who would have absolutely no interest in him or his business whatsoever. He heard her speak exclusively in Spanish, except for the few words she spoke to him. At least it was the part-time housekeeper and not Cecilia, the head housekeeper. He considered whether he even needed two housekeepers. But as was often the case, the new one probably had mouths to feed.

Maya paused before stepping up to the doorbell and ringing it. Afterward, she stepped back and turned around, taking in the ocean view before her, masking her nervousness with deep, conscious breaths. When she heard the door open, she turned back around.

They both stared at each other for a moment. To Maya, Sam Walters was even more unattractive in person than he was in the picture. She wasn't expecting someone so old and, well, raggedy. Sean, on the other hand, had assumed that the new maid would be Hispanic, as the others were. The thought that the maid might be Black hadn't occurred to him. Sean took in the uncombed, unkempt wig, the big, wrinkled shirt, the oversized sweatpants, the cheap tennis shoes and hid a frown. *Lord, does she have to look like a maid just because she's working as one?* Her glasses were so thick Sean honestly wondered what, if anything, she could see out of them. Sean recovered first.

"You're Martha."

"Uh, yeah, sah." Maya had decided to adopt a simple, pseudo countrified accent and avoid looking directly at Mr. Walters as much as possible. Hopefully, especially for her assignment, he'd be gone most of the time she was in the home.

"I'm Sam Walters."

Sean stepped back and opened the door without speaking; her sign to enter. She did so and immediately noted the home's understated elegance. As much as Maya dabbled in interior design, she was sorely tempted to touch several of the home's accessories, sure she knew at least one of the designers or artists. She refrained. *Maybe one day when he's gone . . .* Maya gave herself a mental shake. This wasn't a pleasure visit, this was business. She would do well to keep this in mind.

Sean had walked over to the dining room table and picked up a piece of paper. He handed it to Martha. It was the same list of household duties she'd received verbally from Maria. "They explain this to you?" Sean asked.

"Yeah, sah," Maya replied, taking the paper.

"Any questions?" Obviously Sam was a man of few words, Maya thought.

"Uh, no, sah."

"As you probably know, Cecilia is the head house-keeper. Normally she'd be here but she had a doctor's appointment."

Maya simply nodded.

Sean could see the woman was nervous. Surely this wasn't her first job. He couldn't see a company sending a novice to his upscale neighborhood. As long as she did her work and did it well, it wasn't his concern. Still, something about the woman made him want to put her at ease. "Cecilia is an excellent housekeeper. She'll train you well and be able to address any concerns."

Maya stole a quick glance at Sam over the rims of her eyeglasses. She could barely see anything when looking through them. "Thank ya."

Sean stood there for another second or two, watching Martha. He couldn't put his finger on it but something about her was prickling the investigator in him. Maybe it was her pathetic demeanor, or the way she talked, barely above a whisper, as if every word were a dollar she didn't want to spend. And she looked so insecure, so nervous. Then he got angry. She probably was in her twenties, even though her outdated wig and thick glasses made her appear older. And here she was throwing her life away cleaning someone else's kitchen. Was this really the best she could do in life? Was this really as high as she aspired? And why did he care? It wasn't like Sean to get soft, ever. He really needed to take a vacation.

"Cecilia will be here at two. She'll give you more details on your duties. For now, you can start in the kitchen. I'll be in my office," he said, turning to walk toward a set of closed double doors. He stopped abruptly and added, "The only room in the house that is strictly off-limits."

Maya watched as Sam walked, or a better word might be waddled, to his office. When he shut the door, she let out the breath she didn't know she'd been holding. So she was in; she was the new, official part-time cleaning woman at Sam Walters's home. And as sure as she knew that, she knew that whatever Sam had that could help Zeke was probably in that off-limits office he'd just entered. Maya had always liked a challenge. Before it was over, Maya was going to turn that office inside out. If there was something hidden there or anywhere in this house that would help her confirm that this man was really who he said he was, Maya, as Martha, would find it.

Maya headed to the kitchen. She was glad to be alone. Although the insecure bit was part of her act, she actually was nervous. She'd always been the se-rious one in the group, the no-nonsense business-woman. If she'd thought it once, she'd thought it a hundred times . . . she needed Trish!

Maya placed her purse on the table and looked around the kitchen. Her first job would be easy; there were only a few breakfast dishes in the sink. Obvi-ously Sam ate light; though one couldn't tell to look at him. Maya searched the cabinets, finding dishes up top and cleaning supplies beneath the sink. There was a huge, stocked pantry off to one side of a kitchen that boasted stainless steel appliances and granite countertops. The upscale environment didn't surprise Maya; in fact, with the large portfolio she and Zeke had reviewed, she was surprised he lived even this modestly. *Interesting.* For some reason, this fact felt like information that should be tucked away for future reference. Maya unconsciously reached for her BlackBerry to make a note, then remembered she'd left at home the gadget that was as much a part of her as her right hand, in her *other* purse, the Prada she'd voluntarily traded for a beat-up Wal-Mart reject from Goodwill.

Maya sighed, rolled up her sleeves, reached for the rubber gloves and dishwashing liquid she'd seen under the sink, and started working. "C'mon, Martha," she whispered, with a sarcastic emphasis on her pseudo-name. "Time to earn your eighty-a-year salary."

When Cecilia walked into the kitchen two hours later, she found Maya in the pantry organizing the cans, boxes, and bottles. Maya was extremely organized and old habits died hard. She'd cleaned the kitchen from top to bottom, and was now acting like an organizing fool.

"Oh my, Martha, you do good job. My name is Cecilia."

"Thank you," Maya said naturally, forgetting her accent. *Oh, shoot! You're Martha, stupid, Martha!* Maya turned back to the stack of cans and continued arranging them. Of course she was being paranoid; Cecilia barely noticed her answer. It was a wake-up call, though. *I've got to be careful.*

"I show you house," Cecilia said. "Finish this later, okay?"

Maya simply nodded and followed Cecilia out of the kitchen.

The first thing Maya noted was how impersonal the house appeared. Granted, Mr. Walters had moved to town only recently, but most times one could note some type of personal effect, even if it was minimal. But there were no photos or mementos lying around, no personal effects of any kind. She thought this would change when they reached the master suite. It did not. The furnishings were expensive, yet sparse. Aside from the clothes in his closet—which with the exception of a couple of suits were just like the ones he now wore—and a few pieces of jewelry on his dresser, the room could have been in any hotel.

As they were leaving, Maya noticed another closet, next to the master bath. Without thinking or hesitating, she went to open it. It was locked.

"Oh no, Mr. Walters only," Cecilia said. "We no go in there."

"Oh, uh, 'scuse me," Maya said softly. *Hmm, what's behind door number two?*

The rest of the tour was uneventful and when they finished, it was in the laundry room. A couple of loads of clothes had been sorted and were ready for washing. This and replacing the linens on Mr. Walters's bed were to complete her work for the day. As Maya poured detergent into the machine and began to fill it, there was only one thing on her mind: how in the world she was going to survive this boring madness two days a week. She missed the razzamatazz world of B&A already.

Downstairs, Sean had relaxed his facade behind the comforts of a locked office door. The Afro wig was perched over an unused lamp, and while the fake paunch was still strapped on, Sean was shirtless. He had pretty much finished the minor computer research he'd scheduled for the day, and so far, had come up empty. His clients, the Rosenthal Group, had leveled charges of bribery, coercion, and blackmail, among others, against the man he was investigating. When he'd countered that those were some pretty strong accusations to make against someone, they'd agreed, but hadn't flinched. That combined with the steep fee they were paying him was more than enough motivation for him to keep digging until he found the proof his clients needed to bring their adversary down. For Sean it wasn't a matter of if, but when. If there was any truth to the unsavory allegations about Zeke Brennan and his empire, Sean, as Sam, would find it.

But for now, Sean was just waiting for Martha to leave so he could follow suit. So far she'd seemed harmless but Sean kept his eye on everyone. Another week or two and he'd feel safe in leaving the house with her in it. He reached for the brochure in front of him and perused the suite he'd just rented. Not knowing how long this assignment would last, he knew it was important for him to be able to unwind without fear of blowing his cover. So he'd rented a hotel suite about twenty-five minutes from the house, and was ready to take full advantage of it. He wanted to lose the paunch, the wig and mustache, and hit a gym.

Tomorrow, he needed to be relaxed; so tonight he would work out the tension that had built up over the past few days. Every meeting he'd scheduled was crucial: the first, with the Rosenthal Group, second, lunch with his long-time friend Neil, who had deep connections to Los Angeles' political and social infrastructure, and the third and final meeting of the day, with Zeke Brennan.

5

The Fourth of July was here and just in time. Maya needed this holiday weekend. Two weeks had passed since she'd started being Martha part-time, and she was about to climb the walls. Playing maid was the most boring job she'd ever tackled in her life. So far there had been absolutely nothing of note to be discovered in the house and with the exception of a couple of magazines, nothing remotely personal belonging to Mr. Walters. And she'd been painfully reminded how much she hated housework. When Cecilia had assigned her to the master bathroom, complete with scrub brush and shower squeegee, she'd almost quit on the spot.

That's why she was so thankful for tonight, Magic Johnson's Benefit Fourth of July party. Trish had managed to get two VIP tickets to this exclusive event and had proven what a true friend she was by inviting Maya, instead of new boyfriend Tony, as her guest. Considering she'd barely spoken to Trish the past two weeks, much less seen her, Maya would have totally understood if Trish had given her new man the generous gift.

Maya was ready to get loose; let her hair down. She might have been bored, but she was still stressed. She'd finally gotten comfortable with her Martha persona, complete with the unsure demeanor and simple accent, but she was more than ready to step back into her place at B&A. Word had it that Jade was trying to make Maya's reduced office presence a permanent one, and even though Maya was still in the office a couple of days a week, that was hardly enough to satisfy her thirst for power and prestige. Maya's work was her life. The past couple of weeks had sorely proved she had very little going on in her world without it.

Maya pulled up to Trish's apartment in her newly washed silver Beemer. That's another thing she'd missed on the days she became Martha, her own vehicle. After enduring a two-block walk to the bus stop and then two buses to get to Playa Del Rey, she had a whole new respect for bus riders, drivers, and the things they endured: foul language, foul body odor, dirty seats, and often homeless and demented Angelenos. The bus ride, however, was a necessary ruse. She couldn't afford to be seen driving a luxury car, and riding public transportation helped her get into character. After this experience, she would never look at a bus stop the same way.

"C'mon in, I'm almost ready," Trish said loudly, over the loud sounds of Beyoncé's voice coming from the stereo. "I'm getting in the mood! It's time to get our party on!"

Maya laughed as she joined Trish in a dance around the living room. Trish was always good for a laugh and fun times; things Maya had had far too few of the past two weeks.

"You are looking hot! Is that new?"

Maya shook her head as she stopped dancing and did a model's turn. "You like it?"

"Girl, the way that dress fits, your 'a' might get some tonight."

"My 'a' could use some." Maya laughed as Trish went to finish dressing. She and Trish had adopted this abbreviated form of cursing years ago when Trish had babysat her pick-up-everything-you-say two-year-old niece for a couple of months. The habit stuck and now the only cursing both she and Trish did was the implied word's first letter. *Yes, my "a" could use a big, hard "d."*

Thinking of her love life, and the nonexistent possibilities of said life, almost caused Maya to lose her good mood. Perhaps that's why she worked so hard and so much, so she wouldn't have to think about being lonely. Maya didn't know why she always seemed to be in a catch-22: The men who were attracted to her she didn't like, and the men she liked weren't attracted to her. It had been that way since college and after walking in on her last boyfriend making out with her neighbor, she decided to shift all of her desires into becoming successful and rich.

But she had to admit, lately she had been thinking of how nice it would be to have someone in her life, to have someone to come home to. Especially these last two weeks when she'd hardly talked to Trish. If not for Trish, Stretch, who she talked to almost every day, and coworkers, her phone would rarely ring. And then there was "Mr. ATM," as she'd named the handsome stranger who for some reason wouldn't leave her thoughts. Every now and then his image would drift up into her mind and she'd imagined all kinds of things that could happen with the body that had so perfectly filled out a pair of jeans.

Stretch limos and town cars lined the walk leading up to Marina Del Rey's Ritz-Carlton Hotel. Beautiful people of all shapes, sizes, and colors added to the glamour. Trish and Maya felt right at home among them as they entered the hotel: Trish in her KLS shirred mini, and Maya in an equally short brickred Angali Kumar. The silky fabric teased her naked skin with every step, a lacy black thong and bra set being her only other clothing. With Maya spending most of her days in button-up suits or, as Martha, Goodwill castoffs, this extravagance felt good. She felt fine and foxy; ready to unleash the wild animal side of her that had been tame for too long.

They entered the crush of the ballroom and were instantly swept up into the party mood. Almost immediately, Trish saw someone she knew and left Maya to say hello. Trish knew some of everybody in L.A. and Maya was well aware she'd probably seen the last of her until it was time to go. That was fine, Maya was right at home in this environment. She decided to go to the bar for a cool glass of sparkling water, but before she could get there, she was accosted.

"My, my, my, my, you sure look good tonight," the handsome man said, blocking her path with his buff body and a dazzling smile.

"Thank you," Maya responded. She started to walk around him, believing if she didn't she might not be responsible for her actions. The man looked good enough to eat right there!

"Uh, could I get this dance?" he said, stepping in front of her once more and placing a hand gently on her arm.

The hand could have been an iron, that's how hot it made Maya. Now she really needed something cold, like a shower. "I was on my way to the bar,"

Maya said, realizing she wasn't going to be able to make a quick escape.

"Then allow me to join you for a drink."

Maya looked up into eyes the color of dark chocolate, framed by long, thick lashes. Her mouth watered. Remembering the "lonely single" thoughts she'd had only hours ago, Maya decided to try and relax, enjoy herself. Hadn't she and Trish agreed that Maya needed to get some? Not that Maya would do that tonight; she was a lady after all. There'd be no one-night stands with someone she'd just met, someone who was almost melting her like wax with his sexy eyes, lush lips, and a cleft that made . . . wait! *That's it!* Maya thought, eyeing the handsome stranger more carefully. *This is Mr. ATM!* Maya became even more flustered, remembering the late-night erotic fantasies she'd constructed at this stranger's expense. Maya swallowed hard, and tried to discreetly find where her "cool" went.

They reached the bar and Maya, who rarely drank, decided she needed something to calm her nerves. She asked the bartender for something light, and he suggested a wine spritzer. Mr. ATM ordered a beer.

"My name is Sean," he said, after he'd placed his order. "And what is yours . . . besides lovely?"

Maya sipped her drink to delay an answer. What if this man worked in the Brennan Building or knew any of her associates? Maya fiercely guarded her privacy, always mindful of her professional reputation. But she didn't want to think about work tonight, she wanted to have fun, and forget about Martha. *That's it. I'll adopt another persona, just for tonight.*

An inebriated woman sidled up to Sean and interrupted them with a tired "don't I know you" line, giving Maya another precious second or two to think about whether or not she really wanted to be a clandestine girl gone wild.

Another look at Sean and she decided she did. Maya usually walked the straight and narrow, honest to a fault. But since she'd be adopting a persona, she'd be acting, not lying, wouldn't she? And even though she'd only seen him in the lobby that one time, if he worked anywhere near the B&A offices it was probably best he not know her real name. That way what happened at the Ritz could stay at the Ritz . . . even though she was *not* going to sleep with this man. Well, maybe not sleep with but lie next to . . .

"I apologize for that," Sean said once the stranger left. "Now, where were we? Ah yes, your name."

"It's, uh, Macy," she said, when Sean turned back to her, the name coming to her because she'd listened to Macy Gray en route to Trish's.

Sean nodded, drinking her in. He thought Macy beautiful, from her simple, short hairstyle that emphasized her almond-shaped eyes, to her pert nose, rosy mouth, long, slender neck, and equally slender body. He guessed her to be about five foot four or five, but with the four-inch spikes she was wearing, she almost reached his nose. There was something oddly familiar about her, but he quickly dismissed any chance of having met her. He wouldn't have forgotten a woman like this.

Sean realized he was staring and tried to think of something else witty to say. He had to admit his gaming skills were sorely lacking. Work kept any thoughts of a serious relationship at bay. With the constant travel, secrecy, and sometimes life-threatening situations, he knew it would take a special woman to handle his lifestyle. There were a couple of casual relationships, women with whom he'd obtained a mutual understanding that nothing existed between them beyond good conversation, great sex, and an occasional vacation. The latest, a woman in London named Tangier, was getting a bit tricky; for the first time in their two years together she'd mentioned taking the relationship to another level. He looked at Macy again. *Maybe* . . . No, he had a feeling that this one was anything but a casual lay.

"You're beautiful," he said finally.

"Wow," Maya replied. "Beautiful and lovely. Careful, or your flattery might go to my head."

Something was going to Sean's head also, but not the one he was talking with. He tried to get his act together and ran to safe ground—work. "So, Macy, are you here representing your company tonight?"

The last thing Maya wanted to be reminded of was her dual occupations. "No, and work is the last thing I want to talk about. Tonight, I just want to have a good time."

"I hear that," Sean answered. "Let's do that, then, let's have a good time."

Just then a rumble went through the crowd as Magic Johnson and his wife, Cookie, took the stage. After sustained applause, Magic gave a brief speech about the various AIDS foundations and other beneficiaries of the night's event. He thanked everyone for coming, for being beautiful and generous, and then began the part of the evening everyone had been waiting for, the musical guests.

First on was jazz guitarist Paul Jackson, who gave the crowd a simple yet stunning guitar feast. Next came the legendary Stevie Wonder, who rocked the ballroom for a solid thirty minutes. In between acts, Sean and Maya chitchatted and got to know each other better. She even gave him her phone number,

which he wrote down on a piece of paper. As an afterthought, he decided to give her his too. By the time
Beyoncé hit the stage, they were talking like old
friends and flirting like new lovers.

Beyoncé was dazzling to watch, but in time she encouraged everyone to get crazy on the dance floor. It
was the perfect suggestion and Sean and Maya bobbed
and weaved their way to a spot near the front of the
stage. The music was thunderous, the atmosphere
electric, and Maya was thrilled with how the night was
turning out. Here she was at a banging party, listening
to one of her favorite artists, and dancing with, literally, the man of her dreams. Thinking that, she remembered she hadn't brought up their initial encounter. Just
as well, she decided. She hadn't been on her best behavior that day. And since she'd just recently cut her
formerly shoulder-length hair into a fashionably chic
pixie, he probably wouldn't remember her anyway.
Something about the fact that this man was new to her,
and to the city as he'd mentioned in their conversation,
gave her an unusual freedom to let her pixie'd hair
down. Normally she was all about appearances. After
all, Zeke Brennan's reach was far and wide, and she
never knew who was watching and what might get
back to whom. But tonight, she felt uninhibited, free.
And it felt good.

Sean needed to thank Neil for telling him about
tonight's gala. And to think, he had almost passed on
the invite. When working on a case, he normally kept
a low profile. But since he was costumed during the
day anyway, and set up at another location, he felt he
could be incog-Negro at a big event like this. He
rarely made it to the West Coast, and although his was
a pretty big network, he felt fairly certain he wouldn't
run into anyone he knew, especially anyone he didn't

want to see. It wasn't until he arrived at the party, and especially after he'd met Macy, that he realized how much he'd needed to chill, leave the work behind for a short while. And boy, was he glad he did!

Sean's eyes lowered to slits as he watched the chocolate confection in front of him move her body to the beat. A fine sheen of sweat showed on Maya's neck and arms, giving her an ethereal glow. Her body moved with sexy abandon. Sean's manhood stirred as his eyes roamed Maya's body the way his hands longed to do.

Beyoncé broke into another fast-paced song, her hit "Naughty Girls." It was one of Maya's favorites. She threw up her hands, gave Sean a wide smile, and immediately became a prototype of the song's lyrics. She came close to Sean, cupping his clean-shaven cheek before running her hand down his chest, waist, and thigh. *Feeling sexy, feeling n-a-s-t-y* . . . Maya turned around, rubbing her booty against Sean, grabbing his hips from behind and thrusting back against him. Her kitty began to throb in the excitement of her abandon. Maya had never in her life acted in such an uninhibited manner; she knew after tonight, she probably never would again.

Sean squeezed Maya's hips, moving them in rhythm with her dancing. His rod was throbbing now, aching to be inside her. Maya turned and put her arms around Sean's neck. Before either of them knew it, they were deep inside each other's mouths, tongues swirling, hands exploring, fireworks going off on the dance floor.

Suddenly Maya felt faint. She stopped, and pushed away from Sean. "Stop, I, I can't breathe."

Sean immediately took charge, guiding them through the pulsating throng and out of the main part of the ballroom. He sat Maya down. "Wait here."

Maya's head was spinning. *What's wrong with me?*
Then she remembered. Although she'd only had two
wine spritzers, she'd had virtually nothing to eat all
day. She'd intended to get something in between her
hair appointment and her mani/pedi, but with L.A.'s
bumper-to-bumper traffic, had run out of time. She'd
intended to eat as soon as she came inside the party.
But then Sean happened, and food was forgotten—
until now.

"Here, Macy," Sean said, handing her a glass of
water. "Maybe this will help."

"I need food," Maya said, taking the water and
drinking it down. "And fresh air."

"Let's go." Without waiting for an answer, Sean
took Maya's arm, gently encouraging her from the
chair, and heading toward the entrance.

Maya heard strains of "Irreplaceable" as they
exited. "Wait, I love that song." A wave of nausea
hit her. "Oh, goodness, I think I might be sick."

Sean changed directions and instead of going outside, headed for the elevator.

"Where are we going?"

"My room. You can lie down and I'll get you some
food and coffee."

Maya was too weak to protest. She leaned against
Sean, comforted by his strong arm as the elevator as-
cended to Sean's floor. Once it opened, he quickly escorted her to his room, and opened the door.

All Maya wanted was the bed she saw as soon as the
door opened. "I think if I just lie down for a minute,"
she said. She half sat, half lay on the bed, gingerly placing her head on one of the fluffy, king-sized pillows.

"Here, wait," Sean said. He walked over, untied
Maya's sandal straps, and gently removed her heels.
He couldn't help but notice the silkiness of her skin

as he did so. He fought hard, resisting the urge to run his hand up and between her legs. "Let me get you something to eat," he said with authority, trying to keep his mind on the matter at hand, making Macy feel better.

He went to the desk, opened the guest accommodations book, and scanned the room service menu. After ordering soup, rolls, a 7up, and coffee, Sean went back over to the bed.

During his absence, Maya had crawled up onto the bed. In the process, her miniskirt had ridden up, exposing the bottom half of a creamy round, brown cheek. Sean licked his lips. His fingers twitched. His throbbing shaft strained forward like a Thoroughbred heading out of the gate. He moved from the bed and over to the window, forcing his libido down. Sean thought back to the last time he'd had sex and after realizing it was two months prior, understood why his manhood was protesting so vehemently to explore what was in front of it. Sean wanted to explore it too.

A knock on the door let Sean know that room service had arrived. He took the food, tipped the bellman, and placed the items on the table. He went back to the bed and stood staring down at the lovely creature apparently asleep in his bed.

"Macy," he whispered softly, and then again a little louder. When there was no answer, he gently covered Maya with the comforter and let her sleep.

Maya awoke to the feel of two strong arms around her and a leg thrown over her thigh. Immediately she remembered the past night's events: Beyoncé, wine spritzers, and Sean. His limbs were the weight of dead wood; it took her several minutes to disengage herself from his softly snoring frame. Once she got up and her eyes acclimated to the dark room, she went into the restroom.

She closed the door and turned on the light. Not bad. Her dress was only slightly wrinkled and because of her short hairstyle, she didn't look unkempt. She splashed some water on her face, brushed her teeth with her finger and some toothpaste she found on the counter, and leaving the light on, walked back into the room.

It looked as if Sean was still sleeping. She smiled as she watched him from across the room, remembering how good it felt to sleep next to a man. Maya felt like a voyeur in her own movie, it was so rare for her to do anything remotely out of the ordinary. She thought of Beyoncé's song then. Yes, she still felt like a naughty girl. She thought of Trish too, and went to her purse. Sure enough, Trish had called several times. Maya sent a quick text message and then turned off her phone.

With the light from the bathroom, she noted the food on the table. Although the food was cold, her ravenous stomach still enjoyed the potato chowder soup, rolls, and now tepid 7up. She finished quickly and after returning to the bathroom to rinse out her mouth, lay down tentatively on the far side of the king bed. As an afterthought, she rose, removed her four-hundred-dollar dress, and after securely covering herself in part of the top sheet, lay back down.

Sean held his breath until the movement stopped. He'd awakened shortly after Maya got up and went into the bathroom, and had feigned sleep when she came back out. Now he wished he hadn't awakened. Because if he hadn't, he wouldn't know that she had removed her dress and that only a flimsy sheet separated him from a much-needed release. He was a gentleman and would never take advantage of a tipsy woman who was half asleep. He tossed and turned for about half an hour before making a decision: he only lived once. Nothing beat a failure but a try.

He rolled over next to Maya and gently loosened the sheet. Sean always slept in the nude, and sliding next to her near-naked body was almost his undoing. But he did it anyway. He nuzzled her neck and then began gently kissing her shoulders, arm, and back. Maya moaned softly, before turning over to face him. "I thought you'd never wake up," she said, all thoughts of what she'd never do on the first night forgotten.

Sean was both surprised and pleased. He hadn't taken Maya for the type who'd have casual sex, but he wasn't looking a gift horse in the mouth. He rolled her over and began a frontal assault with his lips and hands, enthralled with the sweetness of Maya's lips, mesmerized by the softness of her skin.

Maya was equally caught up in the wonder that was Sean's body, lean and hard, feeling so strong beside and on top of her. She cupped his backside, firm and strong, and then ran her hands up and down his wide back. She moaned as Sean rolled them over and lowered his head to kiss her neck and breasts. He gently tongued one nipple, and then the other, then moved back up to claim her mouth with fiery passion.

Maya's fire burned bright as well, and she took her turn to kiss Sean's chest, lightly sprinkled with curly black hair. She moved down to his stomach, coming close to but not touching his manhood, before she worked her way back up to his mouth. Both of them knew intuitively that this dance could go on for hours, and it did continue for a time.

But after a while, Sean wanted more; he wanted all of Macy. He stopped kissing her, and sat up, bringing her up with him and placing her in his arms. "I want to make love to you, Macy," he said once his heart had slowed down enough for him to talk.

"I want it too," Maya said. "And that's not like me. I mean, I'm usually not—"

"I didn't think you were. Are you sure?"

Maya didn't know why, but she was, totally sure. She turned to look Sean in the eye. "Yes."

Sean kissed Maya lightly on the forehead, on each eyelid, her nose, and briefly on the mouth. Then he got up, went over to the dresser, and pulled out a pack of condoms. He reached in and turned off the bathroom light, opening the drapes and letting the beginning of the new day light their lovemaking.

Maya's heart beat a crazy rhythm as she watched Sean's naked body move around the room. She was wet for him, her body vibrating with excitement. She couldn't remember ever feeling this way about anyone, and attributed it to the fact that she'd gone so long without sex. When Sean came back to the bed, her stomach flip-flopped.

"Now," he said, taking her in his arms and slowly removing her thong panties. They soon joined the bra he'd removed earlier. "Let me love you."

6

"Girl, you're lying," Trish said simply.

"Swear to God, Trish, me and Sean f'd last night."

"Shut up!" Trish said, a laugh accompanying her incredulity. "You want me to believe that Ms. Gotta-Wait-Till-She-Gets-The-Home-Phone-Number-Meet-The-Mama-Sleep-At-The-House-Riffle-Through-The-Closets-Background-Checking Jamison gave it up on the first night? Within hours of meeting a total stranger?" Trish waved a finger as she shook her head. "Uh-uh. This is your girl you're talking to, Maya, remember? Tell that story to someone who'll believe you."

Maya grabbed a pillow and leaned back against Trish's comfy sofa. "I think I'm in love."

Trish rolled her eyes. "Oh Lord. Talking like that . . . you really may have f'd him."

Maya's eyes shone as she sat up and hugged the throw pillow to her chest. "He was so good, Trish, the best lover I have ever had. He knew just how to hit my button. Girl, I've never had so many orgasms before! Maybe I should call him." Maya reached for her Prada

on the coffee table, thoughts of this encounter being
a one-night stand already forgotten.

"Absolutely not," Trish replied, staying Maya's
hand. "You want a nucka to think he turned you out?"

"He did turn me out!"

"Which is the exact reason why you've got to let
him call you first. Matter of fact, let him get voice
mail the first couple times, make him wonder what
you're up to."

"Trish, you're absolutely right," Maya answered in
a firm tone. Just then her cell phone rang and she
almost tore up her Prada trying to find it. "Hello?"

"Macy . . . it's Sean."

"Hey, Sean!" Maya looked at a chagrined Trish as
she got up from the couch and walked toward the
patio door. Slipping outside, she continued the
convo. "How are you?"

"Are you kidding me? I've never felt better. I
just had to call you and make sure last night wasn't
a dream."

"I had to pinch myself too," Maya admitted. "I
really enjoyed, uh, meeting you, Sean."

Sean laughed. Something about this woman named
Macy filled his heart with joy. "We did a bit more
than meet, wouldn't you say?"

Maya's smile radiated through her voice. "Just a bit."

"Well, would you like to do *a bit* later on this afternoon? I know it's late notice but a friend of mine
just invited me to sail with him and his date. Want to
come?"

Maya most certainly did; in more ways than one.
"Hmm . . . it's been years since I've been to Catalina."

Trish tapped her on the shoulder. *No*, she mouthed.
Maya hadn't heard the patio door open and gave

her friend a "talk to the hand" motion. "What time should I be ready?"

"I can pick you up around, say, two o'clock?"

Maya immediately remembered that to Sean, she was Macy Williams, who lived and worked as a secretary downtown. They'd sounded like innocent enough lies the night before, when she thought she'd never see him again, when she was acting. Now she had to sleep in the bed she'd made. "Uh, why don't I meet you at your hotel?"

"You sure? That's actually better since his boat is moored here in the Marina, but I didn't want you to think for a moment I'm not a gentleman."

"You're a very gentle man," Maya cooed. "See you at two."

It was almost twelve hours later when Maya and Sean walked into their suite on Catalina Island. It had been the best Fourth of July Maya had ever experienced, and the reason could be summed up in one word: Sean.

"I've been wanting to do this all night," Sean said as he walked up to Maya, placed his large hands squarely on her round booty, and squeezed her lusciousness up against his hard, long shaft.

"Um," Maya sighed, as she gently ground her pelvis against Sean's muscled manliness.

"You're a dangerous woman, Macy Williams."

"Me? You're the one with the weapon."

Sean picked her up and walked purposely toward the bedroom. "Let's take a shower," he whispered.

Sean and Maya undressed each other quickly and stepped into the oversized stall. Soon they were rubbing silky, soapy bodies against each other; their mouths hot and wet, tongues thrusting, heads turning, trying to find a position that would give them more of each other. They couldn't seem to get enough.

Sean poured soap onto a sponge and lathered Maya's body all over. He paid particular attention to her breasts, booty, and the apex at her thighs while not neglecting her arms, legs, and face. In turn, Maya soaped Sean all over, turning him around to admire one of his best features: a strong, round backside with a deep dimple just above each cheek and a perfectly positioned black mole at the top of his ass's crevice. She ran the sponge up the length of his hard, muscled thighs, over his butt, around to his rigid manhood, across a six-pack stomach, and between his powerful shoulder blades. There were no two ways about it: Sean Wynn was the finest man on this side of forever.

Sean turned, picked up Maya, and positioned her up against the smooth shower stall glass. Maya wrapped her legs around Sean's midsection, her nana throbbing with anticipation. Sean held her up with one arm, and with the other, gently fingered her nub. He slid a soapy finger between the folds of her feminine flower before thrusting two fingers inside her.

"Ooh," Maya moaned, even as she rocked back and forth, her body craving more, craving Sean. "I want, I want . . ."

Sean knew what she wanted. His fingers worked like magic, playing her g-spot like a guitar. Before Maya knew it she was climaxing and at the height of her orgasm. Sean fastened her against the glass and plunged his eight-inch shaft deep into her warm cocoon. He stroked her steadily, masterfully, as if he'd been custom-made to bring her ultimate fantasy to life. His tongue thrusts matched his hip movements, slow, circular gyrations lavishing love on

Maya's mouth, even as his juicy Johnson lavished the inner walls beyond her lower lips. He turned their bodies slightly, until the water was shooting over them, between them, hot, wet, steamy . . . just like their lovemaking.

Maya stirred lazily, mindlessly swatting whatever was lightly touching her face. She shook her head and swatted again, unwilling to open her eyes and leave the wonderful world of sleep she'd entered after a torrid night of endless sex. But the pesky creature wouldn't leave her alone; there it was again, on her eyelids, her nose . . . Maya slapped hard.

"Ouch!" Sean yelped in mock pain. "You hurt me."

"Bugs get squashed, don't you know that?" Maya replied, yawning as she rolled into Sean's arms. "Good morning."

"Um . . . it is a good one," Sean replied. "And a late one too. Get up and brush your teeth. I've ordered breakfast."

"Oh my goodness, what time is it?" Maya asked, straining to see the clock on the nightstand next to Sean. For a couple of seconds she panicked, forgetting it was a holiday, her mind racing through a list of to-dos for Brennan & Associates.

"Time for my chocolate nymph to prepare for the feast I've planned." Sean tussled Maya's short curls. "C'mon now . . . we've only got a few more hours before we get off Gilligan's Island and head back to the real world."

"Ugh, don't remind me." Maya jumped off the bed, barely missing Sean's playful swat at her lush behind before she darted into the shower.

The real world. Those three words haunted Maya as

she massaged conditioner into her hair while pulsating jets of hot water soothed her sore thighs. While he'd been gentle, Sean was very well endowed, long and thick. It was enough that Macy hadn't had sex in awhile, even more that it was a stallion she'd ridden back into the land of coital bliss. Was it really only two days ago she'd battled feelings of loneliness, and the frustration of her dream job turned housekeeper horror? For forty-eight, no seventy-two, hours, Maya had forgotten "Martha" and the impossible-so-far job of getting the real deal scoop on Sam Walters, the bloated, unkempt, haughty a-hole who barely spat out a hello on the rare times she saw him. That and try and stay on top of a job that her colleague, Jade, would like to edge her out of. Between Sam and Jade, Maya was too through with attitude.

But for two whole days, Sean Wynn had brought out a side of Maya she didn't know existed; one who under the guise of "Macy" could roam free: uninhibited, insatiable, giving herself fully, completely to the experience of making love with Sean. Before, she now realized, she'd only had sex. Sean seemed to touch her very soul, and not just because of his extremely long member. Maya's nana tingled as she thought of some of the things Sean had done to her last night, and how much she'd enjoyed giving him oral pleasure. *My God . . . when he licked my . . .*

Sean tapped lightly on the glass. "Baby . . . your breakfast awaits."

"Okay." Maya hurriedly toweled off, finger-combed her hair, and wrapped her naked body in Sean's large shirt. She didn't bother to button it up.

Sean groaned as she entered the dining area, his butter knife in midair. "Macy, if you don't cover up, this strawberry jam will never see a slice of toast."

Maya smiled and wrapped his shirt around until she was covered. The tantalizing smell of eggs, bacon, hash browns, and coffee made her mouth water. She didn't realize until she'd dug into perfectly scrambled eggs what an appetite she'd worked up the night before. "Thank you, Sean," she said, with a quick kiss on his jam-stained lips. "You're too good to me."

"You think I'm good now? Just wait till dessert."

7

Sean watched Joseph Rosenthal carefully exam-
ine the documents he'd given him. There was no
doubt Zeke Brennan was into some shading dealings
when it came to the lock he had on the Los Angeles
real estate market; the problem was in finding concrete proof.

"Councilman Rollins, the city treasurer . . . I knew
it! I knew Brennan's cock ran the length of city hall.
He's got guys in his back pocket, and an inside track
to winning the most coveted contracts." Joseph
smacked the papers down on his desk, then jumped
up to pace the room. "But how do we catch him?
How do we nail the sonofabitch?"

"These things take time," Sean said evenly. He'd
learned long ago that when it came to private investigations, patience was a man's best friend. "My
sources are one hundred percent reliable, and thorough. But getting solid proof that Zeke Brennan is
behind the corruption is another matter altogether.
We've got to secure wiretaps, cameras . . . I'm working on an inside connection for the council meetings,
and another for the mayor's office.

"But you've got to understand something," he continued, leaning back into the plush leather seats, his calm a purposefully measured contrast to Joseph's barely concealed rage. "You're trying to bring down the top real estate mogul in Los Angeles, and one of the most powerful tycoons in the United States. This isn't going to happen overnight. Just like when constructing a building, the blocks have to be laid in place one by one, piece by piece, with precision. You've got to keep your head, Joseph. If you're looking for a rush to judgment, you've got the wrong situation, and you've definitely got the wrong man. There are a lot of poisonous spiders in this web of deception. One wrong move and the hunter will become the prey."

Joseph returned to his desk. He placed his elbows on top of the polished cherry-wood executive desk. He steepled his fingers and looked into Sean's eyes without blinking. "Listen Sean, the Rosenthal Group has been around for almost a hundred years. We didn't get to where we are without knowing a thing or two. Of course, I'm well aware that these things take time. But time is something I don't have a lot of.

"Projects like this don't come along often. It's why almost every major firm in the world is vying for it. But make no mistake, the Angel's Way project belongs to me, to the Rosenthal Group. We've earned it, we deserve it, and it will be ours!"

From his research, Sean knew Joseph was right. La Manera de Angel, translated Angel's Way, had been commissioned by the state of California and was to be for Los Angeles what the Golden Gate Bridge was to San Francisco, what the Eiffel Tower was to Paris, or what the Twin Towers were to New York: one of a kind. It was to become the jewel of L.A. real estate, a

maze of shops, offices, restaurants, and theatres an-
chored by a cultural center and museum celebrating
the richness of Los Angeles. The top floor of what
would also be the tallest building in the United States,
would house a world-class, five-star restaurant and
viewing arena. The landscaped surroundings were to
include parks, fountains and a large angel statue that
would exceed fifty feet in height. There'd never in the
history of California been a building project this sig-
nificant, and there probably would not be another one
for at least a hundred years. This was all the more
reason why caution, not carelessness, was of the
utmost importance in this investigation.

When Sean remained silent, Joseph continued.
"Our company has been working for over five years to
expose the corruption that's allowing Brennan and his
cronies to gain a monopoly on the permits issued for
the big jobs. Last year we were this close"—Joseph
held his thumb and forefinger close together—"this
close to getting his former general manager impris-
oned for bribery and fraud."

"And the case got thrown out at the last minute,"
Sean interjected, "because the prosecutor got excited. He started eyeing his promotion, maybe a bid
for attorney general. He started seeing his name in
the news, his face on TV. He got in a *hurry*. And
that's why I'm sitting here and you're still trying to
expose Zeke Brennan."

Sean knew all about the former case against Brennan & Associates. It was his business to know. Aside
from what had been headline news, Sean had uncovered insider information about the case, information
that also sullied the Rosenthal Group's squeaky clean
image they tried so hard to maintain. Sean made it his

business to know everything about all the players in his assignment, especially the one who hired him.

"Look, Sean, we know you're one of the best. That's why we hired you." Joseph said. "But I'm going to be honest, I've got to get this contract. And for that to happen, we've got to break the juggernaut Zeke's got on the L.A. market!" Joseph smashed his fist against his desk for emphasis.

"What do you know about Zeke's assistant, Maya Jamison?"

Sean's abrupt change of subject caught Joseph off guard. "Maya? Smart cookie there. Honors grad at USC, majored in business administration with a minor in international relations. She worked her way up from the secretarial pool. Heard it was quite a coup when she knocked Zeke's former right-hand woman off her perch a year ago. Word is Zeke threw money at the situation, his usual answer for solving problems, gave her a hefty severance and an early retirement plan."

"Hmm."

"You've met Maya, right? In the meetings you had with Zeke? Well, of course you have, she's always in his meetings."

"Actually no, I haven't, at least not so far. Both times I've been there she's been out of the office. Another assistant, Jade, sat in on them."

"She's quite the looker, that Maya." Joseph rubbed his chin thoughtfully. "Hey, that might be a way to—"

"Don't even go there, Joseph."

"C'mon, it's perfect. You're a successful, nice-looking man. She's a successful, attractive woman. You're both single, at least, I think she is. What easier way is there to get on the inside than to, you know, get on the *inside*?" Joseph chuckled at his double entendre.

"First, I don't mix business with pleasure and second, she's not my type." Sean's mind immediately went to his type: a freaky, feisty, curvaceous Tootsie Roll named Macy Williams.

Joseph took in Sean's suddenly stern countenance. "Look, I've got faith in you to get the job done. Just make it sooner rather than later, okay?"

"As soon as I possibly can."

Sean left the Rosenthal Group's office a few moments later. But it was he and Macy, not Zeke and Maya, on his mind. Thinking of the two women, he was struck by their contrast. From what he'd read and the picture he'd seen, Maya was a prudish, ambitious, and serious woman while Macy was almost the opposite: fiery, sensuous and carefree. He continued to think about Macy as he headed to his rental car. *I need to call her.* He'd been so busy since the holiday that his personal life had gone neglected. And obviously Macy wasn't the type to hound him. After calling once, the Monday after their trip to Catalina Island, she hadn't phoned again.

The smile that thoughts of Macy put on his face disappeared when he thought about the other women in his life, Tangier and Martha. Tangier had called several times over the Fourth of July holiday, had even suggested flying over from London. Sean adamantly insisted she stay put in England. She responded by increasing her calls to three, four a day. Eventually he stopped answering and for the past couple of days, he hadn't heard from her. He liked Tangier; she was witty, intelligent, and looked good on his arm. But he'd never thought of her in permanent terms, and thought she understood his number-one dating rule: no binding ties. She probably wouldn't call again. After all, a woman had her pride. He didn't know that he'd call her either, or even if he'd return to London once his job was done. He'd lived across the pond for two years; being in L.A. reminded him of all that was good about America. Macy reminded him of all things good too, maybe even someone with whom he could entertain "permanent."

And then there was the other irksome female—Martha. He didn't know what it was about her that bugged him so much, but something surely did. Maybe it was her mousy demeanor, or servile body language. Maybe it was the way she tried to shrink into invisibility whenever he was around, which wasn't often. Maybe it was the fact that he felt she was throwing her life away, when she could go back to school and secure a better job than wash dishes and make beds.

"It's not my business," Sean said aloud as he looked for a parking place in busy Beverly Hills, his next business stop. Besides, he continued to reason, somebody had to get paid to cook, clean, and perform other domestic chores. Sean decided it was just as well the money was going to a sista. He needed to tamp down his annoyance and leave the girl alone.

8

"That's all you've got so far? A portfolio from the Rosenthal Group sticking out of his briefcase?" Zeke leaned back in his chair and studied Maya thoughtfully. "You're normally so resourceful, Maya. I thought you'd have something more concrete than that by now. Something in his personal files, drivers's license, passport, credit cards, correspondence, some way to know this guy is really who he says he is . . . or not."

Maya stanched a heavy sigh. She wasn't happy with her results either; one of two things she was unhappy about. There'd be enough time to stew on that issue later, though; right now she had to focus on B&A.

"In the weeks I've worked in that house, there's never a scrap of paper lying around, not even a napkin from a restaurant, matches, nothing. I've still not been able to access the office, or the small closet in the master bedroom that remains locked at all times. It's going to take a bit more time to gain Cecilia's trust. She pretty much lets me do my work, but still, I never know when I'll turn around and find her

there, making sure I'm tucking that sheet correctly."
Maya's sarcasm seeped through on the last sentence.

"Look, I know this isn't easy. We'll give it a couple
more weeks and if you can't find anything, we'll let
you keep your day job."

"Honestly, Zeke, I'm surprised you tried this as
your first option, especially with all the top-notch investigators who work for you."

"You are not my first option, Maya. I know everything there is to know about Sam Walters, the Sam
Walters I can find on paper, that is. Sometimes, Maya,
you have to go with your gut, follow your hunches.
And my hunch is telling me there's more to Sam than
meets the eye. I'm using various options to find out
what." Zeke sat forward and shuffled the papers on
his desk, his sign that their meeting was over.

Maya stood. "So . . . two weeks and I can return to
work and start removing the knives that Jade has
flung toward my back in my absence?"

Zeke laughed. "Oh, so you've heard what's going
on, huh?"

"You're a great mentor, Zeke. And you always
have eyes and ears everywhere." Maya knew all
about Jade's attempts to head up the administrative
arm on all projects related to Angel's Way.

"Jade's ambitious, but she's not Maya Jamison.
You have nothing to worry about."

"I appreciate that, Zeke." Maya didn't know how
Zeke would handle her inability to get the goods on
Sam Walters. She'd seen people chewed up and spit
out for lesser failures. But this charade wasn't over.
Maya had two weeks to help Zeke solve the Sam
Walters mystery. She vowed to put those days to
good use.

Sam Walters, Maya thought as she stopped by her

office. Her sigh was audible this time. Something
about that bumbling Black man got on her nerves. He
had tons of money. Couldn't he buy a suit that fit?
Get a twenty-first-century haircut? Join a gym? And
why did he have to be so curt and dismissive, as if
she was too lowly to engage in conversation, and all
her instructions had to come through Cecilia? At
least that's how Cecilia made it seem . . . that a direct
look in her lofty boss's eye could get her fired.

Not that she wanted to talk to him anyway.
Hmmph. Little did he know how much she *wanted* to
get fired; she couldn't wait to burn those rubber
gloves and get out of his lifeless, impersonal show
home. Sam Walters wasn't worth the riches God had
given him. The sooner she finished the assignment,
the sooner she could wish Mr. Waddle Walters good
riddance.

She was ready to wish another man good riddance
as well, only this good-bye wasn't as easily done:
Sean Wynn. Sam and Sean couldn't be more dissim-
ilar. Sean Wynn had everything Sam Walters lacked:
looks, style, sexual magnetism, charm. Even so, it
galled her that she'd fallen hard and fast for the sexy
boy with a silky line and golden rod. Was it her imagination that her body still tingled days after they'd
been together?

Sean had called the evening they returned from
Catalina Island on his friend Neil's boat. That's the
last she'd heard from him. Although she'd reached for
her phone countless times, she refused to put in a
second call after leaving the first and only message.
He probably had plenty women who blew up his cell.
No, better to look at the Sean Wynn situation for
what it was . . . a beautiful lovers' holiday like a fire-
cracker's spark: hot, bright, and temporary.

"Gone so soon?" Ester Rios was the "eyes and ears" who kept Maya informed on the office happenings.

"Unfortunately," Maya said with a weary smile.

"That research must be really intense, you've been gone for what, two weeks now?"

"It's a lot," Maya agreed. "But I'll be back in another week or so." She leaned closer to Ester and continued in a low voice. "Until then, thanks for looking out for a sista."

Ester winked. "You know I've got your back, girl."

"And I've got yours. Maya never forgets a favor."

The switchboard lit up, announcing another call. Ester reached to answer it. "That's what I'm counting on."

Maya's phone rang as she headed to the elevator. She found her phone and answered as she always did, just as the doors closed. "Maya Jamison."

Silence on the other end.

"Hello?" Maya looked down to see the call had ended.

"That always happens to me," the other elevator occupant offered. "Every service claims theirs has the fewest dropped calls, yet the calls keep dropping!"

"Hey, happens to the best of us," Maya said, smiling, as the doors opened. The gentleman motioned for her to get out first. As she did, she slipped on her Bluetooth and punched the received calls button to see who she'd missed. Her eyes widened as she noticed the number. *Sean!*

"Dang it," she said, redialing the number and trying to think on the fly. She needed to immediately code Sean's number with a special ring. How was she going to explain that Maya was Macy?

"Macy?" Sean answered quickly. His voice immediately stirred her sugar.

"Uh, yes, it's Macy. You just called?"

"I did, but I couldn't hear anything."

Thank you, God! "Can you hear me now?"

"I hear you just fine," Sean said, his voice a husky whisper.

"Don't give me that wet-a-woman's-panties voice," Maya said, her thoughts of Sean as a "one-weekend wonder" already disappearing. "I called you days ago."

"I apologize," Sean said, his voice unchanged. "Duty called, I've been swamped. And speaking of work, is it working?"

"What?" Maya asked. She punched the button to unlock her Beemer and slid inside.

"My voice. Are you wet for me, Macy?"

"No," Maya lied, even as she squeezed her thighs together to quell her vibrating va-jay-jay.

"Can I make you wet for me, Macy?" Sean's manhood throbbed, and almost doubled in size within seconds.

Maya glanced at the clock on her dash. "Maybe, if you feed me first." Just days ago, nothing could have torn her away from her work, projects that were backlogged because of her time spent masquerading as "Martha the maid."

"I'm just finishing an appointment in Beverly Hills. Can I meet you somewhere?"

Maya was just about to pass the 10 Freeway, but she quickly crossed three lanes and hit the 10 West. "I'll meet you there. There's a nice little bistro, the Porterhouse, on Wilshire Boulevard. I can be there in about twenty, thirty minutes." Maya gave Sean the address, then hung up and called Trish.

"He called," she said simply.

"And?"

"And I'm headed to Beverly Hills to meet him for dinner."

"Girl, did you lose your rule book? The man hasn't called for days and when he does, you meet him just like that?"

"Just like that."

"It must be good is all I'm saying. So, what are you having for dinner, the double 'd' special?" Trish asked innocently.

"Forget you, heifa," Maya laughed. "I might take a lick of that double-dipped 'd' for dessert, though."

"Look, I'm just glad you're getting some," Trish said. "Since brotha man ex showed his 'a' with your neighbor tramp, all it's been is work, work, work. I'm glad you've found someone, Maya."

"I wish he were *the* one. I really like him, Trish."

"Girl, it had been what, six months since you got some? You'd like Flavor Flav if he ate the coochie right."

Maya guffawed. "You're a mess. I almost missed my exit." Maya became serious. "I just have one big problem."

"What?"

"Remember how I didn't tell him my name because I thought it was a one-night stand and was doing the what's done in Vegas stays in—"

"Maya! He still thinks your name is Macy and doesn't know that you work for *the* Zeke Brennan?"

"No."

"It's not like you to be dishonest. But don't trip; just tell him now."

If only it were that simple, Maya thought as she hung up the phone. And why wasn't it? Maya knew the answer. It was because of this crazy duplicitous assignment she was doing for Zeke, the one in which she was sworn to secrecy. Something about Sean seeped into her very soul and she felt if she just cracked the door to truth everything, including what she wasn't supposed to tell, would come tumbling out. Zeke was a generous man, and she stood to make a high five-figure bonus if he secured the Angel's Way project, even more if something she found on Sam Walters helped seal the deal. She could not only pay back what she owed him but also gain clout for future projects, clout that would go a long way when she struck out on her own. Just two more weeks, then she could stop hiding and tell Sean who she really was. After hearing the reason, she was sure he'd understand. But there was too much at stake to tell him now.

Less than an hour later, Maya was enjoying her tender porterhouse steak as much as she was the tantalizing sight before her. It was as if no time had passed since she and Sean had seen each other, talking as if they'd been friends for years.

"Why don't you ever talk about your work?" Sean asked.

Maya shrugged. "Not much to talk about, typing, filing, organizing, things like that."

"Doesn't sound like you like it, Macy." Sean paused to savor his forkful of tender beef. "Have you ever thought about switching careers, doing something you really wanted to do?"

"Sometimes," was Maya's vague answer.

Sean took a break from his dinner, leaned back, and crossed his arms. "If you could have the career of your dreams, be anything you wanted . . . what would that be?"

Maya Jamison, valued executive assistant to real estate mogul Zeke Brennan! is what Maya thought.

"An actress," is what she blurted out, Trish's vocation being the first thing she could actually say that came to mind.

"Really?" Sean asked. "For some reason that surprises me. Not that you don't look like a sexy movie star and all that, but somehow I took you for, I don't know, more the businesswoman type, running some multimillion-dollar business or something."

Maya's mind raced for a way to escape this minefield. Her sudden multipersona life was too tricky.

"What about you?" she asked, to hopefully divert the conversation off her. "You say you're over here from London, on business, but you haven't said what type of business."

Now it was Sean's turn to squirm. He never talked about his undercover work to anyone . . . ever. But something about Macy, he trusted her, and wanted her to be a part of his life, his whole life.

"I normally don't discuss it," he said after a pause. "But I'm a private investigator."

Maya's ears perked up immediately. *Maybe he can help me with this Sam Walters jerk.* "Really? That sounds exciting."

"Well, the excitement part is overrated," he countered. "But I do enjoy what I do, and I'm good at it."

"And if you don't know, just ask you?" Maya said with a smile in her voice.

"No, no, I didn't mean it like that. I said that because enjoying what one does normally leads to being good at it. When it's your passion . . . you want to be the best."

Maya wanted more than ever to tell Sean who she was, that she was living her dream, and of her plans to one day own her own company. But something stopped her, namely the memory of Zeke's stern command. *What we're doing goes no further than this office, Maya. . . .* That, and the fact that Sean was talking to Macy, not Maya.

"So, have you ever acted?" Sean asked when Maya didn't respond to what he'd said.

"Who, me?" Just that quickly, Maya forgot that acting was supposed to be her dream job. "Oh, not really . . . a little, uh, community theater." Actually she'd enjoyed or rather endured her one and only minor role alongside Trish, who'd pulled her in kicking and screaming when the actor scheduled to perform had gotten sick just hours before showtime. She'd delivered one line to the drag-queen-playing actor opposite her: *Right this way, Mr. Ma'am!*

"That's a start. You just have to keep moving toward your goal, if that's what you want." Sean took Maya's hand. "I believe we can do anything, Macy, have anything our heart desires. . . ."

The naked longing in his eyes told Maya that Sean was no longer thinking about careers. It was the perfect segue into what Maya was thinking about as well: becoming naughty Ms. Macy, ready to ride to the Marina and freak her man. "Anything?" she asked coyly, her eyes mirroring his hunger.

"I think we can order up dessert in my room," he said, signaling the waiter for the check.

Maya simply smiled, remembering the "double-dipped 'd'" she discussed with Trish earlier. She'd wanted a special dessert, and she was going to get it . . . all because as Sean said, she believed.

9

Maya peeked around the corner and saw Cecilia humming while busily polishing silver in the dining room. She headed toward the staircase.

"You want something?" Cecilia called out.

Maya jumped. Did the woman have eyes in the back of her head? "No, I was just . . . I'm just . . . headed upstairs to the master bedroom, to clean master." Maya walked into the dining room while stumbling all over her words. She was having no problem portraying the insecure, mousy maid at all! And why was she sounding like Cecilia and talking in broken English?

Cecilia must have wondered as well. She turned slowly and looked at her. "You all right, Martha?" she asked.

Maya bowed her head. "Fine, Cecilia. A little tired, though, and worried about my, uh, cousin. She's sick."

"What's the matter with her?"

Oh Lord, what's the matter with this nonexistent cousin? For as much of it as she'd been doing lately, Maya really didn't lie well. The old saying was true: what a tangled web we weave when first we practice to deceive. One lie necessitated another, and she worked hard to remain the spider and not become the fly. Just a little while longer, she thought before responding. And then truth could reign again. "She's, uh, pregnant." *Yeah, yeah, that's it.*

Cecilia gave a knowing nod and resumed shining the silver. "We do good work no matter how we feel," she said, wiping briskly. "Your cousin be fine. Having babies . . . natural to feel bad sometimes."

"Uh-huh." Maya rushed to get away from this line of lies.

Cecilia turned around abruptly. "You have babies, Martha, yes?"

"Uh, no."

Cecilia frowned. "Why not?"

"No boyfriend."

"Why not? You pretty girl."

Maya said nothing.

"Mr. Walters here on business," Cecilia said, the sudden change of subject rivaling the change in her demeanor. "You here to work only, you try nothing with Mr. Walters." Cecilia wagged her forefinger from side to side for emphasis.

"What!" Maya answered in her regular voice. Cecilia had shocked the Martha out of her.

Cecilia's eyes widened, then narrowed.

"Uh, I mean, I don't do that," Maya said, lowering her voice and scrunching her shoulders in an attempted quick recovery of her servile demeanor.

Cecilia cocked her head to the side.

"What I mean is"—Maya's voice was now almost a whisper—"I keep my body, uh, you know, for husband." The image of her lavishing mad love on Sean's manhood the night before rushed into her mind and almost made her guffaw.

"Ah, a virgin. Good girl."

"Thank you." *Thank you?* But it was the only thing she could think of to say. Hysterical laughter bubbled up inside her and she escaped up the stairs, swallowing giggles.

I can't wait to tell Trish—but no, she couldn't tell Trish, couldn't tell anybody about the crazy episode she'd just experienced. Somehow it didn't seem the thing to share with Zeke. But Sean? She could just imagine his laughing at her, mock sympathy for her predicament in his eyes. She wanted so much to share this with Sean, to share everything with him. . . .

Maya stopped at the linen closet to get fresh sheets and towels. *Getting ready to clean up an already clean room*, she thought sarcastically. It looked like the bed hadn't been slept in at all, but her orders were to change the sheets every day, no exceptions. Her mind reeled. Cecilia thought she might be interested in Sam Walters? Was she crazy, or had she just lost her mind? Maya's humor turned to anger as she replayed the conversation in her mind. *Is that the perception? That every poor, working woman is trying to snag a rich man?* The more she thought about it, the more Maya realized that maybe it was more than perception; maybe it was fact. Who in a dire situation wouldn't want a knight in shining armor to come sweep her off her feet and out of the hood? Maya's mind went instantly to Sean: fine, fit, and financially sound—a fact made obvious by his extended stay at the Ritz-Carlton. Sean's exclusive lifestyle definitely added to his appeal. Maya's anger dissipated a bit and she saw "Martha" through Cecilia's eyes. If circumstances were different, maybe Martha would make a play for the sloppy yet well-off real estate Brit.

But there was no more time for daydreaming; Maya was on a mission. Her talk with Zeke had inspired her to accomplish what she came here for: to unearth proof that Sam Walters was who he said he was, or the imposter that Zeke believed. That the gig was going to soon be up regardless, and that Jade's attempts to usurp her executive position had so far failed, were further motivation. It would be a feather in her corporate cap if she could help Zeke expand his California real estate kingdom, maybe uncover something about B&A's main competition, something about why the Rosenthal Group's portfolio was in Sam's briefcase. Thankfully Sam Walters hadn't been around much in the past week, so snooping around his impersonal palace was easier. Cecilia had lightened up also, finally satisfied that Martha could tuck a sheet corner, fluff a pillow, clean the kitchen, and run a vacuum. At least this was what Maya deduced by the fact she was no longer being subjected to what felt like the white glove test.

Maya finished changing the sheets, but instead of going into the bathroom, she stepped inside the master's massive walk-in closet. She stopped just inside the doors, hands on hips, and looked around. The contents were basically the same as the last time she'd looked there. A few suits: navies, browns, blacks, dress shirts, polo shirts, casual slacks, shoes, and various pieces of underwear neatly folded on the closet's shelves. Martha turned slowly in the center of the closet, willing herself to see something, anything out of the ordinary.

She started at the back of the closet and searched the pockets of each garment. Nothing. Next she took the step ladder from the closet's corner and checked the top shelves, which contained shoes in see-through containers. She opened each container and looked in each shoe. Why she did that was anybody's guess but people hid strange things in strange places.

Maya closed the closet doors and headed for the master bath, picking up the fresh clean towels to replace the dirty ones along the way. Inside the massive room that boasted a Jacuzzi tub, steam and water showers, and a separate vanity area, Maya once again paused and looked around with her best detective eye. As with the bed, the bathroom looked untouched, the towels hanging as pristinely as they had the day before. Clearly, Sam Walters had spent the night elsewhere.

"Interesting," Maya said as she slowly made her way around the bathroom area. She idly touched the few, generic toiletries, ran her hand along the dry marble basin. *Waddling Walters with a woman?* Maya smiled, trying to imagine the geeky, conservative stuffed-shirt Brit getting his swerve on. But she'd never thought of it before, of Sam Walters seeing someone while here on business. Maybe this was a noteworthy development—Sam Walters, supposedly new on the scene in Los Angeles, having personal, romantic ties.

Maya replaced the towels and methodically wiped down the basin. All the while her mind raced. *Who would someone like Sam Walters be involved with? Where would he meet her?* Maya's heartbeat quickened with the intuitive knowledge that she was onto something. But what?

Maya heard Cecilia coming up the stairs and realized she'd probably taken too long to make a bed and change out towels in an already pristine room. She grabbed the old linens and headed toward the door. Just as she was about to exit, a slip of paper caught her eye. She grabbed it quickly, just as Cecilia rounded the hall.

"I'm ready to wash these," Martha said, deftly sliding the paper into her pants pocket. Cecilia simply nodded and continued down the hall to one of three guest bedrooms.

Maya quickly finished the washing and within the hour was headed toward the bus stop. She couldn't wait to lose Martha. Her head itched under the hot, tight wig cap, her eyes hurt from looking through lens as thick as cola bottles, and her back hurt from trying to scrunch down the fiery spirit that was Maya Jamison into the insecure entity named Martha Jones. Maya rubbed her neck to ease the tension there, praying the bus wouldn't be late. The faster and farther she got from Pacific Avenue and Sam's Playa Del Rey home, the more she could relax.

As soon as Maya got seated on the Metro 115, she whipped off the thick glasses, opening and closing her eyes in an attempt to regain clear vision. *I really need to quit wearing these things*, she thought as her vision stabilized. Even though she tried as much as possible not to actually look through them, it wasn't always possible. Maya didn't want to damage her twenty-twenty vision behind this charade.

She plugged in her iPod, pulled out the Black-Berry she finally felt safe enough to carry with her to Sam's house, and settled in for the twenty minutes that was part one of her bus trip. Although she checked her e-mail partly to ward off detractors, she didn't really need to. It was amazing how differently she was treated in her housekeeper getup. Maya wasn't vain, but she was used to getting her share of looks and flirts. But aside from a toothless, homeless man and an overeager dog trying to turn her leg into a humping post at the bus stop, Maya hadn't received so much as a head nod. She was a bit surprised that it mattered, but had to admit, it did. Even homely housekeepers needed love.

Nearing her stop, Maya placed her BlackBerry in her purse and stood up. She placed her hand in her pocket and felt the paper she'd forgotten about. The tension she'd rubbed away earlier returned with a vengeance when she looked down on the paper and saw the last thing she expected to find written there . . . her phone number.

Maya was so rattled she missed her stop and had to walk back a block to catch her connection. When it arrived, it was a jam-packed bus. Just as well. Maya wasn't in the frame of mind to resume checking e-mails on her BlackBerry; especially since one of them had been from Ester, reporting on yet another of Jade's undermining schemes. Maya had something for Jade's "a" later, but there was another level of madness she needed to deal with now. Sam Walters with her phone number scrawled on a piece of paper? What was that about?

Maya pondered the Sam Walters question all evening, ignoring calls from people who usually always got through: Trish and Stretch. But when Sean called and she let him also go to voice mail, she knew this Martha Jones mess was eating up too much of her life. She had to make a breakthrough quickly and take back her life.

"This charade game is getting ready to be over," she announced resolutely to Lucky. Lucky's ears perked up, his eyes fixed on Maya. "First," Maya continued, buoyed by her attentive audience, "I've got one more week of housecleaning, and I've got to make it count. If I can help uncover some unsavory plot against Zeke, led by a role-playing Sam Walters,

I can ride that wave right into my own company, and gladly give Jade what she's trying so hard to steal."

Maya got up from the couch and continued, walking back and forth in her living room. "No, on second thought, I need to handle Jade. She's proven in no uncertain terms that she can't be trusted, trying to move into my office and I'm not even gone yet."

Lucky found something more interesting to focus on at that point: fly, gnat, Maya wasn't sure what. But two swipes of the paw and he was off the couch and down the hall, off to capture what he obviously thought belonged to him.

There's one more thing, Maya thought, as she plopped down on the couch and hugged a throw pillow to her stomach. She had to come clean with Sean; tell him she was Maya, not Macy, and the reason why she lied. She reasoned that would be easier to do once she'd shed the Martha persona and was back into Maya full-time.

This three-persona lifestyle had taken its toll. She was getting ready to kick Martha and Macy to the curb, and roll up on Sean as Maya and Maya only. It was the woman she really was and prayed that for Sean . . . it would be all the woman he needed.

In the meantime, there was something Maya needed. An answer for why Sam Walters had her phone number.

10

"Just be careful," Neil cautioned Sean. "These guys never give something for nothing. If they offer any information of value, they're going to want something in return."

"Nothing in life is free, man," Sean responded. He was well aware of how the game worked; and aside from a tidy sum of "greasing the pipe" money, he had a tidbit of information he felt the men he was meeting with could use.

Neil continued. "Campbell worked for Zeke for years and his partner knows L.A. politics like the back of his hand. I think you'll move your little project along tonight, my friend."

Sean looked at his watch. It was getting close to the time for his dinner meeting. "All right, Neil, let me get moving."

"Sure thing, man, take it easy."

"Hey, if it comes to me easy, I'll take it that way. Thanks for the connect, man."

A little over an hour later Sean, now Sam Walters, sat in a corner booth of the dimly lit restaurant, able to scope out the entire establishment without being seen.

He cautiously nursed a Manhattan and mindlessly twirled the cherry garnish. Without thought, Sean had morphed into a slightly awkward, good ole Black guy who easily blended into the woodwork. His undercover persona was the exact opposite of the real Sean Wynn, who if he'd walked in as himself would already have been accosted by at least two of the three tables full of women surrounding him. Even with paunch, mustache, and beard, he'd received a wink from a forty-something strawberry blonde.

Sam politely waved away the waitress who came over to refresh his drink. He doubted he'd even finish the barely touched Manhattan in front of him. Sean was a very light drinker, but he'd learned over the years that having a drink around gave off a casual, just-one-of-the-boys air. Businessmen he met tended to lighten up with a drink in their hands. They usually ended up drinking much more than he, but with his jovial, self-effacing personality, the imbibers never noticed.

He hoped the men he was waiting to meet would drink themselves into a state loose enough to provide the investigative break he was looking for. He'd been in L.A. a month, and while he'd talked patience to Joseph Rosenthal, he was ready for this case to be over. This wasn't how he usually felt about his work; he usually loved his work, the challenge, the thrill. But something had happened to him, and her name was Macy. Having her in his life suddenly made the million or so he stood to make on this job seem less important. He wanted to hang out with her, spend time with her. He wanted to let her in on his life, on who he really was. Yes, he'd told her he was an investigator but she had no idea about his double identity as Sam Walters. He knew he could never tell her that, not only because of the confidentiality clause in his contract but more importantly, for her own safety. He wanted to share everything of who he was with this woman who'd occupied his mind from the moment she walked toward him in a hot red dress.

He'd have to do that later. Two men, obviously the ones for whom he waited, stepped into the restaurant. One looked to be in his forties, striking but not handsome, clean-cut, businesslike. *He must be the politician*, Sean thought, as he watched the hostess point him out to the duo. The second man was older than the first, balding and portly but still with a commanding presence. Sean correctly guessed this was Phillip Campbell, the man who'd worked with Zeke Brennan for years.

Sean stood with hand outstretched as the men approached. After introductions and small talk, Sean got down to business, confirming what the men had heard, that he was itching to buy some huge chunks of real estate.

"Well, your timing is perfect," Phillip assured him. "Me and my partners are looking for a fourth and final investor to try and break the stranglehold that Zeke Brennan has on the L.A. market."

"Join the crowd," Sean said. "I hear the Rosenthal Group is trying to do the same thing."

"True, but they don't know what I know," Phillip said.

"Nor I," the ex-politician, Mark Dobbs, chimed in.

"And what's that, gentlemen?" Sean asked casually. "Wait, first, let me buy you guys a drink."

Two hours and a couple hundred dollars' worth of drinks and dinner later, Sean pounded the treadmill of his hotel's gym. He'd decided not to call Macy after his meeting; he needed the night to digest the information

he'd uncovered and to strategize his next move. The
information he received was even better than expected, and added a new and lucrative dimension
to what he wanted to achieve in L.A. Getting there
successfully, though; that's what Sean had to figure
out. Exercise helped him clear his head and think.

Mark Dobbs had confirmed what Sean suspected:
Zeke had political insiders in his back pocket, from the
mayor's office on down. Thing was, the system had
been in place for so long, and involved so many people
from so many sectors of the city, it would take a vir-
tual army of attorneys and investigators to successfully
unravel the layers of cover-ups. Even lawyers who'd
normally go after a corruption case like this had been
paid off. That's what Zeke did. He convinced the best
of the best, those who started as opponents, to join his
team. Then he made it worth their financial while to
do so. At least that's what everyone in the world of real
estate suspected. So far, Brennan & Associates had
been too savvy to leave any type of trail that offered
concrete proof. The speculation was rampant, the
belief absolute. The validity of some sort of corruption
was in the numbers. How could one architectural firm
legitimately outbid so many other companies, year
after year? And, as many suspected, even be the blind
partner in dozens of other deals throughout the state?

This was information Sean had expected. What he
hadn't expected was to find out that five years ago,
Joseph Rosenthal had barely missed being indicted on
money laundering charges involving dummy corpo-
rations and offshore bank accounts. There was also a
shady Mafia connection and at least one murder that
pointed, at least indirectly, to the Rosenthal Group.
Sean remembered his last meeting with Joseph, the
barely concealed rage and the obvious contempt

Joseph held for Zeke Brennan. At the time Sean attributed it to simple business rivalry, albeit for billions. But was it more?

Sean pondered this question as he stepped from the gym's sauna into the shower, and even as he returned to his room and ordered room service. He'd mostly picked at his meal with Mark and Phillip, preferring to keep his attention squarely on what they said. The workout had stirred up his appetite. He'd just begun to enjoy a chef's salad and baked potato when his phone rang.

"Hey, you," he said, pleased that Macy had called him. So far, he'd usually been the initiator.

"Hey back. You busy?"

"Not too, for you," Sean replied. "That's if you don't mind a little salad munching in your ear while we talk."

"You're just now having dinner? A bit late, isn't it?"

"Yeah, long day at work. But productive, though. What about you?"

"The same," Maya said, thinking about the things Martha had uncovered at Sam's house.

"Tell me about it," Sean said, digging into his salad.

"Not much to tell," Maya answered. "The usual secretarial stuff, but my boss is, uh, getting ready for a big meeting." She hoped he wouldn't ask for details.

"What type of company did you say you worked for?"

Maya needed to change this line of questioning. "Always the investigator," she answered, putting some sexy into her voice. "Well, Mr. Wynn, I have something I'd like for you to investigate."

"Oh, really?" Sean's appetite quickly went from his mouth to his manhood.

"Yes, really," Maya answered, lying back on her

bed and idly rubbing her nana. "Do you think you're *up* for a job like this?"

"Oh yes, I'm definitely up for the job." Sean shifted in his chair, giving his quickly engorging shaft room to grow.

"Then tell me . . . how would you go about conducting this investigation?"

"First," Sean said, "I'd have to invite the subject of the investigation over to my hotel room. I'm very private, and very thorough. My research would have to be done behind closed doors."

"Okay, so I'd have to come over."

"Uh-huh."

"And then?"

"The first thing I'd have to do is conduct a strip search."

"You mean . . . take my clothes off?" Maya asked innocently.

"Oh yes, Ms. Macy Williams. I'd have to determine there was nothing . . . um . . . up your sleeve."

"Oh . . . so you'd just take off my blouse."

"No." Sean's voice went deeper. "I'd have to check everywhere."

"Is that so?"

"That's so."

"Okay, then what?"

"Now, now, not so fast. Let's get those clothes off you first."

Maya squirmed on her bed, trying to douse the fire starting between her legs. "Okay, go ahead."

"We'd start with those sexy sandals you always wear. I'd take them off and give you a quick foot massage. Your feet are so pretty, I'd also have to suck those toes."

"That's allowed. Massaging and sucking? Are

you sure this wouldn't jeopardize your investigator/client relationship?"

"My darling, the way I massage and suck would ensure the *continuation* of my relationship!"

Maya laughed, enjoying the conversation. "Oh, really?"

"I don't want to sound vain but yes, I think so. And then, only if my client had no objections, I'd continue the massage from her feet to her calves . . . thighs . . . but wait. My client would probably want to become more comfortable at this point, so I'd carefully remove whatever clothing she wore, pants, skirt, dress, whatever."

Sean waited for a response but, hearing none, continued.

"I'd take off her underwear later and if she was wearing thong panties, I might not take them off at all but instead, use them to help enhance my, um, investigation."

Maya moaned audibly, remembering how Sean had used the string of her thong to double the stimulation that first his fingers and later his shaft provided.

Sean chuckled softly. "And then . . . I'd continue the massage, kneading my client's soft, lush buttocks and firm breasts, rubbing the tension from her shoulders, relaxing the muscles in her back. Are you wet for me, Macy?"

"Uh-huh."

Sean pulled his hard penis from what had become a very confining pair of briefs. He rubbed himself casually as he continued. "And then I'd continue the massage, but instead of hands, I'd use my tongue." Sean heard a click on the other end. "Macy? Macy?"

Maya looked at her phone and saw it had disconnected. She'd placed the receiver under her ear and had begun to use both hands on her body. She'd disconnected from him accidentally.

Sean waited for a moment. *Did Macy just hang up on me?* A knowing smile came to his lips. His manhood hardened more as he imagined her pleasuring herself. He began to do the same when his phone rang.

"Are you ready for my tongue?" he murmured in a low, husky voice. He wasn't worried about clients as this was his personal cell phone number.

There was a moment of silence before a voice answered, "I'm always ready for your tongue, Sean Wynn."

Oh, damn! Tangier! Sean bolted upright and his hard-on went soft at the same time. "Tangier, hello."

"Hmm. So that question wasn't meant for me, I take it?"

"I'm sorry I haven't called you. I've been busy." Sean immediately regretted the ill-timed comment.

"So I gather," Tangier replied smoothly. "I know the things you can do with that wonderful tongue of yours. She's a lucky woman."

"I've been busy with work," Sean replied in a clipped tone. "As for what I said when I answered—"

"I'm a big girl and we're not married," Tangier interrupted. "You don't have to lie about your sex life. You're a healthy, hearty, virile male. And L.A. is full of beautiful women. It's only natural you'd find a *temporary* friend while you're there. As long as she stays there when you come home, all is well. And you're using protection, right?"

Sean didn't like the possessive sound of Tangier's statement or her misperceived right to check into how he conducted his sexual affairs, but chose to let it slide. "How are you?"

"Missing you," Tangier replied, wisely following Sean's obvious desire to change the subject. "How's work going?"

"Slow, but I'm making progress."

"How long do you think you'll be gone?"

"I don't know."

"Sounds like it could be a long time."

"Maybe."

"I want to come see you, Sean."

"No, Tangier."

"Just like that, no room for discussion?"

"No. You know I don't mix business with pleasure."

"So doing things with your tongue is part of your investigation?"

Sean's phone beeped. Macy. "Look, Tangier, I've got to go."

"So do I," Tangier replied brusquely. She hung up without a good-bye.

Sean looked at his caller ID this time before clicking over. "What took you so long to call back?" he asked.

"I was . . . you got me all hot, Sean. I had to finish what you started."

"I would have been happy to do that."

"It wasn't planned. The phone disconnected and I, well . . ."

"No worries, my mocha nymph. Why don't I come over and, uh, tuck you in?"

"I'd love that, but I've got a busy day tomorrow."

"Are you sure? I won't stay long."

"Tempting offer, but not tonight. Maybe we can get away for the weekend. Have you visited San Diego?"

Sean and Maya made plans for the weekend and then bade each other good night. Thanks to Tangier, Sean no longer needed to take a cold shower. No, what he needed, he thought as the first wave of sleep overtook him, was a good weekend dose of Macy. Sometimes his most brilliant ideas came when he was away from the grind of investigating. He would take the weekend to step back from all he'd learned, a process that would help him start fresh with a game plan Monday morning. His game plan for making Macy a permanent part of the Wynn enterprise was already in operation.

Sean was on Maya's mind as she went to sleep as well. *This weekend*, she thought as her eyelids became heavy. *This weekend I come clean and tell Sean who I really am.* The timing felt right; Maya felt he would understand. After all, none of the lies had been harmful, nothing that affected their relationship directly. *And then after I tell him about Maya, and once the investigation wraps, I'll tell him about Martha as well.*

11

The shrill sound of her cell phone woke Maya from a deep sleep. "Hello?" she answered groggily.

"Martha, sorry to wake you," Cecilia said sincerely. "Can you work today? I have family emergency."

Cecilia? Maya struggled to a sitting position, while her mind raced. She had meetings, reports, a rarely requested lunch date with her brother. All this before rushing to a last-minute hair appointment that became available only after Maya bribed her football-fanatic hairdresser with two tickets to a Chargers game. And now Cecilia was asking her to be Martha for four hours? "I, uh, I don't think so," she said before she'd finished processing her thoughts.

"Very important," Cecilia said. "My mother very sick. I must go see her."

"Can't you call the agency?"

"Mr. Walters very choosy, must approve all girls who work for him." Cecilia paused, then pulled what she thought was her trump card. "We pay you double."

Whoop-de-doo, Maya thought, even as she remembered that, one, her housekeeper salary was going to charity and, two, and more importantly, this might be

her one and only chance to be in Sam Walters's home
alone. "Okay," she replied quickly, jumping out of bed
at the same time.

"Thank you," Cecilia said, proud that pulling the
wage card had done the trick. She told Maya to pick
up the house key at the agency, and then gave her one
last piece of advice. "Remember, you no likey Mr.
Walters," she said sagely.

What is wrong with this chick? Maya took a breath
and reined in her temper. "Right, no likey," she responded dryly. Maya imagined it was Cecilia who
"likey'd" Sam Walters, and if Maya could, she'd
gladly help Cecilia get an overnight stay in the Walters master suite. Housekeepers needed love too.

After telling him about the chance to search Sam
Walter's house, Zeke gladly rescheduled their meeting and pushed the due dates for her reports. She
spoke briefly with Jade, a little longer with Ester, and
half an hour later, Maya stepped out the door and
headed for the cleaning company's administrative
office to pick up the key to Mr. Walters's house.
From there she caught two buses to Playa del Rey.
She'd briefly considered driving her Beemer today
and parking down the street. But in the end she decided that even though it meant an additional bus and
extra hour of travel time, it wasn't worth the risk of
being seen. She was close to this gig ending anyhow,
and maybe close to it all having been worthwhile.

Maya took in the beauty of the ocean view as she
walked from her bus stop toward the Marina that surrounded Playa Del Rey. She would love to live by the
ocean, and maybe one day, when Jamison and Company was up and running, she'd turn that dream into
reality. These thoughts caused Maya to quicken her
pace. Finding something on Sam Walters that would

help Zeke might make the journey from Brennan &
Associates to Jamison and Company a shorter one.

Maya punched in the code to the wrought-iron
gate. She admired the pristine landscaping before
quickly placing the key in the door lock and walking inside. It felt weird knowing she was alone in the
home. She stood in the foyer for a brief moment and
looked around, for the first time feeling she actually
had the leisure to do so. She admired the intricate
marble work in the entryway, the delicate carvings
etched in the crown molding, the sparkling crystal
chandelier. She was just about to make a closer in-
spection of what she guessed was an authentic Van
Gogh when she stopped herself.

"No, Maya," she said under her breath. "Stay
focused. Get the job done."

Maya walked to the hall closet and as always, set
her purse inside. With one exception: She pulled out
a small, digital camera and placed it in her baggy
pant pocket. She then walked quickly, purposefully
toward the forbidden office doors. Her heartbeat
quickened as she placed her hand on the knob.
Locked, just as she figured. She walked through the
kitchen into a small utility room, and began going
through the drawers. Her hope was that there'd be an
extra set of keys, or at the very least the key that
would let her peek behind door number one.

No luck. Maya went through every drawer in the
utility room and then every one in the kitchen. She
looked in the pantry, the hall closets, and the drawers
in the dining room. Maya eyed the stairway a
moment before heading to the master bedroom.
She'd spent plenty of time in that room, though, and
didn't hold out hope of finding much there.

Maya turned the corner and stopped, a bit taken

aback to see the door to the master suite closed. Her eyes widened with the realization that Mr. Walters could very well be home. She'd assumed since it was midmorning, he would be gone.

"Stop being silly," she whispered, even as she continued to stand unmoving near the top stair. He probably was gone, she reasoned, and maybe Cecilia always opened the door before Maya came to work. There was only one way to find out.

Maya squared her shoulders and walked toward the closed bedroom door like a soldier marching into battle. She stopped just outside it and knocked tentatively. When she didn't get an answer, Maya opened the door. "Mista Walters?" she called out, in her best simple sista voice. And then a bit louder, "Anybody home?"

When nothing but silence greeted her, Maya relaxed. Aside from their first meeting, she'd never had to deal one-on-one with Mr. Walters and she surely didn't want to do so today. She smiled at her unnecessary nervousness and walked through the sitting room toward the actual bedroom area with renewed confidence. Turning the corner, once again, she stopped short. That the bed was disheveled wasn't the problem. The problem was one big foot sticking out from the bottom of the sheets.

Her first instinct was to run—fast. The prospect of seeing Sam Walter's naked fat backside seemed like nothing nice. Having him wake up to find her gawking was an even less attractive prospect. She almost tripped over her feet trying to do a one-eighty. As she turned, however, something out of the ordinary caught her eye. The door was open. The smaller, always locked closet door was ajar. *The key. Maybe the key to the office is in there!*

Maya stood by the wall between the sitting room and the bedroom area, undecided. On one hand, it was incredibly risky to cross the room and attempt a look-see in the closet. On the other, this was her last week at Sam Walters's, and perhaps her one and only day to get inside that office. If she crossed the room and he woke up, she could lie and say she was looking for, for what? Maya didn't know, but she did know this: that it was better to have tried and failed than not to have tried at all. Quickly modifying her plans, she hurried back to the linen closet in the hallway, took out a couple of fresh towels, and headed back to the bedroom. The smaller closet was by the master bath. If Mr. Walters woke up, she'd say she was headed there.

Maya barely breathed as she tiptoed back into the room, through the sitting area, and around the corner where Sam Walters lay sleeping. She took one tentative step, then another. The closet was across and to the left of her, the king-sized bed to her right. Maya prayed Mr. Walters was a deep sleeper, and that she would make no sounds.

Maya took three hurried steps toward the closet—stopped. No movement from stage right. *You can do this, Maya.* Her heartbeat, already frenzied, sped up more. About five or six more steps and she'd be at the closet. She prayed what she wanted, whatever that was, would be clearly visible inside. She took another step, then another. A small creak sounded from across the room. *Oh, God, don't let him turn over. Okay, let him turn over but don't let him wake up. Please, God, please, Jesus.* Maya hadn't gone to church in years, but she'd do a holy dance and donate her next check if God kept Mr. Walters sleeping. She took another step, and then another. *A couple more and I'm there.* Maya smiled. She could almost touch the closet door.

And then she was there. She placed her hand on the knob and before pulling the door open wider, looked back at the slumbering Sam, or rather Sam's ass, because that was the sight that greeted her when she turned her head. What had been hidden when Maya was on the other side of the room now filled her vision in all its round, brown glory.

Maya was shocked into paralysis. She couldn't move. And she couldn't stop staring at Sam Walters's ass! It was, well, it was a gorgeous ass. A stunning ass really, one that seemed unlikely to be found inside the baggy khakis that was common Sam Walters attire. Maya stood transfixed, ass-notized. Those creamy brown cheeks worked better than any swinging pendulum. She drank in the sight of those strong, round buns, the two perfect dimples, and the perfectly placed mole at the top of his . . . *Sean!*

Maya stumbled backward, her hand near her heart. A pointy part of the camera that she forgot she held hit her squarely in the chest. Before she had time to consider the consequences, she aimed and clicked. She held her breath. He didn't move. Suddenly she couldn't breathe; surely she was in the twilight zone or the not right zone or the please-let-me-see-the-sanity-light-on zone. She shook her head slightly and looked again. It was still there, in pristine detail. *Sean's "a." What's Sean Wynn's "a" doing in Sam Walters's bed?* Maya's mind flooded with questions and confusion. Since she couldn't think, she did what any intelligent, successful, brave, strong woman would do—she ran like hell. Maya fled out of the room and down the steps, shoving the towels in the downstairs hall closet as she grabbed her purse. She didn't stop to think about an explanation of her hasty departure for Cecilia, didn't stop to think at all. She fled out of the house and barely remembered to lock the dead bolt before continuing through the gate and down the street. She ran past her bus stop and kept on running, until her heart pounded and her throat burned. Only then did she slow, and realize her face was wet with tears. When had she begun crying? She also realized that somewhere along the way she'd lost her glasses, and her wig was askew. Maya walked another block to the next bus stop, and sat on the bench—stunned. It was crazy; too bizarre to get her head around. There was no doubt in her mind that the ass she'd seen in Sam Walter's king-sized bed belonged to the same man she'd made love to in another bed, one at the Ritz-Carlton Hotel, in the room assigned to her dream man, Sean Wynn. The madness had reached epic proportions; it was time to call backup. Zeke was her boss but Trish was her best friend. Maya had gotten lost in a masquerade and needed some sista-girl help to get out. She reached a shaky hand into her purse for the BlackBerry.

12

Sean's eyes fluttered open, slowly at first and then wide-awake. He jerked his head up, only to have a shooting pain explode inside it. He lay back on the bed and reached blindly for his watch . . . ten thirty. *Ten thirty?* Sean ignored his pounding head and forced himself to sit up. He rubbed his eyes, trying to remember what had happened to cause this pounding headache. And hadn't a sound woken him up just now?

Sean opened his eyes and looked around him. Immediately he saw that all was not normal. The closet door where he kept his disguise materials was ajar. Sean felt his head, his face: clean. So he'd taken off the wig and facial hair. He looked around; good, they weren't lying around, so obviously he'd placed them in the closet. But why was the door open? He always locked that door after putting away his Walters disguise . . . always.

Then he remembered what had happened. On top of the wine he drank at dinner, he'd taken sinus pills when he stopped by the house on his way to the Ritz to pick up some files. The medication made him drowsy, and he'd decided to spend the night in Playa. Because of Tangier's repeated calls, calls that went unanswered, he'd turned off his phone. Had he not, the alarm that was always enabled would have awakened him.

Sean took a quick shower, put on his Sam Walters persona, and walked downstairs. He needed coffee, black and strong. He saw the note as soon as he walked into the kitchen, Cecilia and yet another family emergency. How many people were in that woman's family? And were weekly dramas a prerequisite to belonging? The note said that Martha would be coming in early, yet here it was eleven o'clock and there was no sign of her. He thought about calling the agency and canceling her workday altogether. And then he thought about the fact that it would be money out of her pocket and changed his mind. He was rich now but not a stranger to struggle, having been determined to make it on his own after graduating from college. It had taken him a good five years before he left paycheck to paycheck behind. He tried hard not to forget those days, memories that helped maintain compassion.

Sean took his mug of coffee to the office, and was relieved that at least he'd remembered to lock this door. Once inside, he began a flurry of phone calls. He needed to make sure his investment was in place, that the partners from China were on board with him and Phillip, and that his meeting with Joseph was still on schedule. The faster he wrapped up work, the faster he could wrap his arms around Macy Johnson . . . lose himself in all that chocolate sweetness.

Thinking constantly about one woman was something new to Sean Wynn. He'd never been a player-player, but usually juggled three or four women in as many cities. Tangier was the closest thing to a steady, but even she didn't have exclusive status. What was it about Macy that filled him up, made the thought of another woman irrelevant? Sean smiled. He was getting to spend a long, love-filled weekend finding out.

13

"I knew something was going on with you," Trish said as soon as the waitress had taken their order. "Now, start at the beginning and tell me everything."

Maya began with the morning Zeke had called her into a meeting and announced he wanted her to be a maid.

"A who?"

"Yes, girl, you heard me."

"Did you tell him you didn't know nothin' 'bout birthin' no babies?" Trish asked, mimicking Hattie McDaniels and her famous line in *Gone With the Wind*.

"All one tells Zeke Brennan is yes," Maya replied. She told Trish how she'd immediately copped an attitude toward her temporary new boss, Sam Walters, and how Cecilia thought she might be trying to go from housemaid to housewife. Trish interspersed the appropriate "hmmphs" and "tsks" and "no, he didn'ts" as Maya continued.

"So, last week I found a piece of paper in his bedroom, and guess what was on it?"

"What?"

"My phone number."

"And?"

"What was Sam Walters doing with my number, that's and."

"You're working for him, Maya."

"Yes, but through an agency. He should have the agency's phone number, not my cell."

"Maybe Cecilia wasn't the only one with the housemaid-to-housewife idea."

"Don't make me throw up, and you're missing my point. Sam Walters doesn't know Maya, he knows Martha!"

"Not necessarily. You said he's into real estate. Maybe he's checking B&A out like y'all are checking him out. Having your number probably has to do with your working with Zeke."

Trish putting it that way made perfect sense. What Maya was about to tell her, did not. "Your logic is quite sound except for one thing. . . ." She paused dramatically and Trish, understanding how to follow the script, remained silent.

"Sam Walters knows Sean Wynn."

Trish sat back and crossed her arms. "All that dramatic buildup and that's the punch line? That the man you work for knows the man you're sleeping with?"

"Sleep would be the operative word," Maya said, leaning forward to deliver the punch line. "I saw Sean asleep in Sam's bed this morning."

Trish blinked her eyes rapidly for several seconds, saying nothing. "Uh-uh," is what came out when she finally found her voice.

Maya gave Trish the details of what had unfolded that morning, ending with her running away faster than Marion Jones.

"That's why I couldn't take it anymore," Maya continued. "I had to talk to you about this crazy situation so you can help me figure out what's going on."

"Let me get this straight. You found *your* man asleep in *another* man's bed, and you need *my* help to see what's up? C'mon now, Maya. Miss J didn't raise no fools."

"What?" Maya asked honestly.

Trish looked at her pointedly.

"You think Sean's sleeping with Sam?" Maya laughed nervously. "Uh-uh, no way. There's no way Sean's gay."

"Who knows? He may be traveling on the bi-way."

Maya sat back stunned. Sean gay, or even bi? It didn't make sense. And if he was, how did he play into what Sam was doing in L.A.'s world of real estate? Was he involved? Did he come over from London with Sam? Were they partners, in more ways than one? "I need a drink," Maya said finally. She signaled over the waiter and instead of the tea she'd been drinking, ordered a glass of pinot noir.

Trish ordered one as well and in between sips, they discussed possible reasons behind the Sam/Sean liaison.

"He said he was in town on business, right?"

Maya nodded yes. "I told you he's a private investigator."

"You didn't tell me that!"

"I didn't?"

"You've been seriously holding out on your girl. See what happens when you don't keep a sista informed? You get hoodwinked, bamboozled—"

"Whatever, Trish."

"He's got to be either working for, or sleeping with, or both, your boy Sam."

Maya thought for a moment and then slowly shook

her head. "No. And I'm not trying to be in denial about Sean's possible booty bumping. I just don't feel it, and I think I would."

"Yeah, Terry McMillan probably thought she would too."

"Trish, that is wrong on so many levels."

"I'm just saying . . ."

"And *I'm* just saying Sean Wynn is not gay. Look, this is complicated enough as it is. Let's just go from the premise that he isn't, for now. That would mean he's working for or with Sam. Which makes sense because Sam's trying to get in on the real estate action. He's probably got Sean checking out all the . . ."

"All the what?"

Maya's eyes narrowed as she continued. "All the players in the L.A. real estate game. Which includes B&A, which means Zeke Brennan, which means me. Oh my gosh, Trish, do you think Sean knows who I really am? That all this time he's been playing me just to get the 411 for Sam Walters?"

Maya's confusion turned to hurt and then anger, all in the space of about thirty seconds. It had been enough to find out Sean was acquainted with the very man she'd been spying on. If it turned out Sean had been spying on her for this very same man, and that their lovemaking had been just sex after all, she'd be devastated. She looked at Trish, her expression plaintive. "If it turns out another man has been dishonest, has betrayed me . . ." Her sentence trailed off as she looked away, tried to peer into a tomorrow that didn't include Sean Wynn. Of course, the easiest thing to do would be to outright ask him to tell the truth about who she was and perhaps solve the mystery. She'd been too stunned to do anything but get out of the house the day she'd seen him in Sam's bed.

And she too had been deceptive. Would he even want to talk to her if he learned the truth now, like this? Oh, what a tangled web she'd woven.

"Let's not jump to conclusions, Maya. First, you don't know for sure Sean is working for Sam. And even if he is, you don't know they're investigating B&A. And how would he even know you work there?"

"Please. Just Google me and I come up all over the place, mostly in connection with B&A, and Zeke Brennan."

"Well, even if that's so, and we don't know that it is, he doesn't know Maya, remember? He knows Macy."

Maya rolled her eyes.

"Have there been pictures posted on the Internet since you cut your hair?"

"I don't think so."

"You look very different with short hair, Maya. Unless someone is purposely looking for you to have changed your look, one wouldn't necessarily suspect it's you, unless they have your pictures side by side or something.

"I can't tell you not to be upset because where there's stinky, there's usually doodoo, and this has all the qualities of a funky situation. But you've got to stay cool, keep yourself together so you can get to the bottom of what's going on."

The women were silent awhile, trying to digest a heavy conversation. "What are you going to do?" Trish finally asked.

Maya shrugged. "I don't know. Going to Zeke feels like I'm betraying Sean, and vice versa. If I am wrong about Sean being involved with Sam's investigating the L.A. market, maybe my exposing him will mess up whatever he's really investigating. On the other hand, he was in Sam Walters's bed today!

That house has three, four guest rooms. Why was he
in the master suite?"

Trish started singing EU's "Doin' Da Butt."

Maya tried to keep a straight face, but the atmosphere soon lightened with both their laughter. By
evening's end, Maya still wasn't sure about anything
in the Sean/Sam/Zeke/B&A/housekeeper/hotshot executive assistant situation. But from here on out, she
had a sounding board. Between her and Trish, she'd
keep from being boo-boo the fool.

14

Maya's stomach churned as she waited for Zeke in his office. She'd been a bundle of nerves all weekend and, after deciding to put Sean on hold until further notice, sexually deprived as well. She didn't know how long she'd go without seeing him; she just knew that since seeing his ass in Sam Walters's bed, the trip to San Diego was off. He'd instantly felt something was up. Maya frowned as she remembered their conversation.

"Just like that, you want us to take a break from each other. And I'm supposed to believe it's work? Come on, Macy. You hate your job, have absolutely no commitment to being a secretary, and I'm supposed to believe that that's come between us?"

"You can believe what you want," Maya had responded. "All I know is I can't go to San Diego, and I can't see you for the next whatever because like I said, there's a huge conference coming up that's requiring my undivided attention."

"What's this conference's name, Macy? What's this *conference* look like, huh?"

Like Sam Walters, Maya had wanted to say. But

she held back. She'd learned from Zeke to keep one's cards close to the chest. In time Sean would know what she knew. But not yet.

"I'm glad you asked to meet with me, Maya. I was going to have you come in first thing this morning anyway." Zeke's demeanor was jovial as he walked into the office, bringing Maya back to the present. Instead of going to his desk, he walked over to the conference area. "Have a seat over here, will you?"

Maya walked from where she sat in front of Zeke's desk over to the conference area. The usual spray of exotic flowers had been moved to a back wall credenza. An urn of coffee and a tray of pastries, bagels, and croissants were also displayed.

"We're having a meeting?" Maya asked. She almost always came prepared to take notes but had been so focused on telling Zeke what she knew that she'd forgotten to bring her laptop. It had taken her all weekend to decide that he should know; she wanted to get it over with.

"I have some important information to share with you," she continued without waiting for an answer from Zeke. "I think I've uncovered some things about Sam Walters."

Zeke leaned back in his chair. "Oh?"

"Yes. I believe I have concrete proof that Sam Walters is conducting extensive investigations into the players of L.A.'s real estate market, and it makes perfect sense that B&A is one of the players being investigated. Now, I don't know if the Rosenthal Group is behind it, but I—"

Just then the intercom sounded. "Hold that thought," Zeke said. "Yes, Ester?"

"Mr. Brennan, your nine-thirty appointment is here."

"Have Jade bring him back," Zeke said. "Wait a

moment, Maya. I've just hired someone to help with this whole Sam Walters thing. The information you have could be beneficial to him as well."

Jade tapped lightly on Zeke's office door before coming into the room. Zeke stood as his hire came around the corner. Jade nodded quietly and made her exit. Maya had walked to the credenza to pour a cup of coffee and missed the dagger eyes Jade cut at her back.

"Maya Jamison, I'd like you to meet someone introduced to me over the weekend."

Maya turned with a smile on her face.

"Sean Wynn."

Had Maya not become paralyzed into immobilization, she would have dropped her coffee mug. *Sean!*

"Sean, this is my right-hand woman, Maya Jamison."

Sean's face showed absolutely no recognition as he took a couple of steps toward her. "Nice to meet you," he said cordially, his back to Zeke. But his eyes blazed.

"N-n-nice to meet you." Maya had never stammered a day in her life. There was a first time for everything.

The stammer didn't escape Zeke's notice. He glanced briefly between Maya and Sean before asking Sean if he'd like coffee. "Maya, do you mind?" he asked.

"Not at all." Maya forced herself to regain her composure. She called upon thirty years of discipline and then called upon another thirty she hadn't yet lived to force the tremor from her voice. "Cream and sugar, Mr. Wynn?"

"No, black is fine, Ms. Jamison, correct?"

Maya prayed she could get the coffee in the mug. She gripped the urn as if it were a lifeline. *Deep breaths*, she told herself. The coffee poured into the mug perfectly. *Breathe out.*

Sean joined her at the credenza. "Here, let me help you with that."

"No, no, I've got it." She handed Sean the mug with a barely shaking hand, then forced herself to look him in the eye. "And please, call me Maya."

"Maya? Is that M-A-Y-A?"

"Correct."

"Hmm. I met someone recently with a similar sounding name. Marcy, Myra . . . it was a casual meeting. The name escapes me now. At any rate, please, call me Sean."

It was only because Maya knew Sean that she detected the sarcasm underlying his seemingly innocent comment.

Maya and Sean joined Zeke at the conference table. "I had the privilege of meeting Sean this weekend," Zeke restated. "The moment he told me he was a private investigator here from London, I knew I wanted him on my team."

"Oh," Maya said. "You're a private investigator?" *What were you investigating in Sam Walters's bed on Friday?*

Sean looked at her with smoldering intensity. "One of the best," he said casually before taking a sip of coffee. After drinking, he rolled his tongue across his lips, an action not lost on its intended. *A lowly secretary, huh? Low enough to suck my dick for information? What kind of game are you playing?*

Maya forced her eyes away from Sean's tongue. Her mind didn't cooperate, replaying the "sexual investigation" conversation of a week ago. And then right after that thought, another: *Where else has your tongue been?* The thought of Sean and Sam Walters being intimate cooled her rising libido.

"I'm hiring Sean specifically to check out Sam Walters," Zeke went on. He turned to Sean. "Maya here is quite the multitasker. Because in addition to her myriad of responsibilities pertaining to our multi-billion-dollar portfolio, I've had her on, shall we say, special assignment for the past month."

Sean looked at Maya. "And what assignment is that?" he asked pointedly.

Zeke smiled. "Why don't you tell him, Maya?"

"Yes, Maya. I have a feeling you'd tell the story much better than Zeke. Am I right, Zeke? Is she a great storyteller?"

"Maya's a skillful wordsmith," Zeke agreed. Both men then turned to Maya, and waited.

Maya's navy blue Chanel suit matched the outer calm she conveyed. Inside, she was feeling so many emotions she couldn't have named them all if asked. She was shocked that Sean was sitting in Zeke's office, astounded that he'd lied about his name (*as did you*, she thought, but what had that to do with the price of eggs?), perplexed that Sean would tell Zeke his true profession, amazed that Zeke would trust this stranger so quickly, pissed because of Sean's allud-ing to having forgotten her name and scared as "h" to tell Sean about Martha! She'd wanted so many times to share with him all that she was going through, to tell him about Martha and Macy. This was *not* the scenario she'd envisioned. And as it were, she wasn't the only one with secrets.

Maya realized the room was silent and two very powerful-looking men were waiting for her to speak. *You're in hot water anyway, Maya, might as well swim into the deep end and get totally scalded.*

"I've been," Maya began tentatively, and then cleared her throat, squared her shoulders, and spoke clearly. "I've been working in Sam Walters's employ as a part-time housekeeper."

Sean coughed. He'd been taking a sip of coffee and when Maya said she worked for Sam, he almost choked. "You, a maid," he said, still coughing.

"As I'm sure Zeke has told you, it's our belief that there is more to Sam Walters than meets the eye, or the paper as it were, and Zeke arranged for me to become a part of his household in hopes of digging up additional information. Are you all right?"

Ignoring her, Sean said to Zeke, "You see, already her oral skills have me all choked up." And then to Maya, "Could I have some water?"

"Sure," Maya answered in a cheerful voice, all the while seething at Sean's reference to her oral ability. She went to the credenza, filled a large crystal goblet, brought it back to Sean, and resisted the almost overwhelming desire to throw it in his face.

Sean brushed his fingers over hers as he took the glass. "Thank you, Maya."

Maya refused to show she was flustered, but it was as if she could *feel* Sean's fury even as she felt the heat of his touch. And then it hit her: Sean might have heard her run away on Friday. *Is that possible?* She looked him in the eye, trying desperately to read what was in the mind behind them. She knew the lie she'd offered Cecilia on not showing up had been flimsy, that her cousin had gone into labor and there'd been no one else to drive her to the hospital, but it was the best Maya could do at the time. That she remembered to call at all, after seeing dimples and perfectly placed moles, was a victory in itself.

But was that it, she thought? *If he heard me in the house, in Sam's room . . .*

"Are you all right?" It was Sean's turn to ask the question.

"Yes, Maya," Zeke said, a hint of irritability in his voice. "You seem a bit preoccupied."

"I'm sorry, Mr. Brennan," Maya responded. *Get it together, Maya!* She needed to shift the power in this conversation, get on the offensive, and knew she had the ammunition to do it. Sean knew Sam, but what was the best way to fire the weapon? Guns backfired, and so could ill-timed dispensation of information. She'd have to tread carefully, but tread she must.

"I was just thinking, Mr. Brennan, of the information I had to share with you about Sam Walters. It also involves a private investigator." She resumed command of her voice and control of her demeanor.

"I'd like to finish hearing the story about your housekeeping," Sean said calmly. "If that's okay," he added, to Zeke.

"We've got time," Zeke said.

Again, all eyes were on Maya. "There's not much to tell. I worked part-time, mopped floors, made beds, tried to find something on Sam Walters that's not in our files."

"How long have you worked there?" Sean asked.

"Four weeks."

"And what exactly did you look for?"

"Something to confirm or deny that Sam Walters is who he says he is. His is a billion-dollar company that has flown under the real estate radar. He comes out of nowhere with money to burn. He wants to build an alliance with B&A. We want to know everything there is to know about him. Especially what he doesn't want us to find out," she added, an unblinking stare aimed at Sean as she did so.

"I told you I know Sam Walters, right?" Sean asked Zeke, effectively ending Maya's attempt at one-upmanship.

Zeke leaned forward. "No, you didn't."

"I don't know him well, but our paths crossed a couple times in London. I also knew he was in Los Angeles. And how do I know this? Because the Rosenthal Group hired me to check him out."

"Now, this is an interesting development," Zeke said, his years of experience at playing the game telling him he'd just trumped Rosenthal's ace with a joker. "Whatever the Rosenthal Group is paying you, we'll double it, triple if necessary. I get the feeling you're a highly intelligent man, Sean Wynn. One who will be able to figure out the truth for himself, and discover where the real corruption lies in L.A.'s downtown building boom."

"I'd be happy to discuss your offer over lunch," Sean said. His smug glance toward Maya was imperceptible. But the smile he delivered at her shocked expression was open and honest. *Your move, baby. You're trying to play the player who invented the game.*

15

Hours later, Sean still seethed from the day's revelations: that not only was Macy Williams Maya Jamison, but she was also his homely housemaid Martha Jones! He'd been shocked to turn the corner and see Macy in Zeke's office, and flabbergasted when he found out she'd also spent hours cleaning his home. Sean's highly honed investigative skills had made him a very wealthy man; how had he missed this massive deception occurring not only right under his nose, but in his bed?

Had this been her motive the night they met? Did she already know who he was then? Had she planned to try and coax him into Brennan's camp all along? Granted, he remembered being the aggressor in their meeting, but who's to say she hadn't planted herself in his path, purposely irresistible in that silky red dress and fuck-me pumps. And if there had been no ulterior motive, why had she lied? Why had she introduced herself as Macy Williams, and why hadn't she revealed her true identity after their relationship continued? Sean didn't know the answers to those questions, but he did know this: If she'd used herself as bait, it had been the best he'd ever tasted. He'd jumped on her line and gotten reeled in faster than a striped bass at a fishing contest. And truth be told, she held him captive still.

But not for long. His wildly fluctuating emotions were why he'd purposely trivialized their relationship in the meeting by calling it casual, and why he'd kept his strictly professional demeanor firmly in place. They were also why he hadn't answered her call, or listened to the voice mail he knew she'd left. Today's encounter had thrown him for a major loop; he needed time to sort out his feelings, separate fact from fiction, and get his head together. Nobody, least of all a woman, was going to make him lose control.

But more than anger, Sean felt hurt. Maya had transfixed him like no other woman before her ever had. For the first time in his thirty-eight years, he imagined spending the rest of his life with someone, growing old with someone . . . someone like Maya. The man in him wanted to demand she come over and tell him the truth. No one could deny the intense connection between them; there was no way he would believe their love affair had been a total lie. But the investigator in him hesitated, for more reason than the deep affection he felt for her. Whether she knew it or not, she was caught up in a high stakes situation, a game with unsavory players who played for keeps. Players like Joseph Rosenthal, who'd stop at nothing to be the "winner take all." Sean was determined to find out the truth *and* keep Maya safe. To do this he'd have to plot his next moves very carefully. But plot he would because even after discovering her deception, his need to protect her and, he begrudgingly admitted, to continue to see her remained strong.

Sean admitted there was a somewhat positive

development out of today's events: His "hiding in plain sight" tactic of playing the Rosenthal Group against B&A had worked perfectly, a plan he devised after receiving news of Joseph's underhanded plans where he was concerned. A reliable source had told him to watch his back, and then given him enough proof for Sean to consider it advice well taken. Sean's loyalties ran deep, unless his trust was betrayed. In those situations, his motto became *to thine own self be true*. Joseph Rosenthal now presented such a situation. And even though he hadn't planned to reveal his connection to Rosenthal today, Maya's forcing his hand to do so had worked to his advantage. He would inform Joseph of his inroads into the B&A network, investigate Zeke from an insider's advantage and find out exactly what Maya knew about the Sean Wynn/Sam Walters connection.

Sean frowned as he casually sipped a cup of chamomile tea, his second of the evening. He'd purposely brewed it because of its purported calming effect. It wasn't working. His ire rose even as did a mental picture of the lowly Martha, in oversized clothes, a matted wig and thick, unnecessary glasses, shrinking like a violet whenever he walked into the room. Sean sat straight up as he thought of something else. Was it possible that somehow she'd seen him on Friday, when he was knocked out from taking the sinus medication? He shook his head, negating the thought. He'd checked the house; no one had entered it, a fact confirmed when Cecilia said Martha's cousin had . . . Sean's frown deepened. Maybe there wasn't a cousin, and maybe Maya had seen him asleep in what she knew as Sam's bed. If that was the case, Sean didn't even want to ponder those implications. But Maya wasn't that smart, was she? Sean knew that she was. Her brilliant mind was a part of her allure. Once again he moved to call her, and once again he stopped. If she knew he was not only friends with Sam Walters but *was* Sam Walters, it might jeopardize her safety. He didn't want to burden her with keeping his dual identity a secret and didn't want to jeopardize her job at B&A. Plus, he knew the investigation would end soon. Then he'd tell her everything, including how he planned to make her his forever.

He felt sure about being able to handle his professional dilemmas, but what about his personal ones? Sean felt about Macy the way he'd felt about no other woman. When he thought of her, he thought long-term: of a shared household and the sound of kids. Before she'd canceled their trip to San Diego, he'd even thought of the dreaded "m" word, the "together forever" one, and had looked forward to a weekend of having her around him twenty-four-seven. That's what Macy, no, Maya had done to him.

Sean picked up the company photo of Maya, the one from the folder he'd initially been given regarding B&A. Now, of course, it was obvious that this was his Macy. Even with the severe bun, the dour expression, and sans makeup, he now recognized what he so loved about Macy in Maya's face: the sparkling eyes, soft, luscious lips, high cheekbones. The fire he knew she possessed was carefully concealed beneath a dark suit in the photo, and the no-nonsense persona she portrayed.

This persona was totally unlike the free-spirited, uninhibited Macy Williams he'd met on the Fourth of July, the one with whom he'd shared sensual pleasures within hours of meeting, and whose insatiable passion matched his own. The short hairstyle added to her sassiness, highlighting her face and eyes, features partially hidden beneath the severe bangs Maya wore in the company file photo.

Sean pushed aside the now cold tea, stood, and walked to the balcony of his Ritz suite. Even with all he knew, his body ached for Maya: the feel of her soft, pliable skin, her feminine scent, the taste of her love potion on his tongue. He forced himself away from the patio view, the glorious, red sunset playing out against the ocean's blue waves. It reminded him of when he and Maya had made love out there, her back pressed against the building's cool, stone exterior, his hot shaft plummeting into Maya's welcoming feminine flower, again and again.

Sean forced his mind away from this train of thought. "I've got to get out of here," he said to the empty room. He stripped off his clothes and quickly donned workout gear. After grabbing a bottle of water from the minibar, a small towel from the bathroom, and his cell phone, he headed for the door. Sean felt that after a good workout he'd go to the restaurant for a nice meal and maybe stay to hear the jazz trio that often performed in the lounge next to the restaurant. After a few hours of unwinding, of divesting himself from work and Macy, no, Maya, he'd be better able to strategize his next moves.

Feeling better already, Sean put his hand on the knob, and then stopped. *I won't even take my phone.* Part of his reasoning involved not wanting to take a business call, but an equal motivation was Tangier's constant calling, and fearing his resolve to not call Maya would weaken. He placed the phone on the charger and again headed for the door. This time, there was a decided pep in his step; he almost felt lighthearted. But the feeling was short-lived, gone as soon as he opened the door fully and gleaned what was on the other side.

"Hello, Sean."

"What are you doing here?"

"Is that any way to treat your lady?" Tangier asked, her voice a mixture of sarcasm and hurt. "I thought you'd be excited to see me."

The look on Sean's face suggested otherwise.

"Well, even if that's not the case . . ." she began as she slithered up to Sean, wrapped her arms around his neck, and placed a wet kiss on his unyielding mouth. "Aren't you going to invite me in?"

Sean let the locking door and his brushing past her toward the elevator serve as his answer.

Tangier was shocked into stillness, but not for long. "Sean," she said, running to catch up with her lover's long, strong strides. "I've just traveled five thousand miles to see you. The least you can do is act civil!"

Sean reached the elevator and punched the down arrow. "And the least you can do is retrace your steps, tonight if there's a flight." He took a couple of steps toward Tangier. "I expressly told you not to come here, Tangier, that I don't mix business with pleasure. You think our screwing for the last couple of years gives you some kind of ownership where I'm concerned? Well, think again."

The elevator doors opened and they both entered quickly. Tangier worked to keep her anger under control. She'd known Sean would be upset; fanning the fire served no purpose at this point. "I'm sorry, Sean," she said softly, in what she hoped was a contrite-sounding voice. She wasn't sorry she'd come, just that he was so angry. "But I just had to see you. You sounded so distant when we talked, on those rare times I could even catch you. Yes, I know you're working, but it's never stopped us from being able to communicate."

Silence descended along with the elevator, all the way to the lobby.

"At least let me buy you a drink," Tangier coaxed, once they'd stepped into the hallway. She slid her hands over his tight shoulders. "Looks like I'm not the only one who could use one."

Sean stopped, put his hands on his hips, and stared toward the gym. He was wondering if his day could get any worse. The last person he wanted to deal with at the moment was Tangier. But he had no choice. Not to mention she'd just flown across a continent to see him. Another time, another frame of mind, and he would have welcomed her into his bed. He and Tangier had shared some good times and even with her cattiness, he considered her a friend.

He turned to Tangier and allowed a brief smile. "One drink," he said, putting a finger up for emphasis. "And only if you promise to go back to London."

Tangier smiled.

"I mean it," Sean said, rising to his full six feet two inches. "There's too much at stake for you to be here and distract me." He softened his features and brushed his finger across Tangier's full, red mouth. "And believe me, you would be a distraction."

That's exactly what I intend to be, especially where the L.A. chick who's got your attention is concerned. Instead of voicing these thoughts, Tangier answered, "Baby, it looks like you could use a distraction." She brushed up against him seductively and whispered in his ear, "We can have a bottle of wine and a couple steaks brought up to the room. I'd like to help you unwind, Sean. And I've come so far. . . ." Feeling his anger abating, Tangier pressed against him a little more.

Sean grabbed Tangier's hand and returned to the bank of elevators. Room service and comfortable conversation sounded like a good idea. Tangier could fill him in on the goings on in London and take his mind away from the rumblings in L.A.

As soon as the elevator doors closed, Maya came out from her hiding place behind the huge marble column near the hotel lobby's entrance. She was seething, her desire to apologize to Sean for her duplicities dissolved. After wavering back and forth between being angry at Sean for lying to her and angry at herself for the lies she'd told, she'd decided that what she and Sean shared was worth saving. She'd convinced herself that it wasn't just her, that Sean undoubtedly felt the same way. She'd thought about the last time they made love, and how it felt that not only their bodies, but their spirits had become entwined. She'd come to the hotel with the hopes of rekindling the flame that had burned so brightly between them, and perhaps working with him to solve whatever mysteries existed with B&A, the Rosenthal Group, and the L.A. real estate empires.

Then Maya entered the Ritz and saw the attractive, long-legged woman practically mauling Sean in the hotel lobby. Her first thought was to confront him, but before she could formulate her grand "what the bump's going on?" speech, Sean had grabbed the woman's hand and headed back into an elevator. Maya had taken that trip before, and knew how it ended . . . in Sean's knowing and capable hands.

Maya's eyes narrowed as she glanced at the bank

of elevators once more before spinning on her heel and heading back to the valet. She was angry, hurt and confused, and needed a moment to think before she reacted. She desperately wanted to believe there was an explanation that defied the scene she'd just witnessed but after what she'd already experienced today, she didn't have the energy to find out otherwise. Besides, if she went up to his room and confronted him, what truths would he demand in return? Could being honest in any way jeopardize Zeke's work and the Angel's Way deal? Was she absolutely certain Sean was really on their side, and not Rosenthal's? Her heart felt it knew the answer but her head wasn't sure. And with her financial freedom, future, and family at stake, tonight was not a time to gamble.

"I'm sorry," Sean said as he peeled Tangier's arms from around his neck. "I guess I've got too much on my mind to get in the mood right now."

Tangier tempered her reaction, which, considering this man's usual libido, could have bordered on outrage. "There's a first time for everything, I guess," she said calmly instead.

"Yes, I guess so."

Tangier swung her legs over the side of the bed and got up abruptly. She had just known that after their scrumptious dinner and a bottle of wine, her plan would work. That her seductive, open-legged sprawl on the covers had cooled Sean down instead of heated him up convinced her more than ever that someone else was trespassing on her testosterone territory.

"Tell me, Sean," she said as she reached for the stilettos she'd tossed aside upon entering the room. "All of this stuff that's on your mind. Is it something . . . or *someone*?"

Sean's private life in general, and Maya in particular, was none of Tangier's business. He intended to keep it that way. Instead of answering her question, he suggested what he hoped was a peace offering—in light of the fact Tangier hadn't gotten the "piece" she wanted. "I'll upgrade your ticket for tomorrow's flight to first class. That should help the jet lag a bit, huh?"

Sean's avoiding Tangier's question simply served to piss her off. "What will help the jeg lag is a few days in sunny L.A.; maybe a shopping spree on Rodeo Drive, a night of classical music at the Hollywood Bowl, and some delicious seafood at an upscale restaurant." Tangier reached for her purse and stood. "Since it's clear that I'm of no use to you, I'll just have to find other ways to spend my time here."

"Don't do this, Tangier."

"Do what? Enjoy L.A.?"

"Stay where you're not . . . where I'm not able to be with you as I'd like. This case is complicated. But if there's any chance at all of us being together when it's over, it starts with your being on that plane tomorrow."

"And if there's any chance for me to believe that statement, you'll fuck my ever-loving brains out tonight."

Sean sighed. There was no way he could be with Tangier; at this point he didn't think he could get it up if he tried. He admitted a difficult truth—the only woman he and obviously his body wanted was Maya.

"I've told you already, I will not be distracted. Making love sounds wonderful but not here, not now." *And not with you.* He walked over to Tangier and offered a light hug. "Wait now, better later?"

"I'm going against every instinct I've ever employed where men are concerned," she said, a slight smile playing across her lips. "But I'll take you up on your offer for that first class ticket. The faster I get home, the faster I can start preparing for you to come back there." She hugged him tightly and forced his lips apart for a kiss. And then she was gone.

After closing it, Sean leaned against the door. His friend with benefits of the last two years had broken a cardinal rule; she'd come into his professional territory uninvited. Continued actions such as those could effectively close the door on their relationship. And as much as it pained him to consider, if he found out Maya had used him, he'd close the door on her, too.

16

"I want him out of B&A, out of L.A., and out of my life!" After railing nonstop about Sean to Trish, Maya felt no better than she did when she'd barged into her best friend's home more than an hour ago. She'd already worked through hurt and confusion and was now spending time on anger.

"How could I have been so stupid? It's obvious he was just using me to get to Zeke! All this time I thought we had something special. Ha! Well, I just saw his 'special' tonguing him in the hotel lobby!"

Trish had racked up a few dating doozies in her life, but she had to admit this scenario was crazy even by her standards. Knowing that Maya's immense anger came from her deep feelings for Sean, she tried to go easy.

"I don't know what to tell you, girl. It does look bad. But maybe you should at least talk to him, get his version of what's going on, and who the woman is. Maybe she's just someone he knows from back in the day."

"Do you really think so, Trish?" Maya desperately wanted to believe that once she and Sean had a chance to lay all the cards on the table, to talk everything through, the fire they'd shared would still be burning. Hopefully when this charade was over and the Angel's Way project was theirs, she'd be finished with her financial commitment to Zeke Brennan and could get back to being her true self . . . no more lies.

"Are you hungry?" Trish asked. "I'm getting ready to heat up some leftover casserole, or we can go out if you want."

"Thanks, Trish, but I don't have an appetite. Besides, your girl wouldn't be good company. I think I just need to go home and try to figure out my life, untangle this Martha, Macy mess, and get back to just being Maya Jamison, executive assistant to Zeke Brennan with B&A."

"Okay, but if you need some help with your multiple personalities, let me know!"

Maya knew Trish was trying to lighten the moment. She attempted a smile but failed miserably. "I'll call you tomorrow." And then realizing she'd spent the entire visit focused on herself, she added, "Oh, by the way, how are you and Tony doing?"

"Right now, not good."

"What's wrong?"

"Nothing except I haven't heard from him in two days. We normally talk every day, sometimes several times a day."

"It sounds like you really like him."

"He's a little thugalicious but I'm hanging tough! Maybe I can love the thug out of him, you know?"

"You sure you want to?" Maya knew Trish liked to ride on the wild side.

"No, but that sounded good, huh?"

This time, Maya's smile was genuine. But it was short-lived. She was physically, spiritually, and emotionally exhausted. All she wanted to do was sleep.

Once she arrived home she methodically fed Lucky, walked into her bedroom, removed her clothes and headed straight for a hot shower. Just before she turned the water on, her home phone rang. Her heart sank as soon as she heard the recorder announcing a collect call. It could only mean one thing: Stretch was in trouble. She rushed to pick up before the call disconnected.

"Yes," she said in answer to whether or not she'd accept the charges. She wearily sank down on her bed and wrapped the cover around her naked body.

"Hey, sis." Stretch's voice was low and tentative. "I didn't do nothing, this time. I swear, Maya, I didn't do nothing!"

"What happened, Malcolm?" Maya called Stretch by his real name when things got serious.

Stretch shared with Maya how he'd been busted for consorting with a known felon, an act that violated the terms of his probation. That this felon was his first cousin and best friend from the day they were born didn't matter to the law.

"If y'all weren't doing anything, how'd you get arrested?"

"We got a DWB . . . Driving While Black. Cops pulled us over and said they smelled weed. We didn't have anything on us, but they took me down anyway. You gotta get me out, sis. I can't take this shit!"

"Well, neither can I, Malcolm! I've been bailing you out of one scrape after another since I can remember. And I'm sick of it! You think you're the only one with problems? Well, you're not. I've got my own problems right now, little brother. You need to call your attorney, somebody who can help you."

Stretch was stunned. Maya had never talked to him like this before. His concern immediately switched from himself to her. "What's up, sis? What's the matter?"

Maya sighed. "I've just got a lot going on with the job right now. I'm stressed out. And I can't keep fighting your battles, Malcolm. I'm tired. Talk to your attorney and see if he can get you out on your own recognizance. I don't have a lot of free money right now. You might have to sit there for a minute, and take that time to figure what you want out of life."

"I probably just need five thousand, Maya. You'll get it back, I promise."

It was all too much. Her career was clandestine crazy, she'd just caught her man in a hotel with someone else, and now her one and only close relative in the world was calling her from jail. Maya, usually the strong, stoic one, broke down.

"It's okay, sis, look, don't sweat it. I'll call my attorney tomorrow and see if he can get me out. This is bullshit anyway, Maya. I'm telling you, I didn't do nothing. Stop crying, My-My," Stretch whispered, calling Maya by her childhood pet name. "It's going to be all right. I'll probably be out by tomorrow. Then I'll come over and find out what's making my sister cry."

They talked for a couple more minutes and after she'd hung up, Maya didn't even have the energy for a shower. She curled up under the cover, in the fetal position, and grieved the mother she had lost three years ago, the father she never knew, the brother who couldn't seem to get it right, and most of all, Sean Wynn, her Mr. Right. She just hoped he didn't turn out to be Mr. Wrong.

17

After a fitful night's sleep, Maya got up, showered, and was in her office by seven thirty. She had made a crucial decision in the predawn hours. It was time to get her life back, starting today. She was surprised to see Jade also there and stunned that Zeke too was in his office. What was going on?

Something was definitely up; Jade usually showed up at nine and left promptly at six and Zeke was known for burning the midnight oil, not being an early riser. Not wanting to appear insecure or anxious, Maya decided to go through her mail, e-mails, and in-box before approaching Zeke. While he had been reassuring in guaranteeing her job security, Maya wasn't taking any chances. She had to make sure nothing important slipped through the cracks while she was out of the office, pushing a mop.

Maya hoped this was the day that marked the end of Martha Jones. There were only a couple of days until she would have finished anyway. She would find another way to retrieve documents or information that could verify Sam's identity, but after seeing Sean in his bed, she no longer felt comfortable being in his house. What would happen if Sean showed up there again, especially since he knew the real deal? Now that she thought about it, she figured Sam might know the real deal by now as well. Somebody close enough to sleep in his bed probably wouldn't keep something like that a secret.

A slew of e-mails kept her mind occupied for the most part, but every now and then memories of her ardent lover crept into her thoughts: his smile, cleft chin, dimples, love. Her heart ached to be held by him again, and she willed time to race toward that moment. A few more days, a few more answers, her debts paid and then . . . just maybe . . . lasting love.

With urgent e-mails answered, mail opened, and in-box organized, Maya had one more thing to do before she went into Zeke's office—call Ester. She looked at her watch and, seeing it was nine o'clock, dialed the operator.

"Good morning," Ester answered cheerfully yet in a low voice. "I'm glad you came in today. I was going to call you if you didn't."

"Why, what's up?"

"I don't know the whole 411 but I know it involves the Rosenthal Group, Angel's Way, and Jade all up in the mix. She's been coming in early every day this week, acting like the office diva and meeting with Mr. Brennan. He's getting her a secretary or research clerk or some mess. Watch your back, girl."

Before Maya could respond, her other line beeped. Zeke. "Thanks for the heads-up," she said quickly. "Gotta go." She pushed the button to a second phone line. "Good morning, Zeke."

"Good morning, Maya. I need you in my office for a meeting."

"I'll be right there."

Maya grabbed the small laptop she used to record notes and headed for Zeke's office. Thanks to Ester's heads-up and her own intuition, she wasn't surprised to see Jade sitting at the conference table. A couple of company directors were also there.

Zeke walked over to the table and, after sitting down, began without preamble. "Rosenthal continues to try and sabotage our chances to procure the Angel's Way project. I'm sure all of you know I'm not going to allow that to happen. Chris, I want you to rework our numbers. Alex, go over the building designs and double-check that they're environmentally friendly. Along with our numbers, attention to that detail with everyone going green will give us an advantage."

After giving directives to the remaining departments and requesting additional environmental research from Maya, Zeke turned to Jade. "Get a copy of the statistical report you put together for these guys, Chris and Alex. In fact, I'd like all the directors to have it. Jade's work is impressive," he said to the group. "The information she assembled should make some of your job easier."

Maya watched Jade covertly as she recorded the meeting. She was surprised at the envy that arose as Jade virtually preened in front of the men. The reaction surprised her; Maya was a strong, confident woman who was usually nonplussed at the various antics she saw taking place on the regular in corporate America. She knew all about Jade's attempt to usurp her position as Zeke's assistant. Where was this jealous streak coming from? Maya wondered.

It didn't go without Maya's notice that when Zeke dismissed the meeting, he did not ask her to stay behind as he often did. Instead, it was Jade who remained

seated. Still, Maya played it cool. She'd get her chance
to find out exactly what was going on from Zeke himself, and didn't intend to leave the office until she did.

Eight hours flew by before Maya knew it. Her
growling stomach reminded her she hadn't even
stopped for lunch. She felt good, though; even with
her absence from the office, everything on her desk
was in order and to top it off, one of the agents had
alerted her to a possible B&A sale in swanky Santa
Monica, one initiated by a lead she'd discovered and
passed on. Not only would her part of the commission be a welcome bonus to her bank account, but it
would place her one step closer to financial freedom.
In fact, Maya believed she could close the deal herself, and would love to do so. It was time to put her
real estate license to use.

Maya stood, stretched, and walked over to look
out her skyscraper window. It was a perfect August
day and though her view was unobstructed exter-
nally, Sean's face provided an internal block. Try as
she might, she couldn't keep her mind off him for
long. Whenever she finished a report, a phone call, a
memo or message, Sean Wynn would rush to the
forefront of her mind. If his face didn't appear, then
Stretch's would. Thinking about either of them gave
her a headache.

She sat down at her desk and reached inside the
top drawer for the aspirin inside. Laying her head
against the chair's cool leather material for a moment
and closing her eyes, Maya redirected her thoughts
to the end-of-the-day visit she planned to Zeke's
office. Was now the right time to ask to be released
from her Martha Jones duties? Should she worry
about Jade's seemingly growing importance with

Angel's Way? And just how much should she share with him about her relationship with Sean?

There was only one way to find out. Maya placed her stocking feet back into the Prada pumps that had rested under her desk for most of the afternoon. She stood, finished drinking the water in the glass on her desk, picked up a couple of folders, and headed for Zeke's office. Usually she'd call first but she'd already checked his calendar and seen there were no meetings scheduled—he should be free. Things in the office became more casual after five, and Maya often poked her head in Zeke's door for a last-minute check-in before going home. That her job status was shaky, her nerves were on end, and her head was pounding like a bass drum was no reason for her to alter her behavior. She was trying to get her life back to some semblance of normal; conducting business as usual was a first step.

Maya tapped lightly on Zeke's closed door. When there was no answer, she opened the door gently and peeked inside. He wasn't sitting in the area just inside the door, as he often did as he unwound from the day, so she entered the room, closed the door, and headed around the corner to the more official desk area and conference room. A quick scan of his desk showed that Zeke hadn't left for the day; his partially opened briefcase lay near the corner of the desk and his BlackBerry was blinking missed calls and/or messages. He was probably in one of the agents' offices. Ester would know; it seemed that woman knew everything. Maya decided that instead of using Zeke's phone, she would return to her desk and call. There might be some updated Jade info Ester had to share.

Just as Maya turned to leave, she noticed a platter of pastries on Zeke's credenza. Her stomach growled its pleasure and without hesitation, Maya walked over to the table to snatch a buttery blueberry crois- sant. She bit into her favorite flavor with relish and turned to leave. A soft tinkle of laughter stopped her cold. Maya turned in the direction of the sound.

Zeke had a small, private room just beyond the conference room, one he often used when pulling twelve-plus-hour days at the office. Who could be in there, one of his mistresses? That he dallied from time to time was a not too-well-kept secret. But Maya hadn't known him to entertain them in his office.

Maya silently retraced her steps, just in case she'd missed seeing Mrs. Brennan's purse lying around. Although it was not impossible, Zeke's wife rarely put in an office appearance. But considering Zeke's long hours recently, maybe his wife had decided to surprise him with dinner and then be dessert. Maya did a quick walkaround. There was no evidence that Mrs. Brennan was the owner of the giggle.

Pondering her options, Maya slowly inched toward the door to Zeke's private domain. It would be locked of course; that's if Zeke had any sense at all. But then again, from the sound of things, it might be Zeke's lower instead of upper head in control right now. Maya reached for the knob and turned it. The door was not locked.

Still, Maya pondered what to do. Zeke would not like being interrupted, much less busted. Would she be reprimanded for coming into his office without an invite? Mere weeks ago this wouldn't have even been a question, but the playing field looked much differ- ent now. The easiest thing would be to walk away, forget what she heard, go home, and see about her brother. Here she was worrying about who her boss might be screwing while Stretch languished in jail! *By his own doing*, her inner voice reminded her. Maya pushed the guilt away.

She reached for the knob again. At least whatever happened from what she was about to do would not involve jail time. Short of that, there was no other reason not to feed her curiosity about who was with Zeke.

Maya inched the door open, stopped, listened. Nothing. She cracked it open just enough to peek inside. The couch and recliner were empty. She opened the door farther and stuck her head inside the room. Silence. Maya frowned. There were only two places Zeke and whoever was with him could be, the bathroom or the walk-in closet. Now the risk increased. Once Maya stepped into the room, her chances of exposure were just as high as Zeke's. Even now, if he came around the corner, she'd be busted.

Heart pounding, Maya stepped inside. The room was fairly dark, lit only by a dimmed lamp in the room's far corner. She looked down the hallway. A sliver of light came from the bathroom, which was across from the walk-in closet.

Maya took two steps, stopped, then took two more. She could hear it now, the low, sure sound of moaning and groaning, the kinds of sounds that accompanied sexual intercourse. She slid along the wall to the adjacent doors. The sound of moaning was louder now, coming through the bathroom door, which was ajar.

Maya remembered there was a medium-sized vanity area by the sauna stall, with the main bathroom area with tub and stool farther back. If Zeke was back there, the game would be over. No way was she going to actually go into the bathroom. She strained her neck to see through the small slit in the door without opening it farther. *Shoot, I wish I knew where they were!*

She had to chance it. Using just her index finger, she pushed the door ever so slightly. It opened barely a half inch more. But that was enough. Enough for her to see the mirror that was across from the bench where one could towel off after being in the sauna. Zeke was on that bench, shirt open, pants down. His head was thrown back, mouth open, eyes closed. Jade knelt in front of him, providing skilled oral action as if his member were a hot dog and her mouth the bun. Her long dark hair swung back and forth as her head bobbed up and down. Zeke locked his hands into Jade's hair, twisting some of it around his hands while pushing himself farther and farther inside her mouth. Then Jade rose, hiked up her skirt, and sat down on Zeke's hardened shaft. Soon Jade's murmurs joined Zeke's. Maya had seen more than enough.

Back in her office, Maya quickly gathered her briefcase, laptop, and purse. She'd have to endure being Martha for at least one more day and for once the cover would work to her advantage. She needed time to regroup because knowing Jade had taken the sex bait Maya had rejected just upped the ante. Jade now had a different type of access to Zeke and Maya needed to adjust her strategy accordingly. She needed to move up the time table toward establishing her own business, and to do that she needed one, to be a pivotal player in the Angel's Way deal, two, to find a successful end to the Sam Walters job, three, pay back her debt to Zeke Brennan and four . . . she needed Sean.

18

Sean was not a happy man. Once again his instincts had paid off and the negative feelings he'd felt about Rosenthal and the ulterior motives for hiring Sean had been accurate. Joseph Rosenthal wanted not only to destroy Brennan & Associates the company, he wanted to destroy Zeke Brennan the man. He stood abruptly, walked out onto the patio and stared across the marina, recalling the conversation with Neil that verified what he'd already uncovered.

After a few brief pleasantries, Sean had gotten right to the point. "You have any new information on Rosenthal for me?"

There was a chuckle on the other line. "How much time you got?"

He'd gone on to verify that Rosenthal had friends in high places just like Brennan: an ex in-law on the city council, a college buddy on the state's Zoning and Planning committee, and a silent partner who was helping The Rosenthal Group quietly buy up the main corridor of Century City, a high-end residential and business district popular with law firms and movie industry executive offices. Sean's contact had uncovered sizeable amounts of properties on Olympic, Pico and Santa Monica boulevards, the main arteries through the west Los Angeles community that was purchased by a front but actually belonged to the Rosenthal Group. It was no coincidence that a crony of Rosenthal's, one who belonged to the same exclusive business club as he and other top-level Rosenthal Group executives, was mayor of Century City. What was surprising was discovering possible shadier connections into L.A.'s notorious drug and gang world, where Rosenthal had purportedly turned when he needed muscle or fire power. Joseph P. Rosenthal was not without his share of buried bodies on his way to the top; more than one smaller firm had bit the bankruptcy dust behind their not being able to keep up with the big boys, namely Rosenthal and Brennan. Sean prayed that the deaths at Rosenthal's hands were limited to mergers, not murders. Joseph had once said he'd do anything to get the Angel's Way contract. Did that include putting a contract out on someone's life?

Sean had to find out, and until he did he was more determined than ever to protect Maya. If Zeke was in danger, then she was too, as was Zeke's family, top executives, and everyone else close to him. It would be a tricky road to navigate but he had no choice but head down it. Years of discipline normally allowed a clear separation where matters of the head and heart were concerned but when it came to Maya, both his head and his heart was in turmoil. It would kill him to have to be less than truthful with her, but he couldn't risk telling her that he was Sam Walters, not yet. He'd seen trained military men break down under intense interrogation. He wouldn't put her in a position to have to cover for him.

That said, he could think of several other positions

and ways he'd like to cover her. His body warmed at
the thought, even as he reached for the phone. He
hadn't worked it all out in his head, how he would
keep his professional and personal lives compart-
mentalized in a way that kept Maya safe but he was
sure of one thing: he couldn't live another moment
without her. With gritty determination, he reached
for his phone.

It rang just as he picked it up. His heart jumped at
the unexpected sound, and at the number.

"I was just getting ready to call you. I miss you,
Maya."

Maya swallowed the lump in her throat. His voice
was like syrup over pancakes, warm and sweet. She
tried to maintain a professional demeanor and keep
her mind focused on the business at hand. "I need to
talk to you, Sean."

"Of course. Where should we meet?"

"I'm in my car now and can be at the Ritz in thirty
minutes. Are you there?"

"Waiting for you," he said softly.

The call ended without a good-bye.

Sean looked at the phone as he flipped it closed.
This was going to be an interesting meeting, to say
the least. There was hurt, anger, and mistrust on both
sides. But there was also intense desire and mutual
appreciation. He'd hoped in the end the last two traits
would still be standing.

Thirty minutes later, he answered a firm knock at
the door. He opened it and pure loveliness walked
in. It had only been a few days since their encounter
in Zeke's office, but it had seemed a lifetime ago.
He inhaled her beauty as if it were the very air he
needed to breathe, and forced out the fire that blazed

in his loins within seconds of seeing her. He needed answers, not ardor. And he would get them now.

"I'm glad you called."

"We need to talk." She faced away from him as she spoke, her eyes focused on flying birds and ocean waves. She couldn't look at him, not yet. She thought her anger would prevent her from feeling anything else, anything such as longing or desire. She'd been wrong.

Sean took a couple steps toward her and then stopped as he saw her shoulders tense. His hands clenched and unclenched with the desire to touch her, but he refrained.

"To say I was angry to discover that Macy Williams was Maya Jamison is an understatement," he said at last. "I battled with whether or not to ever speak to you again, but in the end, I knew that what we had between us was at least worthy of an explanation."

"Oh, *at least*," Maya spat out mockingly as she spun around. "It was *at least* worthy of a word or two between us to find out why you have been spying on my company, and probably me in the process, at the behest of our adversary, Joseph Rosenthal."

Maya walked toward Sean as she continued her tirade. "You're angry? Well, suck it up brother because you're not the only one. Are you going to stand there and tell me you, Mr. Hot Shot from London Private I, didn't know I worked at B&A, that I was Zeke's top assistant? And if you can tell me that, then tell me this: who was the jolly Black giant, your new female friend you brought back up to your room the night of your *discovery?* That it took you less than eight hours to find my replacement speaks volumes about what we had between us."

Her breath was hot on Sean's chest as she finished,

and her eyes shot daggers. "You've got a lot of nerve, Sean Wynn. I can't believe I ever thought that coming here was a good idea!" She moved to walk around him, out the door and out of his life.

How does she know about Tangier? That was only one of many questions he was determined to have answered before he allowed her to leave. His hand was an iron grip on her arm as he stopped her, his voice low and deadly.

"You've had your say, and now I will have mine."

They stared each other down for a moment, chests heaving, hot breath mingling. The anger was like fire, stirring, burning, and it mixed with a fire of desire, unwanted yet unstoppable. Each fought to quell the flames from both sources, even as they longed to quench their thirst.

Maya took a deep breath and broke eye contact. Sean loosened his grip from her arm and took a step back.

"No, I did not know that you were both Macy and Maya, and therefore I did not know you worked for Zeke. And yes, I was initially hired by Rosenthal to investigate B&A. But because of information uncovered as the investigation unfolded, along with an unexpected development that has put this whole operation on another level for me personally, I decided to expand my investigation to include both Zeke and Joseph. It still does."

Maya remained quiet as she absorbed what Sean had told her. Purposely avoiding the bed, she instead chose a chair at the table, sat down and crossed her arms. "So you're admitting to continuing to investigate Zeke even as you claim to work for him?"

Sean joined Maya at the table. "It's complicated, Maya, but yes, I'm still checking out B&A and

Zeke's dealings with the state, and specifically with the Angel's Way project. But it isn't to help Joseph Rosenthal bring him down. There are billions of dollars at stake here, and those two aren't the only ones who want to claim Angel's Way as their own. I believe there will come a time when I can tell you more than that, but client confidentiality prevents me from doing so now."

"Does it prevent you from telling me about you and Sam Walters?"

Sean hid his surprise at the abrupt subject change. This is where it got tricky and he called upon years of investigative discipline to keep his cool. He would be as truthful with her as he could, while not revealing any information that could come back to haunt either of them.

He leaned back in his chair and studied Maya, unconsciously licking his lips in the process. *Damn, you are fine, girl. The things I want to do to you . . .* He looked past her to the darkening sky outside to redirect his thoughts back to her question.

"You know how I know him," he answered casually. "Our paths crossed back in London."

"And here too, correct?"

Sean nodded slowly. "Correct."

"Just how close are the two of you?"

"Damn girl, you sound like I'm on trial or something." He picked up the room service menu lying on the table. "Hey, are you hungry? I can order up a light dinner."

Maya had barely eaten all day, but the knots in her stomach choked her appetite. "Are you trying to avoid my question?" she asked with sista-girl attitude.

"No," he answered calmly. "I'm trying to be polite." He continued to eye her as he placed the menu down, and answered as truthfully as he felt possible. "Sam Walters is part of my investigation."

"How so?"

"Maya, believe me, there's nothing I want to hide from you. But at the same time, this is a very delicate investigation of some very powerful and sometimes unscrupulous people. I don't expect you to fully understand this, but there are some things I simply can't share. I will say this though," Sean reached for Maya's hand which rested on the table. He stroked it softly. "I would never do anything to hurt you, or jeopardize your safety. You can trust me on that."

Maya jerked back her hand. "Is that why you invited another woman to your room? I know we haven't been intimate long, and I have no claims on you, but is that how you show how much I mean to you, how much you care? You didn't even call me after leaving Zeke's office."

"Would you have answered if I did? And the phone works both ways you know. Until today, I hadn't received a call from you either."

"Yeah, well my life is complicated and it's not all about you."

"I wish it were," he said softly. His demeanor changed abruptly as he continued. "Tangier Reed is who you saw two nights ago, the night after we 'met again for the first time' in Zeke's office. She's a friend of mine from London, who flew over uninvited. I was as surprised as you to find her here."

Maya's eyes threatened to water but she clamped down on the pain. "A friend, huh?"

"Yes, Maya," his dark brown eyes bore into hers as he continued. "She's a friend."

Maya rose from the table and walked to a large, exotic floral arrangement adorning the dresser top.

She fiddled with a lush bird of paradise stem as she continued. "It's probably silly to ask what kind . . . the answer's pretty obvious."

"Not as obvious as it seems. I've known Tangier for a couple years and we had what I guess you could call an agreement, a no-strings-attached relationship where both she and I were free to come and go as we pleased. Both of us travel quite a bit, and she has a second home in France so . . . we'd see each other when we were both in London."

Maya turned to face him. "That doesn't sound like the type of understanding that would have a woman flying all the way from London to see you, uninvited."

Sean then told Maya what had happened since he'd been here, the repeated phone calls from Tangier, his explicit instructions that she not come over; how it had been three months since he'd been intimate with Tangier and how there had been no one else since he met Maya. He even told her about the time when he'd mistakenly posed a question meant for Maya to Tangier, after their call had been disconnected.

"Remember that," he asked. "When I asked if you were ready for my tongue?"

His voice caressed her soul as she remembered— both the conversation and the feel of his tongue. But she couldn't think about that now, she had to stay focused.

Finally she nodded her head and answered simply, "Yes, I remember."

A quiet moment passed between them and then Sean spoke. "Is there anything you want to tell me?"

That question immediately changed the atmosphere for Maya. She'd been on the offensive but now the tables were turned. There was much she wanted to tell

Sean, but little she could actually share. That was a common reality between them; if only he knew.

"Yes, there are many things I want to share but like you, I can't right now." Without thinking, she went and sat on the bed. Her hand brushed the silky comforter as she offered what little she could: her desire to build up enough contacts to strike out on her own, the mentorship Zeke had provided and how that relationship was now complicated and convoluted by his sexual liaison with her nemesis, Jade. Finally, she told him about Stretch, his jail woes and Zeke's financial intervention. She hoped this information would help him understand that whatever she did she felt she had to do. Her future depended on it.

Sean came to stand beside her and rested his hand on her shoulder. "Baby," he said softly. "You're as tight as a drum. Here, lay down."

"No, Sean, I don't think that's a good idea. I still haven't told you why I came over. It's because I need your help. It may be a conflict, but I have to ask if there's anything you know about Sam Walters that can help me and B&A secure Angel's Way?"

"There are many ways I can help you," he answered, as he lay her face down across his bed. "And I'll do whatever I can, within the confines of my own investigation." He expertly kneaded her shoulders and massaged the tension from the base of her neck. His fingers felt like heaven as he massaged her scalp, then massaged his way across her shoulders and down her back. He stopped only long enough to slide off her sandals and continue massaging her calves and feet. He forced his mind to stay neutral, his thoughts focused solely on easing her stress.

Maya wanted to stop him, knew she should stop him, but what he was doing felt so good. She could feel her stomach unknotting even as the tension left her back. As soon as he finished rubbing her last pinky toe she'd get up and leave. They could finish the conversation later, in a public place where she wasn't in danger. That's right, as soon as he finished with the pinky she would . . .

Sean didn't mean to kiss her ankle. His mind was focused on easing her stress but suddenly it switched to easing his. The opportunity presented itself in the form of her smooth, slender ankle, and before he could stop himself, his tongue was gliding toward the sensitive spot he knew existed just behind her knee.

"Sean, please."

Maya could say no more as his hands joined his tongue's journey and headed to her thighs. She moaned in spite of herself as she felt her dress riding up over her hips, her legs being spread apart. Was this moment what she'd thought of subconsciously as she showered and changed just before coming over, putting on a satiny red thong underneath her silk poncho dress? It may have been then, but now there were no thoughts at all; only the feel of Sean's talented tongue as he buried his head between her legs and released the last of her tension. She rubbed her hands over his soft, cropped hair, murmuring his name, pushing back from the assault, only to be locked in place by strong, firm arms and made to endure his lavish attention to her pleasure. Only after she'd cried out for the second time did he roll over, undress, and then once again take her in his arms. She tried to break the embrace so she could return the love in the way she'd received it, but he held her tight.

"No, my hot chocolate, tonight is only for you." He entered her swiftly then, deeply, completely, and led a dance of love that lasted all night long.

19

"Good, you're home. I'm coming over."

That's all Trish said before she hung up the phone. Maya stared at the receiver a moment, shrugged her shoulders, and placed the headset back on its cradle. She was glad Trish was coming over because whatever her friend had to say couldn't top all Maya had gone through in the past twenty-four hours.

Less than ten minutes later, there was a knock on the door. "That was quick," Maya said aloud. "Hey, girl," she said as she opened the door. "What did you do, call me from the end of the block?"

"Just about," Trish said, oozing excitement as she breezed into Maya's home. "I was on Manchester when I called you, picking up a special outfit for . . . my shoot tomorrow!" Trish spun around before breaking into her best rendition of the '90s running man. "Go, Trish, go, Trish!" she continued. She returned to stand in front of Maya. "This is the break I've been praying for, girl, this is a national commercial! A national ad campaign for Champion's Chicken! And yours truly is the principal actor. Do you know what this means? It means that in about six months I can quit my crazy 'a' job, trade in my hoopty 'a' car, and move out of the gangsta 'a' hood!"

Trish's excitement was contagious and soon Maya was twirling around with her friend, sharing her joy. Trish had been languishing in actor obscurity for almost ten years; an occasional regional commercial here, a video there, but mostly she'd kept her chops honed in local theatrical productions that were long on rehearsal hours and short on pay. If anybody deserved a break, it was Trish. Maya was happy for her and told her so.

"Thanks, Maya," Trish said sincerely. "Can you believe it's finally happening? The dreams we talked about all those years ago, living our lives at the top of our game—vacations in Paris, holidays in Rome; two fine honeys on our arm? We're almost there, girl! Well, except for the honey part." Trish walked over and plopped on Maya's couch. "What's up with you and Sean?"

An excited Trish was hard to follow but Maya did her best, shifting gears as if she were in a '65 Mustang.

"Girl, so much happened yesterday. Let me start at the beginning. Zeke and Jade are screwing."

"Who's Jade? Oh, that girl lying in the cut waiting to take your job?"

"The very one."

"Dang . . . are you sure?"

"Positive, I saw it with my own eyes."

"Girl, stop it!"

"That's what I wanted to say to them, moaning and groaning like pigeons on the coo. She handled his 'd' like it was special delivery, but once they started skin slapping, I was out of there."

"Oh—my—goodness, right there in his office?"

"Not exactly." Maya told Trish about the private

area behind the conference room. She retold the experience down to the last detail, with Trish hanging on every word.

"I went from seeing Zeke and Jade screwing in the afternoon to getting my own groove on with Sean last night."

Trish screamed. "Ooh, I knew it. I knew you wouldn't be able to drop that fine 'd.' Maybe I'll finally get to meet him."

"Yeah, maybe the four of us can go out. You heard from Tony?"

"No, and you know what? Now is not the time to piss me off. He needs to put up or show up before I blow up, because once I turn A-list, it's going to be me and Jamie Foxx, or Terrence Howard, or that fine 'a' Shamar Moore."

"Girl . . ."

"I'm just saying, it's easier to know a man wants you for you when you don't have money. After that you don't know who he likes more, you or Ben Franklin."

Their laughter was interrupted by a knock on the door.

"I wonder who that could be," Maya wondered aloud as she went to open it. She looked through the peephole and gasped. "Stretch!"

Stretch and Maya hugged and rocked back and forth as if it had been years instead of days he'd spent in jail. They were different as night and day but as with many twins, they had an unexplainable bond, one that could never be broken, not even with him in jail. He'd called her every day.

"You didn't tell me you were getting out when we talked last night."

"I didn't know last night."

Stretch came fully into the living room and plopped down on the couch next to Trish. He'd known her as long as Maya and gave her the grief that big brothers reserved for little sisters, even though Trish was only two years younger than the twins.

"What up, girl?"

"Get off me, boy," Trish said, laughing. "You still smell like jail."

"Trish, you know you ain't right," Maya said, laughing. She walked over and sniffed her brother. "You do smell a little like C-block, son."

"Forget both of y'all," Stretch said. He jumped up and headed for the kitchen. "What you got to eat in here, My?"

"I don't know. Make yourself at home like you always do. And how did you get out anyway?"

"How old is this chicken?" Stretch asked, instead of answering her question.

"Just day before yesterday, I think."

Stretch rifled through Maya's refrigerator and when he returned to the living room, it was with two large pieces of chicken, a stack of bread, and a bag of chips. "Thanks, sis," he mumbled through a huge bite of leg.

"Did they let you out on your own recognizance?" Maya asked.

"No, a friend helped me out."

Maya's antennae immediately went on red alert. Nothing came free in Stretch's world, in the one she lived in either for that matter. "Who?" she asked pointedly.

"You don't know him," Stretch replied. "Trish might, though."

"Me? How do you think I could know him?"

"'Cause he's friends with your boy, Tony."

Trish sat up. "I didn't know you knew Tony."

"I know him better now. He was a couple cells down from me."

"What?" both Trish and Maya cried simultaneously.

"You saw *my* Tony in jail? Are you sure we're talking about the same person?"

"Unless there are a bunch of Trishes walking around. That's what he told me his girl's name was. Said she was probably pissed too, 'cause he didn't want to call you while he was locked down. Ah, man, I probably shouldn't even be telling you this," Stretch added with a twinkle in his eye, not at all sorry he was spilling the beans. "But then again, you like a thug." He reached over and tried to kiss the woman he treated like a sister.

Trish couldn't deny that she liked them rough, but she'd rather her man's connection to thug life stop at baggy clothes and gangsta rap. She could do without records of the jail variety. At least now she knew why she hadn't heard from Tony; and unless he was swinging both ways, he hadn't been cheating on her. "What's he in for?" Trish asked. "Which jail is he at? How much time did he get? Can I call him, go see him?"

"Whoa, girl, slow your roll. All of your questions are of an unnecessary nature. Your dude's out now. He's a cool brotha too, has friends in high places." He looked at Maya. "And he knows Cuz."

"He knows Eddie? How? Oh, never mind, I probably don't want to know." Eddie was the felon first cousin with whom Stretch, by mandate of his probation terms, could not hang around and how in doing so he'd landed in jail. It was a well-known fact that Eddie was at one time a major player in the Crips gang. Tony's affiliation with him did not bode well for Trish.

"Look, everybody who knows Eddie isn't gang-bangin'," Stretch said, reading Maya's mind. "I think he and Tony were doing some . . . business ventures together."

"What, selling crack is better than bangin'?"

"Why you got to think a brotha's only hustle is the drug trade?"

"I'm sorry, you're right. What's their business?"

"It's not crack," Stretch said, with an air of annoyance. Then he looked at his sister sheepishly. "It's weed, ecstasy, lightweight stuff." Maya rolled her eyes. "But not that corner-to-corner shit," he continued. "Eddie and Tony are just bankrolling the enterprise."

"Wait, did I hear correctly?" Trish asked, coming out of the bathroom. "Tony is a drug dealer?"

Stretch ate the remaining chips, took the plate from the coffee table, and stood up. "It's getting too hot up in here for a brotha. I think it's time for me to bounce."

Trish stopped Stretch with a hand on his arm. She looked him in the eye. "Is Tony dealing? I need to know. I just landed a good gig and can't be riding around with someone who might be carrying. Well, is he?"

"You need to ask him," is all Stretch said. He hugged Trish, walked over and hugged Maya, and left.

"Well, well, well," Trish said after Stretch left. "We're finding out all kinds of information today."

"What are you going to do?" Maya asked.

"I tell you what I'm not going to do, get caught up in some bullshit and blow my big break. We'll see what's up when he calls me, see how I'm feeling after I talk to him. I mean, brotha man packs a punch, but I'm not letting his ten get me twenty."

Maya laughed once Trish explained she was referring to her man's extraordinary penile length. Then she sobered. "That makes one person who's not choosing sex over sanity. Wish I could say the same for Zeke."

"You think he's a pussy pushover? He doesn't strike me as being that easy, not from what you've told me."

"Zeke is business first, that's for sure. And his wife is certainly not going to stand idly by and watch someone come in and try to occupy the empire her sacrifices helped build. No, I think Jade offered herself up on a silver platter and Zeke decided to dine. It'll be interesting how it plays out, though."

Maya got quiet, her eyes looking far into the distance.

"What else is wrong?" Trish asked quietly.

"I'm worried about Stretch, and whoever it is that got him out of jail. Financial favors are rarely free. I just hope Stretch can afford whatever price he has to pay."

20

Stretch gave a casual nod here and there as he rode down Crenshaw Boulevard. This had been his territory since he was six, seven years old; almost every face he saw was familiar. He sat in a perfectly restored 1980 Cadillac La Cabriolet convertible lowrider: two-toned pearl maroon and cream custom two-door rolling on color-matched powder-coated fourteen-inch spokes with Remington rubber dipping on air suspension. In other words, he sat in one of the baddest cars cruising the block.

If the bounce from the Cadillac's four pumps and sixteen batteries wasn't enough to attract a passerby's attention, then the booming bass from the car's Bose stereo definitely would. Stretch rapped over a beat produced by one of his many wannabe rapper friends. *I got my finger on my Glock, tick-tock, stop the clock, 'cause I'm gonna roll up on ya like I wanna . . .* Stretch pulled an expertly rolled blunt from behind his ear, lit it, took a long drag, and continued bobbing his head to the beat.

"That's fire, huh, Tone?" he asked as he passed the joint.

"Yeah, that's ai-iight," Tony replied in the signature low, slow drawl that had prompted his friends to nickname him "Tone." "I hear somebody in Timbaland's camp liked it. Slip that rhyme up in there and ya'll might get signed."

"That'd be cool right there. Blow the bump up and get out of this madness." Stretch blew a kiss to a particularly hot looking female standing at the bus stop. She smiled and waved back. "Hey, let's go pick up that sista . . . give her a ride home."

"More like to your place," Tone said between puffs of the joint. "Ain't got time for that today, cuz. There's somebody you need to meet."

Tony turned off Crenshaw on to Martin Luther King Boulevard and continued his slow trek through the streets of south Los Angeles. Seeing a police car elicited a string of expletives from his otherwise placid demeanor. He turned off MLK abruptly and continued toward his destination, a chic community called Baldwin Hills, in a circuitous fashion, one that could only be driven by someone who'd grown up navigating these streets. He reached a gated cul-de-sac at the very top of the hill. After having the gate buzzed open, he pulled into the circular drive of a stunning white brick mansion.

"Who lives here?" Stretch asked.

"Your benefactor," Tony replied.

"The dude who bailed me out?"

Tony nodded and opened the car door. Stretch followed suit.

A housekeeper opened the mansion's unusual steel door and ushered Stretch and Tony inside a massive foyer housing an equally immense crystal chandelier. Just beyond it, Stretch could see a living room with large, floor-to-ceiling windows that looked out on a picture-perfect view of Los Angeles, a view that on this clear day included the famous Hollywood sign more than five miles from where they stood. Stretch prepared to comment but turned back around at the home owner's greeting.

"What's up, dogs? What up, Tone?"

Tone walked over and gave a brotha's handshake to the handsome, fifty-something stranger.

"And you must be Stretch," the stranger said. "As for me, you can just call me Money."

Stretch gave Money dap. "Man, for springin' my ass out of lockdown . . . I'll call you whatever you want!"

Money smiled and motioned the men into the living room. The housekeeper made no sound as she brought in three glasses of iced tea.

"You want anything with that?" Money asked both men.

"You got any Courvoisier?" Tony asked.

Money nodded toward a fully stocked bar positioned between the living and dining rooms. "Help yourself." He turned to Stretch. "What about you?"

"Naw, I'm good," Stretch replied. "I'm not too much into the dranky-drank."

Money smiled. "I like that. It's good to keep one's wits about him."

Once Tony returned to the pristine, elegantly appointed living room, Money continued speaking. "Tone gives me a good report about you," he said to Stretch. "You're loyal, smart, know the game. You're also well connected street-side. That's a huge asset for those who join my organization."

"Your organization?"

"Yes. I run a diversified business that stretches across the United States and into Mexico and Canada."

"Drugs?" Stretch assumed.

Money smiled. "A variety of enterprises," was all he offered by way of response. "Should you decide to work for me, you'll soon find out that the job you're working on is the only one you need to know about . . . regarding my varied businesses."

"Cool dat," Stretch said, no offense taken. "I might be interested. . . . What you got?"

Money smiled again, the patiently enduring kind a father might give a child. "Let's be seated, gentlemen, shall we?"

He walked them over to an oversized black leather sofa, love seat, and chair ensemble, positioned in a style perfect for intimate conversation. A uniquely shaped stainless steel coffee table between the furniture pieces was softened by a lit, scented candle sitting in a vase surrounded by colorful stones: in Zen-like style. Brass coasters were already on the table, ready for their tea glasses. What could have been a dark, manly setting with all the black furniture was muted by accent colors of beige and powder blue, blond wood floors, and three large, genuine white tiger rugs. Stretch casually took in the understated show of wealth in Money's home, his eyes stopping on the only thing that looked out of place: an attractive yet outdated velvet style painting of a Black guitar player hanging over the fireplace.

"That's Robert Johnson," Money offered with pride in his voice, sitting in the large recliner while offering the couch to the two men. "But I bet y'all don't know nothin' 'bout that, about the blues."

Tony and Stretch looked at each other.

"No," Tony drawled slowly as he chose the love seat over the couch. "Can't say I do."

Money looked at Stretch, who sat at the end of the couch nearest Money's chair. "What about you?"

Without hesitation, Stretch replied, "Of course I know about the blues, I'm a Crip!"

Money laughed at Stretch's attempt at humor. He liked this young man's intelligence and charisma. If he could take direction, be discreet, and stay out of prison, he might have a solid, prosperous future within Money's empire.

He proceeded to give Tony and Stretch an abbreviated history of the Delta blues in general, and Robert Johnson in particular. "He was the most influential bluesman of all time. The popular music that came after that, rock, pop, soul, even the foundation of your hip-hop music, rests on the strings of that man's guitar.

"But that's not the only reason that particular piece of art is so valuable," Money went on. "It's a collector's item. There are only two of these that exist in the world. Eric Clapton's got the other one."

"That picture must be worth a grip!" Stretch said, getting up to take a closer look at the artwork with a new appreciation.

"Its value would surprise you, but you can't put a price on a piece like that."

"So, yeah, man, about this job?" Tony said, trying a soft prompt for Money to get to the business at hand.

"Are you in a hurry?" Money asked.

"Not especially," Tony said. "Just, I know you've got other business and all."

"My other business will wait," Money countered easily. "I haven't spent a lot of time with you and am just meeting Stretch. Since I'm looking at both of you for more than this particular job, I'd like to take a little time getting to know you. Is that all right?"

"Cool," Tony said, feeling slightly uncomfortable. Neither Money's voice nor his facial expression had changed. Yet Tony got the distinct impression he'd just been reprimanded . . . and reminded of who was in charge of this meeting. "I think I'll refresh my drink," he said, to cover his sudden nervousness.

"You want your tea freshened?" Money asked Stretch.

"No, thanks, dog, I'm cool." Stretch relaxed against the back of the premium leather sofa, stretching his arms across the length of it. As he did so, a movement caught the corner of his eye. He turned and beheld one of the most beautiful women he'd ever seen in his life. Hers was a smoldering, dark beauty: long, wavy brunette hair, dark olive skin, full, naturally pink lips, thick eyebrows, and long lashes. The year-old or so baby she held in her arms didn't hide the voluptuous curves behind it: packaged to perfection in a black, fitted knit dress. Her shapely calves tapered down to slender ankles and manicured toes inside three-inch-high sandals. Stretch's relaxed position didn't change, his head barely moved, and he didn't look at her for more than three, four seconds tops. But he'd drunk in this vision of lovely in an instant, and she was more potent than anything Money had at his bar.

Money walked over to her, and they conversed in low tones. He pulled out his wallet and placed a considerable amount of bills in her hand. Then he kissed her lightly on the forehead, kissed the baby, and walked with them toward the foyer as they headed out. The woman never once looked in their direction.

Tony looked at Stretch, put his hands out in front of him, and made a pumping gesture. "That's what I'd like to do to that," he whispered, taking a sip of straight Courvoisier. "That's a fine mamacita right there."

"Watch yourself, son," Stretch said in an equally low tone. "Money saw you checking her out and he looked none too pleased."

Tony's response was interrupted by Money walking back into the room. "Excuse that interruption, gentlemen," he said, once again taking his seat.

"That was a beautiful interruption," Tony replied. "What is she, Latina or Middle Eastern? I couldn't tell."

Money gave Tony a look that was hard to discern, tinged with the merest hint of a smile. "She's mine," he said simply.

"Bet you're proud of that baby," Stretch said, shifting the subject to safer waters.

Money's chest almost visibly swelled, as if to prove the truth of Stretch's statement. "That's my baby girl," he said, his smile unapologetically broad. "I waited ten years to get a girl. My son lives with his mother in another state."

"Well, she's a beautiful baby, man," Stretch replied.

Money's posture changed quickly; he sat up, to the edge of the chair in which he'd been reclining, put his elbows on his knees, and linked his fingers together. "Okay, here's what I have in mind, gentlemen. I've just come across a rare opportunity, one that could set me up as a major player in the Los Angeles real estate game, especially in this area and further south. Inglewood, Gardena, Hawthorne, Long Beach . . . One of the biggest dogs in the business has a problem. He's looking for someone who can bring some heat and . . . solve . . . this problem." He focused his attention on Tony. "Understand what I'm sayin'?"

Tony nodded that he understood. Stretch didn't say or do anything, but he understood too.

"As you can imagine," Money went on, "this client will be extremely grateful for our eliminating the competition and in addition to the six figures he's offering for the job itself has agreed to help ease me into the biz. I'm willing to spread the wealth and help set up legit business fronts . . . if you're interested. It's a high risk for a high reward."

The meeting ended about fifteen minutes later, after Money had given additional specifics on the job required. Plans were made for a second meeting after which Stretch and Tony exchanged Money's air-conditioned interior for the hot August sun.

"How long you known that dude?" Stretch asked Tony, once they'd driven out of the affluent, gated community.

"Two, three years," Tony replied. "He was good friends with my uncle, who did a job for him one time, similar to the one he wants us to do."

"Where's your uncle now?"

"Doing twenty-five to life."

"Damn."

"This is not a game, son. The stakes are high,which is why the payoff's so good."

"How much is that?"

"A hundred g's apiece."

"That makes no sense, man. You can get somebody offed for a couple g's."

"Not like the somebody Money's talking about."

"You know who it is?"

"No, but it's somebody major with that price tag. The risk goes up, and so does the time if you get caught. Court may even try and throw the death penalty in and shit."

Stretch looked out the window, saying nothing.

"You in, son?" Tony asked after a long pause.

"Man, I don't know. A hundred g's is hella money but doing life is hella time . . . feel me?"

But then he thought about Maya and all he owed her. This payoff would go a long way toward paying her back.

"Man, one of these days I'm gonna put Trish in a place like that," Tony continued, as he turned from Martin Luther King Boulevard and entered "The Jungle" a neighborhood that was the exact opposite from the one in which Money lived.

Stretch was glad for the change of subject. "Trish would look fly as hell in a house like that, no doubt. But then, baby girl looks fine whenever. And speaking of your girl, man, you need to call her. She's freaking about where you at."

"I been calling her ass all day. You seen her?"

"Last night, over at Maya's."

"You tell her I was locked down, man?"

"She figured it out."

"Damn, dog, why didn't you cover for a brother?"

Stretch looked at Tony. "That's my sister's best friend, dog. Trish is family. Go on and tell her what's up. She ain't all highfalutin' and shit . . . she'll be down with you. But lie to her and . . . well . . . I don't know."

"Now, that Maya, that's a highfalutin', fine piece of—"

"That's my sis, son, watch yourself."

Tony smiled and turned up the bass as a gangster rapper spewed curse words and death threats across the neighborhood. "Oh, I know she don't go slummin' . . . I'm just saying she's fine."

"Hey, man, let me off on the corner. I need to cop

a hookup." Stretch kept his posture casual as he
bobbed his head in time to the beat. But he needed to
get away from Tony, needed time to think. He'd been
waiting for a break to take him out of the little
leagues and into the majors. To pocket a hundred g's
would feel like an out-of-the-park home run, but if he
struck out, there wasn't enough money in the world
to justify life without parole . . . or worse.

21

Stretch was out of jail, but Maya still worried. She'd tried to call him last night after Trish left, wanted to find out more about the friend who'd bailed him out. As much as Stretch and his hoodish ways got on her nerves, she didn't know what she'd do if anything happened to him. He'd gotten caught up in the lifestyle of their old neighborhood, where he still lived. But at the heart of it, he was a good man.

She tried him once more as she exited the first bus and waited on the second one to arrive. After again getting his voice mail, she texted him with a message to call her that night. Then she checked her e-mails, both work and personal. By the time she finished a quick scan of both addresses, her second bus arrived.

Maya couldn't believe how quickly one's perspective could change. One day she vowed to never enter Sam Walter's house again and today it felt like an escape from the B&A office madness. Even the Martha outfit was a relief, the oversized top and baggy pants helping her further distance herself from the tenseness of her current corporate state. Today her biggest worry would be folding a towel properly and not leaving spots on glasses. What would it be like to have such a simple life for real? Maya wondered. And if faced with the dilemmas of Maya's world, what would Martha do? Maya laughed out loud at the thought. What would a lowly housekeeper, with no high-profile, high-paying job on the line, do about her brother, her promiscuous boss, and her love life?

She'd probably trust her intuition, follow her hunches, and go with the flow. Simple people didn't overcomplicate situations; life was what it was. Maya remembered what Cecilia had said about her pretend cousin's pregnancy. *Your cousin be fine. Having babies . . . natural to feel bad sometimes.* Just like that, no big deal. Joy, pain, sunshine, rain . . . all a part of life. Maya would make a conscious effort to adopt a similar attitude regarding the things that were taking place around her.

After coming in through the side entrance by the laundry room, Maya placed her purse in the closet and walked into the kitchen where Cecilia often left instructions on the day's chores. Instead of a note, she was surprised to see Sam Walters himself standing in the middle of the room.

"Oh, uh, excuse me," Maya said hesitantly. She'd been so busy focusing on Maya's mess, she'd almost forgotten Martha's accent! "How you doin'?"

Sean drank in Maya's beauty, shrouded yet evident behind the wig and oversized clothes. Now it seemed unimaginable he'd ever been fooled by a disguise that now looked transparent. And with his attraction to her at an all-time high, it was more important than ever that he not blow the Sam Walters cover. He'd heard underground rumblings of violence that didn't bode well for the company he was keeping. If anything happened to Maya because of him . . . well . . . he couldn't even finish that thought.

"Why do you do that?" he asked in a brusque, British accent.

Maya bristled. Sam Walters always rubbed her the wrong way. But now was not the time to make waves. This was the job she'd looked forward to, a day she thought would be fairly routine.

"What, sah?"

"Talk like you're a slave from *Roots* instead of a native Californian. You were born in California, right?"

Maya nodded.

"So what's with the nauseous, southern accent? You do your ancestors a grave injustice by not speaking proper English!" Sam's accent became even more clipped, if that was possible.

Maya longed to give Sam a taste of her extensive English vocabulary, using more than the first letters, but she kept her cool and answered with a shrug of the shoulders. She didn't even look up.

"Look at me," Sean insisted.

Maya took a deep breath, straining to keep her temper under control. For not the first time that day, she was thankful for the disguise, thankful that she'd barely be able to see Sam through the thick glasses, almost as thick as the first pair she'd lost.

"Take off your glasses," he ordered.

"I can't see without—"

"Take them off!"

Maya's head shot up before she could stop herself. Her face fixed into a frown, but she covered it up by acting like the scrunched-up face was to help her see. "Why you want me to take off my glasses?" she asked in a soft, subdued voice.

Forget Trish being the actress; Maya could have

won an Oscar in that moment. For all her subservient posturing, she was seconds away from pimp-slapping her billionaire boss.

Sean struggled to keep the smile off his face. How could he have missed this smoldering fire, this sensuality-charged force barely hidden inside baggy clothes? His stern countenance in place, he answered her tersely, "I like to see what my employees look like."

What the "h"? Maya couldn't believe what she was hearing. She had come to this house for six weeks and Sam had barely acknowledged her existence. Now all of a sudden he wanted to "see what she looked like"? She kept her face scrunched up, trying to disguise her features as Sam Walters gave her the once-over.

Sean knew he should leave her alone, but he couldn't. He wanted to be around her all the time, any way he could, even in the caustic role of the man she despised. With a recklessness he seldom displayed, he pushed on.

"What size are you?" he asked, as if he were inquiring about the time of day, or the weather.

"'Scuse me?"

"What size do you wear, you know, in panties, bra, pants, and top . . . especially panties?"

Maya's mouth dropped open.

"I'm thinking of ordering maid uniforms for you and Cecilia, dress, underwear, shoes, the works." Sean's expression remained blank, casual, but his blood was quickly warming at the thought of Maya in a skimpy French maid uniform.

Maya was stunned. What the bump was going on? Was Mercury retrograde or something, that time of the year when the alignment of the planets sent communication all out of whack? Surely she hadn't heard what it sounded like she heard; surely Sam "Waddling" Walters hadn't just asked her about her panty size?

"Where's Cecilia" she asked abruptly. Somehow she'd walked into the twilight zone, and she needed to quickly make her way back to Real World.

"I, uh, I don't feel right talking to you 'bout this," she said, with more southern drawl than she'd ever used. She was going from Kizzy in *Roots* to Celie in *The Color Purple*, but was too discombobulated with Sam's line of questioning to notice.

Sean figured it was enough badgering for the moment. "I guess you're right," he said after a pause. "Cecilia's running errands. I believe there's a mountain of laundry to be washed and then the linen in all the bedrooms need to be refreshed. Once that's done, all relevant floors can be mopped, the silver shined, and then . . . well . . . just come see me after that."

The silver shined? Cecilia had just done that two weeks ago. Maya decided to remain silent. All the joy she'd felt for coming here today had vanished. She would talk to Zeke first thing tomorrow and tender her resignation; if not to her role as Martha Williams, then to her position as executive assistant at B&A. Nothing was worth this aggravation.

Maya entered the laundry room and for the first time since she'd started working in the Walters household . . . locked the door. She leaned against the cool walnut exterior and inhaled deeply. Her heart was pounding, but until now, she'd been too busy trying to maintain her Martha persona to notice. Slowly, she opened her eyes and looked around. Here, things looked normal. The detergent, bleach, fabric softener, and other cleaning products were in their normal place on the top shelf. The iron, spray bottle, dryer sheets, and other laundering items occupied their normal spot on the second tier. A huge pile of linens, which looked to represent all the sheets and towels in the house, was in the middle of the floor. As Maya took in the familiarity of her surroundings, her breathing calmed and her tense shoulders relaxed.

She began sorting out the whites from colors and while doing so, tried to sort out the meaning behind Sam's strange conversation. He'd never shown the slightest interest in her as a person, much less what she was wearing. And now that he was talking, it was about panties? None of it made any sense.

As she loaded the two washing machines, Maya began to see the humor in what had just happened. That fat, stuck-up Brit had tried to come on to her! What's more, he'd done so with a lame "a" line about panty size! Was that as creative as he could get? The more she thought about it, the more she wasn't surprised. He was a man and she a woman after all. That he would test the employer/employee boundaries was bound to happen. Just look at Zeke and Jade. She only hoped her reaction served as fair notice: There wasn't a chance this side of forever that Sam Walters and Maya, or even the lowly Martha, would do a bump and grind.

Maya worked uninterrupted for almost half an hour, steadily thinking about how to get control of her life. She hoped Sean would help her prove Sam Walter's identity, the easiest solution being he was exactly who he said he was, a rich man wanting to buy real estate. "And a pervert," she muttered aloud. Then there was B&A and how to make a well-timed exit. When it came to Jade, she wasn't running from a fight as much as avoiding one in which she didn't care to win. Jade was welcome to whatever she wanted from Zeke, as long as it didn't involve stepping on her in the process.

And then there was Stretch. Although he affectionately called her big sis, Maya was just a few minutes older than her thirty-year-old brother. He was past grown, and as hard as it was for her to cut the mama-type umbilical cord, Maya knew she needed to do just that. Maya had fulfilled the promise she made to her mother, as they'd talked casually one evening while preparing dinner.

"Look after your brother, Maya," she'd said. Their mother, Janet, knew he and his friends ran afoul of the law. "I know he's hard-headed but he listens to you. One of these days I won't be around for y'all. Just keep an eye out if you can."

"That's my twin, my heart Mama. You know we'll always have each other's back."

The words spoken so casually proved prophetic. The next night her mother was struck head-on during a police car chase. She died instantly.

A rattling of the doorknob, followed by a loud pounding on the laundry door made Maya jump. She'd totally forgotten about locking the door, but was once again surprised at Mr. Walters's uncharacteristic behavior. Then again, maybe it was Cecilia. Maya rushed over to open the door.

"What on earth are you doing in there that you need the door locked?" Sean demanded. He'd vowed to stay away from Maya for the remainder of the afternoon, but his body had refused to listen.

"I—I'm sorry. I must have pushed the button by mistake. I didn't know it was locked."

Maya forced herself to not squirm under Mr. Walters's penetrating stare. His unusual behavior was unnerving, but Maya had gone up against bigger guns than Sam. He had no idea who he was messing with. She might be playing the part of a lowly maid, but if he kept acting crazy, Maya was going to have to introduce him to another side of her. She fixed her eye on a spot just over Mr. Walters's shoulder and waited for him to speak.

"Don't ever lock any of the doors in my home," Sean said finally, once again appreciating Maya's fire, even as she tried to dampen it under the guise of Martha Jones. "And hurry up in here. I'm leaving the house for a couple hours, but Cecilia will be back before then. If you actually work instead of day-dreaming, you might be able to finish most of the responsibilities we've given you."

Maya just stood there, imagining her hand grabbing the iron to the left of her and smashing home-boy upside his snooty face. He really didn't know how close he was to a postal moment. Sam Walters was really pushing her already tightly wound buttons. Was it a full moon or what? Thank God, he was leaving. That's all that mattered. She'd have a little time by herself in his home. Focusing on that fact helped her blood stop boiling.

"Thank you, Mr. Walters. Sorry about the door. Yes, I think I can finish everything." To emphasize her point, Maya turned to the washer that had just shut off and began hurriedly placing the wet items into the dryer and refilling the washer with a new load of clothes. "Yes, suh?" she asked, when Mr. Walters continued to stand there.

He didn't reply, just shook his head curtly and left.

Five minutes after she'd heard the front door close, and with both washer and dryer going strong, Maya ventured out of the laundry room. She hurried to the garage, double-checking that the BMW 720 sedan that Mr. Walters drove was gone. It was. She looked out front. Cecilia's Toyota was nowhere in sight. She walked back into the house and quickly riffled through her usual haunts, the guest rooms, master suite, kitchen and den. As she suspected, nothing different, nothing new. The place looked as much the hotel as when she'd first arrived; there was nothing to be found here. As she walked towards the laundry room she thought about Sean, and hoped he could help her gain the information she needed.

Just before turning the corner, she had a thought. *Try the office.* She almost ignored this niggling; that door was always locked. But because she hoped it was her last day, she saw no reason not to exhaust every option. She turned and walked back down the hall, to the forbidden double doors. She reached up casually and turned the knob, fully expecting the usual resistance. To her surprise, the knob turned. Finally, access to door number one. She opened the door slowly, tentatively, and then, sure the room was empty of occupants, let it swing open wide. Here it was: the off-limits domain of Sam Walters's office. It looked like, well, an office. She didn't know what she'd been expecting . . . a torture chamber maybe?

Maya took in the surroundings quickly: a large desk that faced the window, looking onto a fabulous view of the Pacific Ocean; a large, low-slung file cabinet that ran the length of the side wall; two earth-tone wingback chairs; a black leather love seat; and a colorful rug that covered a major part of the hardwood floor. Its vibrant shades of blue, teal, rust, and gold warmed up an otherwise stark, yet tasteful environment. And she was almost positive that the portrait hanging over the file cabinet was another Van Gogh.

At any other time, Maya could have taken hours to

study the ardent swirl of color in the nighttime scene captured by Van Gogh's talented brush. But Maya didn't have that kind of time today. With renewed resolve, she virtually marched over to the file cabinet, placed her hand on the handle, took a breath, and pulled. The cabinet drawer flew open as if the hinges had just been oiled. She jumped back in surprise.

"Oh my goodness," Maya whispered to herself. The good news: The drawer was filled with multi-colored file folders; the bad news . . . none of them were labeled.

Maya's ultraorganized personality was immediately incensed. "How on earth does anybody work like this?" she hissed angrily as she picked a file at random and pulled it out of its place. Mindful to not leave any clues to her presence, she also pulled up the folder just behind the one in her hand, so she'd be able to put each folder back in its rightful place.

A quick scan of the folder's contents showed a variety of restaurant menus. Thinking she'd probably stumbled onto the food area of the files, she placed that folder back and checked the one behind it. Maya frowned. The folder contained several papers with what appeared to be a bunch of random numbers. She looked at the next folder without totally taking it out of its place. It was filled with computer printouts of California museums, and behind it a folder of . . . purebred dogs? What the "f"? What in the world could Sam Walters need this type of seemingly random information for? And why was it filed so haphazardly? At this rate she'd have to look into each and every one of these files; what she was looking for, whatever that was, could be in any or none of them. It could easily take the rest of the week, let alone the rest of the day. It was one more reason to despise the bumbling Brit.

"Stupid, sloppy, stuck-up, uppity . . ." Maya continued to mumble to herself as she pulled one folder up after another only to find what seemed to her totally irrelevant materials for a man trying to grab the Los Angeles real estate world by the tail: luxury cars, weather reports, world atlases—okay, maybe that one made a bit of sense—and Broadway shows. Disgusted, Maya slammed the top drawer shut and decided to try the bottom. She needed to hit the real estate info jackpot, she needed to find the files that would point her to where Sam Walters's head was. Absorbed in her mission, Maya sat cross-legged on the floor, her head almost buried in the myriad of colored folders. She opened one with a directory to downtown businesses, with several of them highlighted in different colors.

"Yes!" Maya whispered enthusiastically. "Now, Sammy, let's see who you've got your eye on." She quickly ran her finger down the list of names.

"Find what you're looking for?"

Maya gasped, dropping the folder and its contents as she stumbled to her feet. She didn't even want to turn around, to witness Sam's disgruntled face, the last thing she'd see before being literally kicked to the curb. How could she tell Zeke she'd gotten caught, had failed the assignment? *Well . . . you said you wanted to get fired. Here goes. . . .* Slowly, resignedly, she turned around. Her heart was in her throat, and she closed her eyes, waiting for the railing. When nothing but silence greeted her, she opened her eyes.

"Sean!"

Knowing he'd lost the battle to keep his hands off Maya today, Sean had left only long enough to lose his Sam Walters facade. He'd given Cecilia the rest of the day off and planned to give "Martha" some good loving in the master suite's king-sized bed. He was surprised to walk in and find the office doors wide open, another sign of how when Maya was on his mind, he thought of little else. Even though there was nothing incriminating in those files, it was the principle of the thing: he was slipping.

"What if Sam had walked in here, Maya?" He walked fully into the room. "Huh? What would you have told him about breaking into his office?"

"I didn't break in, the door was open. Besides, you know what I'm doing in here. Something I wouldn't have to if you'd help me. Is Zeke beating a dead horse here, Sean? Is Sam Walters really some provocative player set to upturn the L.A. real estate apple cart, or is he just some rich fool from London with money to burn?"

Maya stood there so vulnerable, her eyes pleading for his assistance. He ached to tell her that he was Sam, and to let her in on the deal he had working with Neil, Phillip Campbell, and a firm in China. But it was just too risky, for everyone involved. So he sought to diffuse the situation instead.

"As far as I know, he's who he says he is. He owns a nice home in London and a country estate, travels in elite circles . . . I think the man just wants to get in on the action stateside. Why does Zeke think differently?"

"It's something he feels instinctively, in his gut. But considering what's been happening with Jade just a few inches lower, his radar may be off a tad."

Sean's laughter stopped abruptly as he heard the sound of the side door open followed by Cecilia's familiar hum. What was she doing back here?

Her footsteps in the hallway told him he didn't

have time to find out. The office doors were still wide open and he couldn't chance trying to explain what a strange man named Sean was doing in Sam's office with the maid.

Maya had scooped up the dropped files and held them to her chest as she looked at him with wide, questioning eyes. He grabbed her hand, quickly opened the room's closet door and pushed her inside.

Maya's chest heaved with the breaths that rose and fell rapidly. She didn't know whether her heightened state was from being moments away from getting caught in the closet with Sean, or from his arm now draped possessively over her left breast. He took his right arm and pressed her even closer against him, and carelessly brushed her nipple with his left thumb. Maya shivered, afraid to push away lest she bump into something and make a noise that would get them both discovered.

Sean closed his eyes, savoring the feeling of his woman next to him. She felt so good, smelled so good. He hugged her tighter, becoming bolder with his movements. He let his hand drop down to the hem of Maya's oversized T-shirt, then slid his hand up under it. Maya's hand and adamant shake of the head weren't enough to stop his lustful wandering. After a second attempt to push his hand away, she stopped trying. If he removed his hand now, she might die.

Maya's huge sweatpants gave easy access to the paradise Sean loved. He heard Maya's faint intake of breath as he pushed his fingers gently against her love bush. His tongue flicked against her ear, and then her neck, as his fingers continued their journey downward. All the while he listened, heard Cecilia slowly walking the perimeter of the office, knew when she'd stepped onto the carpeted area, knew when she went to the window, and knew that even now she was looking out at the magnificent ocean view.

Maya's body pressed against Sean's involuntarily. Her legs parted of their own volition. It had been hours, it had been a lifetime, since they'd been together. She turned, wrapped her arms around his neck, and devoured his mouth.

Sean gave as good as he got. He clasped Maya's round butt and pushed it toward his hardening shaft. He wanted her desperately; it took everything he had to keep his wits about him, to remember where he was and everything that was at stake. He kissed Maya passionately and dipped his head to take her hard nipple into his mouth. Maya's gasp was audible then. She reached for his belt buckle just as he heard the outside door close. Sean stopped abruptly.

Sean turned from lover to professional Private I in a heartbeat. "You need to go," he said, straightening her clothes. "I hear Cecilia's footsteps upstairs now. She's probably looking for you. Hurry out, go through the kitchen and come back through the garage. Tell her you thought you heard something." He pressed his lips against hers one last time, caressing her booty at the same time. "Now go!"

Sean opened the closet door and pushed her out. Maya barely had time to think, let alone react. She hurried to the door, which she noted Cecilia had locked. Looking quickly to the left and right, she ran down the hall, out the kitchen, through the garage, and back through the door that led to the laundry room. Sean was right. Cecilia came around the corner just as she stepped inside.

"I'm off the rest of the day but forgot my cell phone. What are you doing out there?"

"I, uh, thought I heard something," she said, not having to act much to adopt a scared, frantic tone. "In the garage." Maya continued, catching her breath. "Sounded like a rat or something!" Thinking of Sean, she realized the last statement she made was the one closest to truth.

"A rat?" Cecilia repeated, immediately looking at the mounds of clothes around her.

"I didn't find nothin'," Maya continued, looking around as well. "But I better hurry up with this washing, get these clothes off the floor. We wouldn't want to give a big rodent like that a place to hide!" Maya reached into the dryer, put those items on the folding table, placed the wet linens in the dryer and a fresh load in the wash. When she looked up, Cecilia was nowhere in sight. Guess the talk of a big rat squelched any questions she might have had about where Maya was or why more hadn't been done in the time Cecilia had been gone. Thank God for small favors. Maya's mind was mush: Sean's stopping by had totally unnerved her; she would have totally failed a Cecilia-style interrogation.

Maya's mind was on Sean the whole time she folded the towels. Was he still in the house? If not, how had he gotten out? She'd been listening, and had heard no door open or close since returning to the laundry room. And what about his car? Had it been parked right outside? Did Cecilia know what it looked like? Did she know Sean? How had Sean gotten into the house? And how had he gotten out?

Sean leaned his head back against the car's headrest. While Cecilia was in the laundry room talking to Maya, he'd eased out the side door next to the ocean, the one that intersected with the bike path. Then he'd crossed over to the condo building, staying close to the shrubbery until he reached the sidewalk, where he casually unlocked and stepped into his Mercedes, the car he switched with the BMW when going from Sam to Sean.

He dialed Maya's number and got voicemail, as he'd expected.

"Baby," he said after the beep, "you know we've got to finish what we started. Call me when you leave there, let me know everything is okay."

There was a smile on his face as he drove towards the Marina. There was still confusion surrounding B&A, Rosenthal and his potential Angel's Way connection, but one thing was crystal clear: he was back on track with Maya. With her in his life no matter what else, his world was right side up.

22

Trish lugged her large carry-on bag inside the door and kicked off her heels. She was sore, tired, dehydrated, and if anybody asked her to eat another piece of chicken, they'd get a beat-down. She'd never been happier in her life.

After taking a long, hot shower, Trish came out and checked her phone messages. She'd purposely not done so while driving home. She figured since Tony was out, he'd be calling and wanting to come over. But since she knew she wouldn't have the strength for his all-night lovemaking sessions after the long hours on the set, she'd put off trying to talk to him . . . until now.

He picked up on the first ring. "Hey, baby, where you been? I've been calling you all day."

"Yeah, I've been calling you for the last few days."

"I know, I know, I've been rather unavailable."

Trish closed her eyes, hoping Tony would come clean about being in jail. If he couldn't be honest with her, there was no hope for the relationship. "Tony, where have you been?"

There was only a slight pause before he answered.

"Aw, baby, they had me on lock for a minute, some bullshit about a past warrant and some old gang-related nonsense. They were just sniffin' out a brotha, trying to see what they could find out and whatnot." His speech became even lower and slower than usual. Trish loved it when he talked like that.

"I been missing you, baby . . . feel me?" he asked.

"Yeah . . . I feel you."

"So, can a brotha come over? Get some lovin?"

"You know I want you. But I've had a long day, Tony. See, I got this commercial and—"

"Commercial . . . for real? You gon' be on TV and thangs?"

He sounded impressed. It made Trish smile and reminded her why she was crazy about this man, police record and all. "Yeah, I'm going to be on TV. It's a national ad."

"What you selling, baby?"

Trish hesitated for only a second. "Champion's."

There was absolute silence on the other end.

"Tony? You there?"

"That new chicken chain? Aw, baby, not fried chicken."

"What, you said you loved their chicken . . . said it was way better than KFC. Wait a minute . . . we've hit their drive-through plenty of times. We can eat it but I can't sell it? We can spend our money there but they can't spend money on me?"

"C'mon now, that's not what I said. It's just that they should have you selling some designer wear, diamonds, furs, shit like that. Not no damn chicken! I don't want you doing that, baby."

The same voice that moments ago had stirred Trish's love juices was now grinding on her last nerve. Who was he to tell her what she should and shouldn't do? True, his "d" was long, but his paper needed to be longer before he could start calling these kinds of shots.

"Excuse me? Do you know how hard it is to get a commercial, a national ad? Do you have any idea how long I've been waiting for a break like this?"

Trish tried to get Tony to see her point of view, explaining that this chain was the first to come along in years to give the number-one fast food chicken chain serious competition.

"Don't trip, baby, I know this is cool and all. I'm just sayin . . . I don't know if I want my woman selling chicken on TV."

"Well, until you are paying your woman's bills and all of her other responsibilities, you're just going to have to let your woman make it do what it do. And for what they're paying me, I'll turn *into* a 'd' chicken . . . know what I'm sayin'?" To prove her point, Trish started squawking.

Tony was upset, but Trish's craziness calmed him down. This was a good woman and he was going to try to keep his temper under control, a trait that had blown relationships with other women. After this job for Money, Trish would be able to do whatever she wanted to, hell, maybe he'd eventually bankroll a movie with her in the starring role. He could finally go legit. He and his boy Stretch were getting ready to suit up.

"So . . . can I come over?"

"Tony, baby, I have to be up in, like, four hours. Can I make it up to you this weekend? I had just got home when I called you, am tired as 'h,' and still need to practice lines. We're doing three different commercials, and this is just the beginning of a campaign that's going to run for almost a year!"

"Yeah, okay, whatever." Tony didn't try and hide his disappointment. "I'll holla later." He hung up without good-bye.

Trish sat in her darkened living room, wondering how one could feel so elated yet so empty at the same time. She'd hoped Tony would be as excited about her project as she was; ask her questions, offer to help her run lines, be there for her. Maybe that was asking too much. Tony had never tried to be anything other than what he was: a thug out of Long Beach, smart enough to be the CEO of any company, yet a man who'd gotten his GED while in prison. She spent most of her time looking at the good things he had to offer: his wit, charm, intelligence, a body L.L. Cool J would envy, and a penis that should be trademarked it looked and felt so good. If it weren't for the fact that he'd have to sleep with so many women, she would have suggested he give adult movies a try. He definitely had the physique and stamina for it, and maybe he could get out of the illegal games he played that, while risky, paid so well.

Trish got up from the couch and headed toward her bedroom. The phone rang. It was Maya. "Hey, girl."

"Hey, how did it go? You ready to give the leading ladies some competition?"

"Child, those sistas are a long way from needing to worry about my 'a.' I had fun, though."

"You sound tired. Feel like talking about it?"

Trish gave Maya a brief rundown of her day. "I never thought I'd be a vegetarian, but after eating all that chicken . . . give me a 'd' soy burger, okay? Some beans, a salad . . . I don't want anything that resembles an animal at this point!"

"Oh Lord, girl. I never thought I'd hear of you not wanting meat. You must be tired and full!"

"Girl, you know I'm playing. Somebody trying to take meat off my plate will get forked!"

"Now, that's the Trish I know," Maya said, laughing. "I was wondering where she went. Speaking of whereabouts, have you heard from Tony? I still haven't heard from Malcolm and I've been calling him since you left last night."

Trish filled Maya in on her and Tony's conversation. "I love me some Tony," Trish said in conclusion. "I just don't know if love is enough. I want it to be . . ."

"Don't let love for his loving blind you," Maya warned. "No man is worth your getting in trouble with the law, Trish. Tony needs to be straight with you about what he's involved in, at least as it affects you. And every time he comes over to your house, you're indirectly affected."

"I know I need to find out just what's going on. We're going to have that talk the next time he comes over. I knew better than to bring it up over the phone."

"I'm glad to hear that, Trish. I know you're a big girl but I worry about you."

"Well, you worry too much. But I appreciate it. So is it on for us this weekend, you, me, Tony and Sean?"

"It was so crazy today, I forgot to ask him, Trish. He's all caught up in the work he's doing."

"You said some detective work, right? Sounds mysterious, adventurous, my kind of fun."

It was Maya's kind of fun too, she thought after saying good-bye and hanging up the phone. The kind that had her wet and panting in an office closet. Sean had been busy when she called him back, an unexpected meeting with someone from China. She was glad to not have to hide the whole Martha charade anymore, and felt even better about her plans to tell

Zeke she wanted out of the assignment. Sean said there was nothing shady about Sam Walters and she believed him.

She went to sleep imagining herself wrapped in Sean's arms.

23

Sean was unaware of the admiring stares as he strode confidently through the lobby of the Brennan Building. The last time he walked through, he had admired the refined architecture, flawless marble, contemporary design, and even an attractive executive or two. But not today. Today, a woman could have passed Sean buck naked and were that woman not Maya . . . he wouldn't have noticed.

There were three reasons why. One, Maya. He'd seen her again last night and as usual, her beauty and brains combo had left him satiated and wanting more. Two, he'd spoken with Tangier and hadn't liked the tone of the conversation. He thought he'd placated her enough to deal with their situation once his business in LA was over but their conversation proved that wasn't the case. He didn't need the extra hassle of her nonsense because three, word was out on the street about a high level hit, one he thought might be aimed at someone in the world of real estate. That brought him back to reason number one, and why he was at the B&A offices. Zeke had scheduled a meeting to discuss Sam Walters. Sean was more than interested to hear what he had to say.

Ester greeted Sean warmly as he stepped into the reception area. "Hello, Mr. Wynn," she said without him having to introduce himself. "You're here to see Mr. Brennan?"

"Yes . . . Ester, correct?"

She was surprised and flattered he remembered, not knowing that Sean's near photographic memory was one of the things that made him an ace investigator. "That's right!" Ester answered, unaware that her body language had turned flirtatious.

One of Zeke's assistants came into the lobby. "Mr. Wynn, Mr. Brennan is ready to see you."

Sean smiled politely at Ester and followed the assistant down the hall. Just as he passed an office door, an attractive, dark-haired woman rushed out of it. His quick reflexes prevented a collision.

"Oh my goodness, I'm so sorry," the woman said, the surprise on her face quickly replaced with admiration. "You must be Sean Wynn, here to see Ze— I mean, Mr. Brennan. I'm Jade," she said, holding out her hand. "Jade Laremy." Had it not been for the hunger in her eyes and the way she straightened her back, straining her breasts inside the tight sweater she wore, her demeanor would have been totally professional.

Sean smiled, shook her hand, and went on his way, reading Jade's mind like a magazine. Maya was right, he could see treachery in the brunette's eyes. She'd do anything to get what she wanted, and it looked like she wanted Maya's right-hand woman position. If things worked out the way he wanted, Jade could have it. Sean had his own plans for both Maya's personal and professional futures.

"Sean, good to see you again!" Zeke's handshake was hearty and his smile sincere as Sean was escorted into Zeke's office.

"You too, Zeke," Sean replied.

Zeke motioned toward the conference room area. "Would you like anything, Sean? Coffee, croissants . . . ?"

Sean shook his head. "No, thank you, Zeke. I'm on a tight schedule today."

Zeke nodded his understanding and motioned to the chair on the other side of his desk. He began to speak as soon as Sean sat down.

"I've got a plan I want to run by you, get your professional investigator input, if I might. It's regarding Sam Walters and the project I've got Maya working on."

"I'm listening."

"Well, Maya's been in that house for over a month and hasn't been able to find anything substantial on the guy, but I just can't seem to shake the feeling that there's something fishy about him."

Sean relaxed. This was something he'd be able to handle. "Oh, so you want me to step in, investigate the guy? I could do so discretely, being that I know him and all."

Zeke leaned back and studied Sean while he tapped a pen on the desktop. "Well, that's just it. I've had background checks done and other screenings conducted. Nothing out of order comes up on the guy. It seems that Sam Walters is who he says he is, owner of a successful, international real estate company.

Sean shrugged his shoulders. "Then what's the problem?"

Zeke rose from the desk, jammed his hands in his pockets and strolled over to admire his thirty-third floor view. "The problem," he said slowly, "is that I don't trust people I don't know. There are few players in this game that I don't know about, and I'm not comfortable with the fact that I didn't know about him."

Sean resisted the urge to squirm in his discomfort. He had a feeling he wasn't going to like what Zeke was planning, but remained quiet as Zeke continued his spiel.

"Now Maya's a beautiful woman, wouldn't you agree?"

"I would."

"And, uh, that Walters fellow is new here, doesn't know anybody. I bet he'd love to get to know somebody like Maya, don't you think?"

"I don't know, why don't you ask him?" Sean knew his answer was curt, but he didn't care. Nor did it matter that he was Sam. Where did Zeke get off treating Maya like property?

Zeke held up his hands. "Now just wait, hear me out. I'm not thinking about asking her to be an escort or anything like that. Maya would never go for that and I'm not that crass."

Knowing what he did about Zeke and Jade, Sean almost snorted.

"But," Zeke continued. "I do know Sam's a businessman and as such, could probably use an assistant. Maya could use this ruse to develop a friendship and . . . who knows what might happen?"

Zeke placed his hands on his desk and leaned towards Sean. "And who knows what secrets could spill out during a little pillow talk if an attraction of the physical nature did develop between those two."

Sean didn't yet trust himself to speak.

"He's rich, powerful . . . not the fittest man in the world but he's intelligent—might be Maya's type."

Sean leaned back in the chair, rubbing his chin thoughtfully, his emotions in control. This was an unexpected development that had to be handled with the utmost care because it involved Maya, his MVP.

He wanted to reject the plan outright, but he knew that wasn't wise. Zeke was already paranoid and Sean didn't want to do anything to heighten his suspicion. Plus, because of Sean's supposed London connection with Sam, he was sure Zeke was suspicious of him as well. But if he went along with the plan, that meant spending time when Maya in the guise of Sam Walters, a gruff, bumbling Englishman who "Martha" couldn't stand and he didn't think Maya would like him much either.

Then it occurred to him, Sam couldn't wine and dine Martha, but he could definitely show Maya the respect she deserved. It would be hell to pay if she found out about his charade before he was prepared to tell her, but with them working together in a more professional capacity, he might be able to pull it off. He'd meet with her three, four times tops, enough for Zeke to think his plan was working. Sean smiled, beginning to warm to the idea. He always liked a challenge. And it would be one more way he could keep an eye on Maya, make sure she was protected until the Angel's Way deal closed and a firm to head up the project was selected. That should be in the next few weeks. Surely his decade plus of undercover work would allow him to keep his true identity hidden for that long.

He was now on board with Zeke's ridiculous plan, but didn't want to seem overeager.

"Since you don't know Sam, why are you willing to risk Maya getting involved with him?"

Zeke chuckled. "Because I know Maya, and you don't. She's tougher than she looks, grew up on the south side, pulled herself up by her own bootstraps. The greater risk will be to Sam getting involved with her. I can't think of any man who'd turn her down if given the chance to get close."

"Including you?"

Zeke leaned back in his chair. "Including me."

Sean looked at his watch and stood. This meeting was over. He had to leave Zeke's office before he lost his cool. The thought of this character trying to roll up on Maya . . . it was time to go.

"I've got to get to my other meeting. But keep me posted on how everything work's out."

Zeke's eyes narrowed as he watched Sean leave his office. Sean seemed miffed at the thought of Maya being with Sam Walters. Could it be because Sean was interested in having Maya for himself?

Zeke was still pondering his options from that possibility as he reached for the phone and rang Maya's office.

"I got your message. You wanted to see me, Zeke?"

"Come on in, Maya," Zeke said. "I hear the Santa Monica deal is about to go through. You're helping with the close, right?"

"I've been invited to the meeting, yes." Maya smiled. She was very proud that this venture, something she'd discovered and then nurtured indirectly as the company's top producer used his skills to bring all the players on board, was now ready to close. Her first sell, not single-handedly but close enough for jazz. She'd believed it all along but now she knew . . . she could do this!

"I'm very proud of you, Maya, knew you had it in you to do well in this field. However, the Santa Monica deal isn't why I wanted to speak to you."

Maya nodded, waited.

"I think we need to switch tactics where Sam Walters is concerned. You've done well to try and get information as his housekeeper, but it seems clear that this ruse isn't delivering what we need as fast as we need it."

Maya fought the urge to squirm in her seat. She had nothing to be ashamed of; if there had been any way for her to find something on Sam Walters, she would have done it.

"I won't tell you I'm disappointed at ending this assignment," Maya said truthfully. "I'm actually relieved that you want me to end that housekeeper charade. You know I'd do almost anything for the company, Zeke. But that assignment was really starting to wear on my nerves, and I'm really antsy to get back into the full swing of things here at the office."

"Don't worry about that," Zeke countered. "Even with your extracurricular activities on my behalf, you're still doing a great job. Which is why I think you'll be perfect for what I have in mind."

Oh God, not another crazy-"a" harebrained idea of yours, is what Maya thought. "Oh?" is what she said.

"Sam Walters is looking for a temporary assistant. I'm thinking to recommend you for the job."

"Me? Work with Sam Walters? Am I missing why this would be a good idea?"

"I know this last month has been a strain on you, Maya. But that's partly because you were out of your element, working as a housekeeper. This assignment should be easy. You're meeting Sam as Maya Jamison, trusted assistant to Zeke Brennan. I think it will be great. He's looking for a research assistant. You'll know everything about him, what locations he's scouting . . . what properties. Most important is for you to find out if he's snooping for someone we don't know about for the Angel's Way. It will be your job to find out."

Maya sat and gazed out the window. Would this nightmare ever end? Just when she was about to celebrate taking off her rubber gloves and putting back on her suit, it was only to find out the suit would be worn while once again working for Sam Walters. Why couldn't she get away from this man?

"How long and how often am I supposed to do this temp work?" Maya tried and failed to keep the weariness out of her voice.

"Not long."

"What if this guy is who he says he is, a successful real estate tycoon with money to burn? Look at all this time and effort we're putting into trying to dig up dirt, when maybe it would be better used developing a partnership."

"That's why this plan can be so effective," Zeke countered easily. "Your developing a friendship with Sam will be beneficial either way. If he isn't who he says he is, your work will be invaluable to helping B&A stay ahead in the game. If he is who he says, then your working with him can only help you in setting up additional deals, and developing valuable friendships with some of this city's power players, all of whom, I can assure you, are trying to become friends with Sam Walters."

"But aren't these same people already your friend, Zeke? Why can't I do the same thing as your protégé?"

Maya made a good point. But the situation wasn't that simple. One of the reasons Zeke was trying to move Maya up in his company was to make room for Jade as his executive assistant. It would give them the perfect cover for their in-office trysts and business trips. He appealed to Maya's ego.

"I want the industry to recognize you on your own merits, Maya, not as someone who was given what they have because they were my assistant. After you get some nice deals under your belt as a Realtor, my plans are to make you a manager. That way you can use both your sales and your organizational and managerial skills to their fullest potential."

Maya couldn't disagree with anything Zeke had said. She should have been elated that he wanted to make her a manager in the firm. Some people had been with him ten years and hadn't been given that title. But was any of that, or all of it, worth having to put up with Sam Walters on a regular basis?

"If you're totally uncomfortable with this," Zeke continued after Maya didn't respond, "I guess I could see if there was someone else in the office who might be interested in this opportunity. Jade's busy with another project, but maybe she could—"

"I'll do it," Maya interrupted.

Zeke smiled. As he'd hoped, mention of Maya's stiffest competitor in the office had the desired effect. "I'm glad to hear that. Now, here's the plan. . . ."

Maya was thankful that her day had been too busy to stay focused on her morning meeting with Zeke. She'd spent the rest of the morning going through her in-box, filled with correspondence, reports, memos, and phone messages. Her afternoon had flown by, spending most of it with Rusty, the Realtor set to close the real estate property tomorrow. This, her first sell, was the one bright spot in an otherwise chaotic, confusing, stressful life, all thoughts of which came rushing back to the forefront as she squeezed into the five o'clock rush-hour traffic on the 10 Freeway.

She needed help sorting it all out, and reached for her cell phone. "Hey, Trish."

"Ooh, girl, you scared me. I wasn't expecting my phone to ring."

"What were you expecting it to do, fly?"

"Oh, you're Comedy Central now, huh? What I meant was, I didn't expect the phone to ring while I was checking messages just now. We're on dinner break, otherwise I would have missed you. What's up?"

"Same 's,' different day. You want to hear the latest?"

"Do I have a choice?"

"Zeke wants me to stop working as Sam's house-keeper."

"Uh, isn't that good news?"

"And start working as his research assistant!"

"What the 'f'?"

Maya gave Trish the one-minute version of her meeting with Zeke.

"Well, that's not so bad, My. I'm surprised you don't see the benefits. You're not usually one to shy away from a challenge, and I definitely think you can handle one fat 'a' Brit. It was one thing when you were a maid, but now he's going to see you as some-one valuable, someone who's working for the top real estate man in Cali. I say you change the way you're looking at this whole thing . . . turn it around to work in your favor."

"That's why you're my best friend, Trish, because

during those rare times I act like I have none, you share your common sense."

Maya exited the freeway onto Manchester Boulevard but instead of going home, decided to go by the mall. She planned to look her absolute best the next time she saw Sam Walters. If she was going to do this, she was going to do it to the best of her ability. A smile broke across her face as she imagined meeting Sam for the first time as Maya Jamison. Trish was right. This was the opportunity of a lifetime, an even better, more productive way to take the leap from assistant to top Realtor. And Maya intended to take full advantage of it, and of Sam Walters. After the "h" he'd put her through as his housekeeper, she was going to work on a creative way to return the favor.

24

Maya stepped out of her BMW with confidence. It had been two days since her conversation with Zeke about Sam Walters, enough time for her to develop a game plan and have a few confidence-building conversations with Trish. That was after the very first conversation she'd had regarding this new employment, a call to the house-cleaning agency with her resignation. That was one of the most satisfying calls she'd ever made.

She'd also talked to Mr. Walters over the phone. But now he was Sam, as he had insisted at the beginning of the conference call between her, him, and Zeke. Sam was quite appreciative of Zeke's generosity in offering one of his top employees to help S.W.I. Maya felt better after the phone conference, during which Sam was pleasant and gracious. Maya imagined he limited his "total a-hole" persona to lowly housekeepers, and maybe stray dogs if any dared cross his portly path.

Maya held on to thoughts of the person with whom she'd quipped over the phone, the "sane" Sam Walters. She was determined to lose the hostile feelings she'd developed toward him while working with Cecilia, and intended to put her absolute best foot forward during their first meeting. To this end, and her game plan, she had added some new, sexier suits and a couple of party dresses, courtesy of her hefty commission on the Santa Monica deal, to her wardrobe. She meant to wow not only anyone they met with, but Sam Walters as well. Knowing that men's lower heads often overruled their higher ones, she decided to take Trish's advice and appeal to Sam's sexual, manly side. Get him hot for her; then she'd be in control, and at the same time remain the epitome of professionalism. If Trish was right, he wouldn't be able to resist a combination that appealed to both his intellect and what Maya guessed was probably his pencil-sized manhood. Someone as snooty as Sam Walters couldn't possibly carry a big stick.

Maya rang the doorbell and waited for Cecilia to answer. As she did, she remembered a day not long ago when she'd rung this doorbell, under very different circumstances. She shook her head as she thought about what a crazy ride she'd been on for the past month and a half.

"Ms. Jamison?"

Maya turned around at the sound of Cecilia's voice.

"Yes." She resisted the natural inclination to hold out her hand. Shaking the help's hand was not something one in her position would do.

"Come this way."

Maya walked with authority through the foyer she'd often admired with a dust mop in her hand. She felt she looked exceptional in a formfitting chocolate suit, beige knit blouse with a V neck that offered just enough but not too much cleavage, and spiked heels. Her brown leather Coach briefcase was the perfect accent, and she'd had her hair freshly done over the weekend, along with a brow wax. A mani/pedi had been the last step in what she hoped was the perfect outfit for this latest assignment regarding one certain Brit. There were very few challenges where Maya Jamison didn't end up victorious. She expected this time to be no different; she had every intention of wowing not the pants off, but the information out of Sam Walters.

Cecilia led Maya toward a side of the house she'd rarely ventured into when she worked there. She didn't even think Sam used it, and as she thought of it, she realized that aside from Sean, she'd never seen a visitor come to the house. Interesting that he had asked her to meet here. She didn't have time to think about that now, though; they'd reached what looked to be a study/library. Sam, his gray-streaked Afro looking unkempt with his bushy mustache and beard, obviously not wanting to go against the grain, was seated behind a massive desk. *To go with his massive ego*, Maya thought, but kept a pleasant smile plastered on her face as she walked toward him with outstretched hand.

"It's nice to formally meet you, though I must say after our conference call, I feel as if I know you already."

Sam gave a curt nod, barely looking at her as he sat back down behind the desk. "Have a seat, please."

Maya sat, wondering why Sam the stuffy Brit had shown up, and where was the affable gentleman who'd conversed easily during the conference calls? He looked like the same old Sam she'd grown to know and despise during her time here as Martha: trademark khaki pants, a wrinkled shirt, and a tacky tie that lay askew over his unsightly potbelly. But she had to keep her eye on the prize. She would not be deterred from her vow of remaining pleasantly professional, even sexy, at all times, even if it killed her—which, if Sam was going to act like this during the entire meeting, it just might. Still, she kept the smile on her face as she sat, placed her briefcase on the floor beside her, and waited for him to speak.

It seemed to take forever. For a moment, Sean was speechless, drinking her in as if she were water and he were dying of thirst. He hadn't expected her to show up looking so fine. Where was that conservative, frigid-looking woman he'd seen in the B&A employee portfolio, the one with the severe bangs and dour expression devoid of makeup? The woman who sat before him was stunning: hair and makeup flawless, lips kissed ever so rightly with a pearl-pink lipstick that matched the knit top that was hugging her breasts the way his hands itched to do. He hoped she didn't turn around any time soon; he was positive the slim, fitted skirt she wore caressed her booty with the same perfection as he did the last time she rode him into ecstasy. This crazy scheme Zeke concocted once again seemed a bad idea.

Wait a minute. She doesn't know it's me. She's meeting Sam Walters. So why is she showing up looking this sexy? Is she thinking of using her feminine wiles to get to me . . . I mean, him? Sean wasn't aware that he was frowning, or that he had yet to say anything further as Maya waited.

"Mr. Walters, Sam, are you all right?"

"Why wouldn't I be?" Sam snapped.

What is this fool's problem? He'd been friendly during their phone conversation, she was being friendly right now . . . why couldn't they all just get along? Maya took a deep breath and decided to try a different tactic.

She reached down and opened her briefcase, purposely taking a moment before pulling out two folders and sitting up. Her breasts pressed together and ridged the top of her blouse like two chocolate bonbons. Sean's frown deepened, even as blood rushed straight to the tip of his shaft.

"I brought some information that I thought may be of interest to you," Maya said. "The top folder contains information about the Century City corridor, a really hot real estate area right now. You might already be aware of the recent purchases made there by the Rosenthal Group. Admittedly, those were some nice buys, but we, B&A, are focusing further west, in Santa Monica." Maya wondered whether or not to tell him about her involvement in one of those sales, and decided to do so, figuring it might up her professional stature in his eyes. "In fact," she continued, "I just helped close my first deal there, the Esperion Building on Wilshire." Maya smiled broadly, not even trying to keep the pride out of her voice.

Sam peeped over the folder he'd been holding up to his face to block Maya from his view and recapture control of his member and his mind. He knew he was being a cad, and knew that for Maya Jamison this was totally out of the character he'd exhibited on the phone. He was normally the epitome of professionalism; he could change characters and demeanors on a dime. Now, he knew, needed to be one of those times.

"Why, Maya, that's just smashing," he offered, putting down the folder and folding his hands across his stomach. "I didn't know your, uh, myriad of talents extended outside the office."

Did he just try and insult me? Maya took a breath to keep her composure. What was it about this man that rankled her so? She squared her shoulders as if preparing to go into battle and reminded herself who she was: the woman who by sheer will and a mother's love had escaped South Central, graduated with honors, held her family together after her mother died, and landed one of the most coveted jobs in real estate. If she could do all that, then surely she could handle Sam Walters. *Pull it together, Maya!*

She sat with perfect posture, slowly crossed her legs, and smiled. "Yes, Sam, I have many talents that are exhibited outside the office." After a moment's pause she continued. "I've had my Realtor's license for a little over a year now, but this is my first, multimillion-dollar deal. In addition, I belong to several professional organizations and sit on the board of the Boys and Girls Club located in my old neighborhood. I believe one should use one's . . . talents . . . in as many ways as possible, in a . . . variety of positions. Don't you agree?"

Sean knew it was ridiculous, but he was jealous of his alter ego, jealous of himself! How was it that Maya could flirt shamelessly with who she referred to as the bumbling Brit Sam Walters. Well, if she thought to do this job on her back, he'd be more than accommodating. "Yes, Ms. Jamison, I couldn't agree with you more." Sam licked his lips. "I believe in filling a . . . variety of . . . positions . . . myself."

Maya resisted the urge to gag. She didn't want her flirtations to work too well, too fast. Her voice became authoritative. "The second folder has information on a few key professional organizations that may be of interest to you, as well as members-only clubs that are frequented by real estate professionals, and one that seems to be a favorite among British transports."

Sam picked up the second folder and slowly flipped through its contents. As he did so, Maya's attention became fixated on his hands, particularly his fingers. They were long, with tapered, manicured fingernails, totally out of character with the rest of Sam's bumbling persona. Her eyes ran the length of Sam's arm up to his face, where, for the first time, she carefully studied it. Granted, the Afro gave his face a rounder appearance, but were it not for the mustache and beard, it could be quite angular. His lips were barely visible underneath the bushy mustache, but when he'd licked them . . . Maya's eyes narrowed as she tried to imagine Sam without all the facial hair. That's when Sam looked up.

"That's some fairly thorough scrutinizing you're doing," Sam said, narrowing his eyes as well. "As if you're sizing up your prey. Shall I be one fortunate enough to witness your . . . hunting skills, Ms. Jamison?"

"Someone of your stature and intelligence could hardly be called prey, Mr. Walters," Maya retorted. "Actually, I was trying to figure out who you remind me of. There's something about your nose and eyes but"—Maya shrugged—"nobody I know of comes to mind. Excuse me for making you uncomfortable."

"Hardly," Sam said, placing the papers back inside the folders and putting the folders in a desk drawer. "I plan to become very comfortable with you, Maya. I'm very glad Zeke suggested you for my research and to help me get better acclimated here socially."

Sam rose from his seat, went to look out the window, and spoke to Maya without facing her. "What are you doing tonight?"

"Excuse me?" Maya wasn't ready for the rapid change of topic.

"Tonight," Sam said, turning around. "What are you doing?"

Maya reached for her BlackBerry, and after a quick check replied, "I have a meeting at six o'clock that will last about an hour."

"Good. Let's say dinner at . . . seven thirty?"

"Dinner?"

"Or should I call it a dinner meeting? Will that make *you* more comfortable?"

Maya hid her chagrin behind a laugh. "Dinner is fine." She glanced at her watch, picked up her brief-case, and stood. "Where shall I meet you?"

"I'll send a car for you. Leave your address, please."

"That's quite all right, I'd rather drive."

"And I'd rather you be chauffered. You don't want to upset Zeke's client, now, do you?"

Maya was seething but when she spoke, her voice was smooth as silk. "I wouldn't dream of it, Sam."

She reached for the pen and pad on his desk, rap-idly wrote down her address, and once finished held out her hand. Their handshake was strong and very businesslike.

"It's been a pleasure," Sam said. *But not half as pleasurable as when I'm pounding that tight pudding of yours.*

"I look forward to tonight," Maya responded. *About as much as a pig looks forward to becoming sausage.*

After cordial good-byes, Maya turned and left, putting just enough sway in her hips to tease Sam with just how well she could move them. She felt she'd walked the line perfectly, part temptress, part top-notch executive. Tonight would be trickier to navigate, but with round one under her belt, she was more than ready for round two.

Sean's eyes stayed glued to Maya's backside as he watched her glide from the office in her high-heeled pumps. As he'd imagined, the suedelike material hugged her body like an overeager lover, while staying just inside what qualified as professional attire.

Sean slowly sank back into the large leather chair behind the large, impersonal desk. *This is madness. How am I going to keep my hands off her?* His best-laid plans had flown out the window the moment Maya walked, or rather flowed, into the room, a chocolate Aphrodite come to steal his soul. His were the best intentions in devising the plan to keep Maya close, and safe. But he didn't know if it would go as he'd planned. She was supposed to be the one fidgeting right now, the one out of sorts and off-balance. But Maya was the picture of poise and while she'd ridged a bit when he came on to her in his sloppy, Sam Walters style, she'd recovered quickly and proceeded to give him a dose of his own medicine, with her clever banter and discreetly displayed assets. Sean knew he needed to step up his game, and he needed to do it quickly.

25

"Did you put the pepper spray in your purse like I told you?"

"Trish, please, what do you think waddling Walters is going to try and do?"

"Light his 'a' up with that pepper spray and it won't matter. Don't you remember anything from your hood days?"

"Yes, which is why I left, remember?"

"Girl, some lessons you should keep with you."

"Trish, I'm not taking my pepper spray or a steak knife, and I don't plan on having to take off my earrings. I've handled bigger, badder wolves in my day. I can handle Sam Walters."

"Yeah, but insisting he have a car pick you up? It just seems funny, Maya."

"Not necessarily, not in these circles. Anyways, I'll tell you all about it when I get back, which, if he's still in the foul mood I left him this afternoon, will be sooner rather than later. Besides, it won't take me long to implement my plan."

"What plan is that?"

"Oh, just a little test to satisfy a nagging curiosity I've got."

"Oh my goodness, are you going to venture down there for a look-see?"

"You never know. . . ."

"Ooh, you bad, girl, you didn't tell a sista you were taking that route to the information highway!"

"I didn't say I was, I just said you never know."

"Listen, you call me—"

"The moment I get in . . . I will!"

"And how long should I wait before I call the police if you don't call?"

Maya laughed. "Being an actress is perfect for you, because you're straight drama!"

"Whatever, girl, you just check in before midnight or I'm ringing the po-po."

"Deal, sista, I'll give you a call."

When the town car arrived promptly at seven, for her seven-thirty dinner with Sam, Maya was glad that her meeting had been less than ten minutes from her house and that even so, she'd left fifteen minutes before it was over. She'd showered and changed into a simple black silk cocktail dress that cinched at the waist and flared at the hips. She'd kept her jewelry simple as well: a thin gold necklace with a locket that contained a miniature picture of her mother when she was about Maya's age, and a single, gold wrist band. While the weather was hot, the dinner was formal, so Maya compromised by wearing thigh-high stockings with the Christian Lacroix shoes she'd splurged on over the weekend. She'd barely been off the phone with Trish for two minutes when the car pulled up.

Maya used the time on the way to wherever to try and calm down. Normally her nerves wouldn't be so on edge, but "normal" hadn't stopped by to see her for over a month. Instead "crazy," "trippin'," and "you've got to be kidding" were regular visitors, lately showing up in her life day and night. Even now, as the driver wound his way through the L.A. streets, she heard "you've got to be kidding" whispering in her ears. Because the car in which she rode was headed to Playa Del Rey, an area of Los Angeles not known for its plethora of restaurants. *Surely he wouldn't . . .*

"Excuse me, driver, but which restaurant are you taking me to?"

The driver looked at her in the rearview mirror and smiled appreciatively. "No restaurant, ma'am."

No restaurant? This man did not just say that I wasn't going to a restaurant. "Well, where exactly have you been instructed to drive me?"

"To Mr. Walters's residence, ma'am." The driver kept looking between her and the road as he easily navigated the streets.

Maya calmly turned and looked out the window. The driver's smile had told her he expected an outburst; well, she most certainly was not going to give him one. So Mr. Walters thought she was some naive assistant ripe for seduction, did he? She'd surely give him something else to think about once she arrived at his home.

Not that she could totally blame him. It was not her style to be overly flirtatious in her line of business and she had to admit that had purposely happened earlier today. In fact, the entire meeting had been . . . weird. She wondered if her plan would shed any light on the unsettled feelings that had cropped up where Sam Walters was concerned. The driver turned on to Pacific Avenue, two minutes away from her destination. It looked like she was getting ready to find out.

Maya's second clue that the night would be unusual, after finding out the dinner would be at Sam's house, was the butler who answered the doorbell. She'd expected Cecilia. But a distinguished-looking older gentlemen, with silvery hair, a ramrod-straight back, and a pleasant demeanor greeted her instead.

"Ms. Jamison," he said, bowing low. "Please, come this way."

Maya stepped into what looked like a page out of *O At Home* magazine. The chandelier lighting was set on low, casting thousands of shards of light against the polished, bronzelike ceiling. White, lit candles adorned the sconces and were placed throughout the living room. An elegant display of orchids dominated the marble coffee table and their delicate aroma filled the room. Maya suddenly felt shy, vulnerable. This was a setting for a seduction, not a sales meeting. Her stomach flip-flopped. And why? Certainly not because she was meeting Sam Walters? She couldn't stand the man. Maya's hand went to the locket around her neck. *Be with me, Mama.*

Instead of taking Maya to the dining room, he led her to a set of double doors that opened onto a patio facing the ocean. White candles of all shapes and sizes illuminated the area, along with two dimmed sconces affixed next to the doors. A stark linen tablecloth lay under bone china, stemmed crystal ware, and sparkling silver, ironically, probably the silver she'd shined! Maya had to admit, it did look good! A soothing sound came in from the ocean as the waves ebbed and tided, and a gentle breeze lent an island air to her surroundings. There was no denying it; Sam Walters had outdone himself with the setting. Now she'd have to outdo herself in setting him straight.

"Would Madame care for white wine?" the butler asked.

"No, thank you, I'd rather wait for Mr., for Sam."

"Wait no more lovely, lady. Sam is here."

Maya turned and almost stepped back. It was indeed Sam, but she'd never seen him look like this before. He wore a black, double-breasted suit that deemphasized his portly middle and enhanced his broad shoulders. Broad shoulders? Until now, Maya didn't even remember Sam having shoulders. Of course he did, but she'd never noticed. His hair, mustache, and beard were groomed to perfection. Why had she never noticed how brown his eyes were? *Brown like . . . hmm . . .* With his mustache cut down, Maya could detect the lips that had been hidden beneath it; soft, kissable-looking lips. *Lips like . . . no. I'm insane for even thinking such madness.* Maya shook her head and tried to clear its cloudiness. She needed her intellect, expertise, and every ounce of people skills to navigate the web Walters had woven with linen, crystal, white candles, and a comb!

"Sam! You look . . . different."

Sam gave the hint of a smile. "It's been said that I clean up nicely."

"I didn't mean—"

"I understand your statement was a compliment and take it as such."

Sam's clipped British accent topped off the night's formality. Maya almost felt she should have one herself and as it were, found herself standing as if she were a contestant on Miss America: left foot positioned slightly in front of the right one, toe pointed outward, neck straight, chin tilted. All she needed was a crown. She felt the nerves coming. She could use that glass of wine.

"My statement was a compliment. You look nice, Sam."

"And may I say you look stunning?" Sam replied, his velvety eyes taking slow inventory of Maya's ensemble. "Yes, simply stunning," he repeated. He turned to take the two glasses of sparkling wine the butler had brought out on a silver tray.

"May I interest you in a glass of Armand de Brignac?"

"Sounds fancy," Maya said, taking the glass he offered. "What is it?"

"A bubbly blend of Pinot Noir, Pinot Meunier, and Chardonnay." Sam continued to gaze at Maya as he held up his glass. "Things got off to a rather bumpy start this afternoon," he began. "So let's toast to us, and new beginnings," he said.

"To new beginnings," Maya repeated as they clinked glasses. She had no idea what "us" had to do with it.

Another stranger Maya had never seen, a chef, brought out two soup bowls and a basket of warm rolls.

"Shall we?" Sam asked. He placed his hand near the small of Maya's bare back. An involuntary shiver went through her.

"Cold?" Sam asked, although the night was balmy.

"Hardly," Maya replied, her tone sarcastic but her face smiling.

Sam gave her a knowing smile and Maya immediately knew he had misconstrued her words. He thought she was hot for him? She was not! Was she?

Maya was thankful for the few moments of quiet while eating the soup. It was delicious: a chicken consommé with fresh vegetables and hints of lemon running through each spoonful. The rolls were flecked with rosemary and thyme, a perfect complement to the soup's contents. On the way over, Maya had been starving. Now she could barely eat.

"It must be nice to have a chef," she said.

"He's not full-time," Sam countered. "He's my on-call chef, for special occasions."

"Oh."

They continued to eat in silence. After a few more sips of the sparkling bubbly, Maya's appetite thankfully kicked in and she finished a good portion of the soup.

Sean studied Maya covertly as she ate her soup. She looked even more beautiful this evening than she had this afternoon, if that were possible. He'd stepped up his efforts to have the deal he was working on finalized, and end his investigations with Zeke and Joseph. He'd met his match in Maya and couldn't hide his true self from her much longer. But tonight he was Sam, not Sean, and as such needed to ask questions common to people who'd recently met. "Tell me about yourself, Maya. I know a few things, that you've been with Zeke for about five years, and that you graduated with honors from USC. But aside from that, I don't know much. Since we're going to be working together, closely, I'd like to get to know you."

Maya's mind raced quickly. What should she tell, what should she leave out? True, she was enjoying this Sam Walters more than she'd ever enjoyed the one she left this afternoon but not enough to trust him with too much information. "What specifically would you like to know?"

"Whatever you'd like to tell me."

Maya gave a brief rundown of growing up in south central Los Angeles all the while dreaming to get out, of high school and college years filled with sports and debate tournaments, and about a onetime stint at acting from a friend's prompting. She didn't mention Trish's name, and she didn't talk about Stretch. She figured the less he knew about her family, the better. Let him think she was an only child; maybe he'd trust her faster if he felt she didn't have a slew of close friends and family to go back and run off at the mouth to.

Sam listened quietly and with seeming interest. "And how did you end up at B&A?" he asked, when she'd finished.

"I'd interned there my senior year in college. That's when I first met Zeke and expressed my interest in working there. He said I didn't have enough experience but to come back in a few years. I worked a few administrative and marketing jobs before spending three years with an Internet marketing company. But ever so often, I'd check in with B&A, see if they had any openings. Four and a half years ago they did, an entry-level clerical position for less pay but more benefits than I had where I was. I jumped at the chance, worked hard, and now here I am."

"About to become one of their top-producing Realtors?"

"How did you guess?" Maya said, smiling. He didn't need to know she intended to use what she learned at B&A growing a business of her own. "And now you. Everyone is wondering who Sam Walters is *really*."

"What you see is what you get," Sam said, with

a straight face. The irony was the distance that statement was from the truth.

As the second and third courses were served, arugula salad followed by perfectly baked halibut served with herbed rice and homemade sour cream, Maya learned about Sam Walters: his childhood in various parts of Europe, and how he cut his real estate teeth in South Africa, a wide-open market for Blacks once apartheid fell.

Even though it was hidden by disguise, Sean enjoyed sharing a bit more of himself with Maya. While some of what he shared was fabricated, much of what he said was true. That his varied business interests and talents were all coming together in this assignment was a coupe he couldn't have orchestrated if he tried.

Maya noticed that Sam also avoided much talk of his personal life. She decided to pry a bit. "I'm amazed there is no Mrs. Walters," she said. "All of this success and no one to share it with?"

"Not yet," Sam countered smoothly, his eyes meeting hers over the rim of his water glass.

Maya raised her eyebrow in question, but remained silent, her eyes once again drawn to his slender, strong fingers.

"It's hard to maintain a relationship in my line of work," Sam continued. "It takes a strong, confident, self-assured woman. My job calls for a great deal of travel, often for long periods of time. It isn't easy for someone to be happy with a continually absent partner for long."

"Why can't she travel with you?"

You could, is what Sean thought. "It would be difficult," is what Sam said.

The chef served dessert, homemade vanilla ice

cream topped with a blueberry crumble and served
in a large martini glass: uncomplicated elegance.

Maya closed her eyes as she took a bite. It was delicious.

Sean watched as Maya's tongue darted out of her
mouth to catch the drop of ice cream that had escaped
it. He'd remembered blueberries were her favorite
fruit; she'd gone on and on about it when they had a
similar dessert in Beverly Hills.

Maya swallowed the bite and opened her eyes,
glazed over in confectionary ecstasy. "Sam, this is
delicious."

"I thought you'd enjoy it."

"Really?"

Sean, momentarily distracted by Maya's sheer en-
joyment of her dessert, even as he thought to make
her his, had caused him to drop his guard. He almost
forgot it was Sam, not Sean, she was talking to, and
Sam had no idea how much she loved blueberries.

His recovery was quick, nearly flawless.

"Okay, it was a lucky guess. Who doesn't like
blueberries?"

As they enjoyed dessert, Sam shared with Maya
his plans for gaining a foothold into the L.A. real
estate market. That instead of focusing on what the
major players considered prime—downtown, West-
side, Beverly Hills, Malibu, etc.—his concentration
would be on surrounding areas, including central and
northern California. Conversation became effortless
as they discussed a world that both enjoyed.

Coffee was served, and along with it, a brilliant
West Coast sunset. "Join me, Maya" Sam said, as
one used to giving commands. But his was a gentle
persuasion, a hand on her chair to prompt her up.

"Bring your coffee. We're just going down the path a ways."

There it was again, that vulnerable feeling as she walked next to Sam, his bulk seeming to swallow up her svelte figure appearing even smaller in the little black dress. Thanks to the high heels, at least he didn't tower over her. They took a short yet winding path that ran down and around the curve of the house. At the bottom of the incline was another sitting area with a glass bird fountain and an old-fashioned swing supported by a U-shaped steel beam.

Maya's heart warmed at the sight. On the few times she and Stretch went to visit their grandmother in Texas, the swing on her front porch had been the favorite attraction. She and her brother would hop out of the car, miraculously revived after a twenty-four-hour drive, hop up on the wooden swing, and keep it moving until they fell asleep. Without thought, her hand went to the locket around her neck, the one with her mother's picture inside. Inexplicably, she began to tear up and before she could wrap herself up in the professional persona she wore so well, a couple of drops spilled over onto her cheeks.

"Maya?" Sam asked as he turned around. He'd been watching the sunset and hadn't witnessed her initial reaction.

Maya quickly brushed the tear from her cheek.

"Maya, are you all right?"

Maya sat down in the swing, looked out over the sunset, and tried to find her jovial nature, the sassy one who was supposed to be going toe-to-toe with Sam. And the one who needed to remember why she was with Sam Walters—because she was on a mission. "If I didn't know better," she purred, "I'd think you're trying to set a certain mood, Mr. Walters."

Sean sat down and placed his arm across the back of the swing. "It's Sam, remember?" His voice was low and comforting when he spoke, the British accent not so pronounced.

Maya shifted so she was facing Sam. "Right, Sam." Her voice was as whispery as the orange, pink, and purple streaks of color painting the western sky.

It took Sean about zero seconds to decide to kiss Maya as Sam. In fact, there was no thought process to it at all. It was the most natural thing in the world.

Maya kissed him back. As the kiss deepened, so did her intuition. She'd dismissed the disturbing thoughts during dinner but could no longer deny what was right in her face, actually on her lips: his kiss. There couldn't be two pairs of lips like this. She continued to kiss him, her rising anger at his duplicity matching the heat from his swirling tongue.

But she kept her cool. She had to be sure. Turning slightly, she ran her hand up his arm and around his neck. The kiss deepened and Sean forgot all about the tentativeness he should have put forth as Sam. Their tongues did a familiar dance, even as he felt Maya's fingers on his neck, moving toward his hair.

My hair? Damn! She'll know it's a wig!

Sean ended the kiss and pulled back from Maya. But when he did, he left something behind. She jumped up angrily, shaking Sam's afro in his face.

"Why didn't you tell me, Sean? All this time, when you knew I was trying to find out about the mysterious Sam Walters, driving myself crazy to end this insanity. And all the time . . . this?"

She threw the wig on the still swinging swing. "You know what? It doesn't even matter. I'm done with the madness. And with you."

She turned and hurried up the walkway, as fast as she could run in three-inch heels.

Sean hurriedly followed, leaving the wig behind to watch the sunset by its lonesome. "Maya! Maya, wait!"

He didn't catch her until she was inside the house. She rushed to her purse, and was calling 4-1-1. "Yes, give me the number to a cab company. Any cab company! Quick!"

Sean raced toward her, struggling to take the phone.

"Get away from me, Sean!"

He snatched the phone. "Not until you hear me out."

"There's nothing for me to hear."

"You may not think so but I've got something to say. All you need to do is listen. Then I'll give back your phone."

Maya stood with back straight, legs apart, arms crossed, and a glare that would melt an Iceland glacier. Sean had never seen sexy look so good.

"Maya, it's been agony to keep this from you. But it's because of how much I care about you that I've had to be so cautious. The most important aspect of my assignment is not B&A or Rosenthal or uncovering corruption or securing real estate. It's you."

"You keep talking this way and it only confuses me more; about my protection, my safety. What's going on? Is someone after Zeke? Trying to destroy the B&A offices? Is there a potential bomb threat or a kidnapping plan?"

Maya paced the room as she continued talking, partly accusing, partly thinking out loud. "I know this involves Angel's Way, and I know that when you're talking about a multi-billion dollar project, the competition is fierce, fearless, ruthless. But is there something even more dangerous going on with these players? And if there is, don't you think it best that I know?"

Sean sighed. "Come sit down with me, Maya."

"That's okay, Sean. I can hear fine standing."

Sean walked over to the couch and sat down. He was silent for a long moment and when he did speak, chose his words carefully.

"There are rumors about a hit being put out on somebody high up in the business community. My sources haven't confirmed that it's one of the players in this real estate game, but instinct and experience tells me it very well could be. I've uncovered some pretty unsavory practices with the Rosenthal Group and know from personal conversation that Joseph will stop at nothing to get that job."

Maya walked over and sat in a wing-backed chair opposite Sean. "What about Zeke? What have you found out about him?"

"Look, nobody gets to where Zeke is without stepping on heads. He's done his share of dirty dealings but I have to give it to him, he's a smart businessman, knows how to handle his maneuvers to where he stays within the shadows of the law. And where he doesn't, well, money can talk pretty loud to someone you want to keep quiet."

"So you're investigating B&A and Rosenthal? Are you investigating me too, Sean?"

Sean leaned back. There was no way what he had to say would sound good. "I looked into your background a bit, in the research I conducted before coming here. It was part of my job, Maya."

Maya was crushed, but refused to let Sean know how much he was hurting her. She allowed the anger that accompanied that hurt to prevail. "And what about after I became more than a job, Sean, why couldn't you tell me all of this? What do we have if we don't have trust?"

It was Sean's turn to get angry. "Do we have trust, Maya? Is that why I didn't meet Maya until weeks after I'd fallen for Macy? After the holiday weekend, and all the nights we spent together? There were plenty of times you could have told me who you were, and that you worked for Zeke.

"And what about your charade? You seem to forget that Martha wasn't revealed during a private conversation between us, but during a conversation that Zeke initiated. That's when I understood how caught up you were in all of this, and how dangerous it could be if the wrong person thought you had information they needed. I figured the less you knew about my investigation, the better."

Sean walked over to Maya, pulled her up from the chair and looked her straight in the eye. "The announcement of who got awarded the Angel's Way project and my investigation will be over very soon. I was going to tell you everything then, when all of this madness had ended and I knew you were safe."

Maya couldn't think when she was so close to Sean's heat; his velvety chocolate bedroom eyes and lush lips. She tried to step back but Sean held fast to her hands.

"Don't you believe me, baby?" he asked.

"I'm so confused, I don't know what I believe. Why are you here as both Sean and Sam? Since you're an investigator, why are you trying to connect so solidly with the real estate crowd? Couldn't you have done that as Sean? And speaking of real estate, what about the files in that office?" She tilted her head in the direction of the once off-limit space. "When I was in there I saw information on buildings downtown and elsewhere. I'd only begun to scan them when you busted me that day, but they looked legit. Are those files merely window dressing, or are you really in the game?"

"I'm in the game," he said simply. It's all he could say. He didn't want to lie and for now, couldn't tell the total truth. "Trust me for just a little while longer, Maya. And then I'll tell you everything."

"I want to trust you, Sean. But I have to ask. Professionally speaking, whose side are you on, Rosenthal's or B&A?"

"I'm on my side, Maya. And if you're smart, which we both know you are, you'll be on your own side as well. At the end of the day, everybody is looking out for number one. Zeke would sell you for a dollar if he thought it meant a billion more."

"You don't even know him!"

"But I know men *like* him. I'm not saying he doesn't appreciate you, Maya. I'm sure he does. But he didn't hesitate to pull you out of the office and into a maid's uniform, did he? I'm just suggesting 'to thine own self be true.' No one is going to care for you as much as you."

"But how can you sit there all self-righteous when you're playing two companies against each other?"

"Everybody's grown in this game. All my cards are on the table. Rosenthal knows I'm dealing with B&A and vice versa. I also know they have no loyalty where I'm concerned, hence your temporary side job. Speaking of which, you saw me here the other morning, didn't you? In the master bedroom?"

Maya didn't know how much she should share of what she knew with Sean. Hadn't he just basically said to trust no one?

But her face must have told the story. Because

Sean's laugh started out as a chuckle and ended in a guffaw.

"What's so funny?" she asked.

"You," he said, wiping his eyes. "I can only imagine what you thought when you came up those stairs and saw my naked ass in another man's bed. What, you thought I was gay, didn't you?"

"I didn't know what to think."

"Yes, you did," Sean said, laughing again. "You thought me and old Sam were homos. I remember it now, your sarcastic comment in that meeting, asking just how *close* I was to Sam Walters."

"Yeah, well, now I can see you're closer than any of us would have guessed," Maya retorted. But she couldn't help smiling. This conversation was starting to feel too good, too much like the kind she had shared with Sean when they first met. From the beginning, they could talk about any- and everything, in conversations that flowed like water. She started remembering other things that felt good between them, other areas of their relationship that happened effortlessly. She looked up to catch Sean watching her intently. Her eyes drifted to his lips, which he licked unconsciously.

"I've got to go, Sean," Maya said, getting up from the sofa. "Should I call a cab?"

"No, I'll call the driver."

There was an awkward silence after he placed the call. Maya returned to the wingback chair while Sean sat on the sofa; a coffee table, a spray of orchids, and a long list of lies between them.

"Are you going to tell Zeke what you know? About me being Sam?"

Maya stood and paced again. "To think Zeke's instincts were spot on. He just knew there was something about Sam Walters that wasn't quite right. And now that I know it's true, and it's *you* . . . this is all so complicated. And it's not just about me and you."

She turned and looked at him. "Okay, maybe there are a few things you still don't know about me. And one of them is that I owe Zeke, in more ways than I can explain right now. Helping Zeke secure the Angel's Way deal is about more than my ambitions."

"Is it about Malcolm?"

"How did you know my brother's real name?" Then she remembered. He'd background checked her.

"Look, Sean, just leave my brother out of this."

"You better make sure he leaves himself out of it."

"What are you talking about?"

Sean's phone beeped. "The car's here."

"What do you know about my brother, Sean? Talk to me!"

"Trust works two ways, Maya, and so does this relationship. You can't have everything your way, you've got to give to receive. And you've got to decide who you're going to trust."

Maya's mind was spinning. What could Sean possibly know about Stretch? Would her brother talk to her, tell her what was going on? She stood, took her purse from Sean, and started to walk around him. He stepped in her path, so close she could feel his breath on the side of her face.

"Even with all that's happened, I'm glad I saw you tonight. And I'm glad you know about the Sam Walters persona. I trust you, Maya. And I hope when this crazy mess is over, you and I will just be getting started."

He enveloped her tightly in his arms but resisted the urge to do anything further. He'd told Maya everything, laid his cards on the table. The next move would have to come from her.

Maya closed her eyes, basking in the feel of Sean's arms around her. She hated to admit it, but she was in love with this man, had known it since the fireworks they created in July. But being with him might mean risking everything she'd worked so hard for. Erasing her indebtedness to Zeke and securing her future financially were tangibles she felt she could somewhat control . . . love was not.

26

"Is this good to you, baby, is this the way you like it, huh?" Tony's drawl was low and slow as he continued his rhythmic assault on Trish's body. Her guttural moans were her only answer. He placed his hands beneath her, pressed them tighter, plunged deeper, withdrew to the tip before plunging in again and picking up the pace. Trish felt an explosion building, starting at the balls of her feet and pooling deep in her soul as she matched Tony's movements thrust for thrust. They both cried out and rode the wave of ecstasy together.

"Ooh, baby," Trish panted, trying to catch her breath. "That was amazing. I love it when you do it to me like that."

Tony turned to face her and sat up on one elbow. "Don't I always do you like that?"

Trish kissed his face, now covered with a slight layer of sweat from their exertions. "Yes, baby, you're always amazing."

After her breathing returned to normal, Trish pushed the sheet back and prepared to get up.

"Where you going?"

"To take a shower. And then I'm going to fix you breakfast."

Tony swatted her booty as she walked by him, then watched as she pranced naked into the bathroom. He lay back and smiled, thinking about how he and Trish had almost been twenty-four-seven the last few days. He was glad they'd gotten their relationship back on track; he'd almost ruined it by badmouthing Trisha's chicken-selling gig. Now that they'd talked about it, he had a better understanding of what she was trying to do . . . of how this job was helping her paint the big picture. He wondered whether she would understand the gig he was painting on his canvas.

If everything went according to plan, she'd never know. And after this job, he was getting out of the game for good, maybe move him and Trish to the valley, the suburbs; live like regular folks.

"Dang, baby, you smell good," he said as he passed Trish on his way to the bathroom. He tried to grab her but Trish scooted past him.

"Uh-uh, Tone, I just cleaned up."

Trish turned on the stereo and danced into the kitchen, jamming with India.Arie's new single note for note. She busted a quick dance move in the kitchen before reaching in the refrigerator for bacon, eggs, frozen hash browns, and milk for pancakes. She was going to make a feast for her and her man; between last night and this morning they'd worked up quite an appetite.

Trish was happy; for the first time in a long while, everything seemed to be going her way. She'd shot her first national commercial and secured an agent in the process, was mere months from being able to leave her temp agency and the string of low-level jobs they sent her on, plus she was dating one of the finest brothas in all of L.A. She'd even begun thinking they could be long-term. True, he was a gangster and as such probably dabbled in a few illegal activities from time to time. But it was hard to find good, gainful employment with a felony record. Sometimes it seemed hard to find work as a Black man period. She'd shared her concerns about his lifestyle and he promised her he "wouldn't bring trouble to her house." There was something he had brought to her, however, happiness. And that was something she hoped would stick around.

Trish stopped daydreaming long enough to not burn the bacon, then went back to thinking about Tony. He seemed excited about some new venture, one he said would change both their lives for the better. When she pressed, he clammed up, said it was a surprise. Trish smiled. She loved surprises, as long as they were good ones.

"Baby, you've got it smelling good in here!" Tony said, as he walked past her with pecs rippling and teeth gleaming. "Are those from scratch?"

"Uh-huh, from me scratching open that Aunt Jemimah box and adding milk and eggs! Here, Tone, before it gets cold."

Tony devoured half of the food on his plate and washed it down with a glass of orange juice. He rocked back in his chair, looking appreciatively at Trish.

"What?" she asked, tingling from his stare.

"What would you think about living in the valley?"

"I don't know. I guess it would be all right, except in the summer when it hits triple digits over there. And earthquakes happen over there too."

"Earthquakes don't just hit in the valley, baby."

"The last one did."

"Which is why the next one will probably split south central down the middle."

"Tony, don't talk like that. I won't be able to sleep at night."

"I'll make sure you're good and sleepy every night . . . trust me on that one."

Trish laughed, taking Tony's hand, dipping a finger in the syrup on her plate and then licking the gooey juice off, nice and slow. "I trust you," she said coyly. "So what part of the valley would you like to live in?"

"Out there by Woodland Hills maybe, or Calabasas. One of those big-ass houses with a pool and basketball court."

"But not too close to Simi Valley. We'd be getting pulled over every five miles."

"*I'd* get pulled over. You're too fine for them to pull you over. Besides, they don't stop females, only brothas."

Trish couldn't argue with that point. She'd never gotten pulled over but male friends of hers were stopped all the time.

"What kind of car do you want, baby?"

Trish didn't hesitate; she thought of a new car every time she saw the oil stain under the one she now drove. "An SUV, either a Toyota, or the other day I saw this cute Kia . . ."

"A Toyota or Kia? Baby, you gonna roll with the big boys you need to be stylin' in a Lexus, Escalade, something like that."

"Yeah, and then I'd be stylin' in those four-hundred-dollar payments and one-fifty-a-month insurance payments. No, thank you. I'm not trying to spend my money as fast as I make it."

Tony didn't tell her, but he didn't plan on Trish

spending her money on the ride. It was one of the first things he wanted to buy for her, after they moved. Then he planned to buy her some diamonds . . . he wanted his baby dripping in bling!

"Hey, Trish, when does your commercial come out?"

"In a couple months, I think."

"Is that when your mad cash starts rolling in?"

"I wish. It will take six, seven months before I see some really good money, but I'll get a pretty good check in about two months. That one will at least allow me to quit the temp agency so I can put all my energy into auditions and stuff. You want some more pancakes?"

"Yeah, baby, just a couple more. No, make that three!" He followed her into the kitchen, watched as she poured three equal amounts of batter to form circles on the grill. "You know what would be cool? For you to be in a movie like, what was that movie with Jada and Queen Latifah and, uh . . ."

"*Set It Off*?" It was one of Trish's favorite movies.

"Yeah! It would be cool if you would be in a movie like that! Pulling off a bank heist and shit! Those were some cold-blooded sistas!"

"Yeah, but look what happened to them in the end."

"But Queen went out gangsta like a mothafucka, all Al Capone like, some Bugsy Siegel–style shit!" Tone stood in the middle of the kitchen, twitching back and forth the way Queen's character, Cleo, did in the movie.

"Vivica Fox—"

"She was Frankie."

"Yeah, Frankie shouldn't have died, though."

"You would have surrendered?"

"I don't know? She was looking at hella jail time. And she had all that paper!"

"None of which she could spend dead."

"But if she'd escaped, like her girl Jada did? She would have been home free then. What was Jada's character's name?"

"Stony. I was glad she got away."

"Homeboy gave her a break. Shows there are a few dudes with heart behind the badge."

Tony finished the last of the pancakes just as his cell phone rang. He gave Trish a kiss as he walked away and answered the call. "Yo, dog, what up?"

Trish began cleaning up, her mind in turmoil. Was Tony thinking of robbing a bank? Was this the path to a new beginning he was talking about? And was Stretch involved? Maya would die if anything happened to her brother. The elation Trish had felt all morning turned into a strange foreboding. But she forced herself to shake it off. For the first time in her life, all the pieces were in place. She was getting ready to live the life she'd always wanted. She wasn't going to let her penchant for paranoia mess up her happy mood.

27

"Maya . . . Maya!" Ester whispered. "Can I hide out in here a minute?" She tiptoed in before Maya could say no. "I'm on my break and don't even feel like being bothered with Jade and her silly requests. I don't know what's gotten into her, but that girl is getting on my nerves!"

Maya knew what had gotten into her . . . Zeke's wild woody. But Maya wasn't in the mood for office gossip right now . . . her own dramas were enough to fill the day. And to top it off, stress had brought down that time of the month almost a week early. Cramps were kicking her "a."

"Maya, you all right?" Ester asked. "It looks like you lost your best friend."

"I'm okay, just a lot on my mind."

"Is it Stretch, is he okay?"

Ester was one of the few people in the office who knew about her brother's activities. She had family members in gangs too, and a cousin who had been killed because of the lifestyle.

"He's okay, as far as I know," Maya responded. "But I'm worried about him. He's smart, talented. I wish he would go to college, or even a trade school. He used to fix all kinds of things around the house, and he's a natural with computers. I just wish he would, you know, do something with his life."

"He is doing something," Ester countered. "He's living it, the way he wants to. It might not be what *you* want for him, but everybody has their own path, Maya. They've got to walk theirs, like we've got to walk ours. I know it's hard, but you've got to let Stretch be Stretch. And hope that everything turns out okay for him. But that's not all that's bothering you, is it?"

"Here you go, trying to get in my business." Maya smiled.

"It looks like somebody needs to. Besides, I hate to see you sad."

Sometimes Maya believed Ester was psychic. She had a mothering instinct, and knew just the right thing to say to get a smile. That's why she made such a great receptionist and Maya thought, in time, would make a great salesperson.

"What would you do if the man you were dating had a secret? And what if in disclosing the secret, it could help you, but possibly hurt him? Would you tell it?"

"I don't know. What do you mean by help you?"

"I didn't say me, we're speaking hypothetically here."

"Oh, okay," Ester said with an exaggerated wink. "I mean, help this *hypothetical* executive assistant."

"Forget it. I'm not even going to ask you."

"No, please. I'm sorry, Maya. You said the secret could help this person but hurt her friend?"

Maya nodded.

"Hurt him how?"

Maya shrugged. "His career maybe, financially . . ."

"Do you, does this person still care about him? Or does she not give a damn what happens to him?"

Maya thought for a moment. "She'll probably always care about him, you know, doesn't wish anything bad on him. But she feels she has to look out for number one."

"Then I'd say this person better be sure they can handle the consequences of whatever happens, to her and to him. That's if she cares. If she don't, and it's going to help her career or whatever, then she might as well go for it."

"You're too smart to be a receptionist," Maya said.

"That's what I keep trying to tell these clowns!" Ester looked at her watch. "Oh well, duty calls. Thanks for letting me hide out."

"You're welcome. Let me know if Jade continues to be a problem. She shouldn't even be giving you work. It should go through the office manager."

"I know, but Jade's on a crazy power trip." Ester ran back to Maya's desk and whispered, "You ask me, I think the girl is doing some office cock sucking!" She laughed and ran out of the room.

Maya stared at the door for moments after Ester left. Maybe girlfriend was psychic. She'd hit the nail on the head with Jade and come close with her assessment of her and Sean.

There was no denying it; Maya loved Sean and would never do anything she felt would destroy him. But Zeke already knew that Sean *knew* Sam. Would it be an insurmountable tragedy for him to know that Sean *was* Sam?

And what about her? Sean knew that anything affecting B&A directly could affect her indirectly. Yet he continued to investigate Zeke and the company.

For what? Why couldn't he tell her what he knew, whatever it was?"

Her thoughts were interrupted by her cell phone ringing. She smiled.

"Hey, Stretch. Are you still coming over for dinner?"

"That's why I called, My. I'm going to have to do a rain check, baby girl."

"That's the second time this week. What's up with you?"

Sean's words about Stretch staying out of things floated through her mind. And she could almost feel something about her twin's spirit that was unsettled.

"Stretch, I hope you're not into anything crazy. I don't think I could handle it if you got locked down again."

"I'm handling my business, My. Don't worry about me."

"But I do, baby brother. I love you. What hurts you hurts me. Each other are all we've got."

"I love you too, sis. And I'd never do anything to hurt you, believe that."

She thought about Stretch for several moments after their conversation ended. True, she'd helped him out of many jams, but he'd always been there for her too, through messy break-ups, childhood scrapes, keeping her safe when she lived in the hood, surviving their mother's untimely death. The financial freedom that could come from Angel's Way and all that went with it was not only for her, but for her brother too. She could buy a home and maybe they could share it. Getting him out of the old neighborhood and his poisonous friends might be the fresh perspective he needed to turn a positive corner.

She was in love with Sean and her brother was her heart. Her eyes watered as she pondered the situation and tried to come up with alternative solutions. She was in too deep and a new life was too close to back out now. Her only hope was that once Sean knew everything, he'd understand why she had to do what she now knew she must. She had to follow her head instead of her heart. She had to finish her assignment . . . and tell Zeke.

She finished the report Zeke had requested, printed out the last meeting's minutes, picked up a "just in case" folder, and headed to his office. His wide-open door told her Jade was working else-where, maybe on work even. He was on the phone but waved her in. She set the report on his desk, placed the minutes on top of it, and took a seat.

Zeke put down the phone as she walked into his office. "I was just about to call you, Maya."

Now that Maya had decided to tell Zeke about Sean being Sam, she just wanted to get it over with. But something in Zeke's demeanor told her to wait. He seemed agitated, and finding out about Sean's alter ego wouldn't put him in a better mood. So she waited.

"What is your impression of Sean Wynn?"

It was an unexpected question. All of their previous discussions had always centered on Sam Walters. She couldn't begin to guess what was on Zeke's mind.

"I don't have much of an impression," she an-swered. "Other than the first meeting where I, uh, met him I think I've only seen him here at the office one other time. We shared simple pleasantries and that was it. Why do you ask?"

"I think that sonofabitch might be trying to screw me."

Oh, 's.' Does he already know? "Why do you say that?" she asked.

"I have my reasons. Suffice it to say I'm not sure

where his loyalties lie; and that he's not just acting like he's on my side to funnel information to Joe Rosenthal. And if I find out he's trying to double-cross me . . . that news won't bode well for his professional future."

There was a long moment before Zeke continued. "How are things going with you and Sam?"

Maya was still trying to absorb Zeke's veiled threat against Sean. She fought to keep any emotion from showing on her face, even as she struggled for an answer. "We met a few days ago. I gave him a couple reports. I guess he's been busy since then because he hasn't called."

"Well, you need to call him. I want you to stay close to him, gain his confidence. Sean told me the two of them traveled in some of the same circles in London. I want you to find out what those circles were, anything you can about family, female friends, you know, just casual stuff. I've got some guys on the ground in London but I want to exhaust every possible avenue to making sure Sean's investigation is limited to The Rosenthal Group and no longer on us. Matter of fact . . ."

Zeke didn't finish the sentence. Instead, he changed the subject abruptly.

"What do you have for me?"

A knock on his office door was followed by the sound of heels walking quickly across exposed marble in the foyer of Zeke's office.

"Zeke, I've got the tickets for our, oh," Jade stopped talking when she saw Maya. "I'm sorry. I'll come back later."

"Leave them on the table," Zeke answered.

During the interruption, Maya quickly switched the folder on top, the one she'd intended to give Zeke

about Sean with the "just in case" file she brought
along in case Jade or someone else had been meeting
with Zeke and he'd insisted she leave the information
on his desk. She would be forever grateful for the
angel who'd inspired that idea. It just may have saved
Sean's life.

"Actually, what I have is for your wife and her charity event." Maya said after Jade left the office. She
passed a beautifully designed portfolio to Zeke. "The
design choices for everything: program, brochures, in-
vitations, is all there. I told her I'd drop them off to her
but she's meeting with the volunteers this afternoon
and asked that I give them to you to bring home."

Zeke's hard stare suggested he did not like being
used as a delivery boy.

"You've got a lot on your mind. If you want, I can
just meet with her tomorrow. I need to pick up a
couple more tickets anyway."

"No, Maya. I'll take this to Vicki." He placed the
portfolio in his briefcase. "You focus on Sam. Give
him a call and try and set up another meeting. I have
a feeling they're close to choosing a firm for the project. Time is running out."

Maya walked quickly to her office and closed the
door. She leaned back against it and took slow, deep
breaths, trying to calm her rapidly beating heart.
Sean had been right, about Zeke, about everything.
How could she have entertained the thought to betray
his trust and reveal who he was to Zeke, even for a
moment? How had she justified that in her mind?
She knew Zeke had a ruthless side, but his words
about Sean had chilled her blood. Could the information Sean had be correct about a hit? And if so, was
Zeke the one ordering it? Ten minutes ago, she would
have rejected the notion out right. But after what

she'd heard today, she'd no longer stake her life on it. From now on, she was going to take Sean's advice and look out from number one.

Sean. She sat at her desk, reached for her briefcase and pulled out her cell. As she did so, she carefully placed Sean's file inside of it, the contents of which she was going to destroy as soon as she got home. Even though she had a high powered shredder, she didn't want to leave a single trace of evidence at B&A. The evidence that she was now ashamed to admit she'd even considered revealing: the picture taken the day she'd seen Sean in Sam's bed.

Instead of Sean, she got his voicemail. She left a succinct message about needing to see him as soon as possible, placed a few folders in her briefcase and prepared to leave. She used to be excited to get to work every day. Lately, leaving made her happy, and the exit felt more like an escape route.

She rolled her eyes as the phone rang. *Please don't let it be Zeke.* "Maya Jamison."

"Maya, it's Vicki."

"Oh, hello Mrs. Brennan."

"We just took a break from our meeting and I can't reach Zeke. Did you give him the materials?"

"I did and witnessed him putting them in the briefcase myself. All of the designs are wonderful. Your biggest problem will be deciding which one you like best."

"Thank you, Maya. I appreciate your help. Oh, and Maya?"

"Yes?"

Vicki Brennan paused. "That's okay; I'll just try and reach Zeke again later."

On her way out, Maya passed Jade's work area. No one was there. She continued toward the lobby, thinking back on Jade's interruption while she was in Zeke's office. She'd been too frazzled to make much of it at the time but now, thinking back, she's almost certain Jade had said "our tickets" when she entered the room. Maya had thought nothing of the tickets from the travel agency lying on the table as she left Zeke's office. Was Jade accompanying him on his business trips now? And was Jade's empty office and Zeke's closed door the reason Mrs. Brennan had been unable to reach him?

The plot thickens, she thought as she stepped on the elevator. *Jade might be getting ready to learn a lesson about working with high-powered moguls. Don't piss off his wife.*

28

Maya hurriedly pushed her Bluetooth talk button when she saw Sean's number. She began without preamble. "You were right, Sean. About everything."

"What's the matter, Maya? What happened?"

"Are you in your suite?"

"Yes, but what's going on?"

"Zeke's on to you. I'll tell you everything when I come over."

"No, baby, don't come here. Meet me at the house instead."

Maya didn't see Sean's car when she arrived. She sat for just a moment before going to the gate. She guessed correctly. He'd parked in the garage. The buzzer had barely sounded when the gate clicked open.

As soon as the door opened, Maya rushed into Sean's arms. "Oh, Sean," she said, tears she hadn't felt coming now rolling down her cheeks. "I'm so sorry I ever doubted you; that I didn't believe you fully. You were right about everything. Zeke's only out for himself. He doesn't care about me, not really, but only as much as what I can do for B&A. It's too much, Sean. These lies, Angel's Way, it's too much."

Weeks of tension poured out of Maya along with her tears. Sean silently walked them over to the couch, pulled her onto his lap and held her while she cried. He rubbed her back and wiped the tears he didn't kiss away. After several long moments, she sat up.

"I don't know what came over me," she said, still trying to regain her composure. "I never break down like that."

"Baby, a lesser woman than you would have broken down long ago." He placed his finger underneath her chin and raised her head to look directly in her eyes. "Are you ready to tell me what happened?"

Maya recounted the conversation she'd had with Zeke, including his directive that she increase her contact with Sam Walters.

"After everything I've done for the company, done for him, it's still not enough. I owe Zeke Brennan a large sum of money," she went on. "Almost seventy-five thousand dollars, money he loaned me when Stretch was in trouble. That's the main reason I've worked so hard to secure the Angel's Way deal. Zeke said he'd remember the work I've done and if nothing else, Zeke has always done right by me when it comes to money. I figured the bonus he'd give me would almost wipe out that debt, if not erase it completely.

"And then there's the prestige that would come from being connected to a project that gets international attention, as this one will. Contacts and leverage I want to use to open my own business, buy a house, help my brother, so many things I've tied into the success of this venture. But nothing's worth changing who I am.

"I almost did something terrible, Sean." She continued to sniffle and new tears threatened to flow. "I almost told Zeke you were Sam."

"Shh, shh, baby, it's okay. Everything is going to work out, Maya. Don't cry."

"Did you hear me? I almost betrayed your trust; I went to Zeke's office to tell him who you were but he started talking before I had the chance. It would have ruined everything Sean: you, me, us. I don't like what's happened to me since taking on that assignment for Zeke. I don't like who I've become, what I almost did."

"You were getting ready to do what you thought you had to, baby. And you've been under tremendous pressure lately. I'm just glad things worked out the way they did."

"It would have been horrible if I'd blown your cover."

"But it didn't happen. So let's move on."

"Is there any way you can forgive me?"

"Not only am I going to forgive you, but I'm going to help you forgive your debt to Zeke. I'll give you the money to pay him back. Just give me a few days to get it wired from my bank in London."

"I could never ask you to do that, Sean. It's way too much."

"It's my gift to you. Don't turn it down. I've been very fortunate in my career and in my investments. Please, Maya. Let me do this one thing for you, Free you from the chain that keeps you bound to that man."

"How can I ever thank you?"

"You already have. From here on out, we work together, baby. Give me just a little time to work out a plan."

29

An hour later, Sean was heading toward Baldwin Hills in an understated, rented Honda, chosen purposely so he'd blend in with the rest of the workweek crowd. He wore casual jeans, a black silk T-shirt, and a Raiders ball cap. As he drove, he went back over the crucial information that had come to him, information he'd shared with Maya before they left the house in Playa del Rey. His street team told him the buzz among those in the know in the hood had intensified, that a former gang member and ex-felon was bragging about being able to leave the neighborhood soon, that he'd gotten a gig and was about to leave town. Sean put that with other information he'd recently gathered—that somebody had been snooping around the offices of B&A, had hacked into a company computer and tried to lift parts of Zeke's itinerary. Both Zeke and Joseph had proved they would employ underhanded tactics to get what they wanted; and they wanted the Angel's Way contract. Sean knew something else: that they weren't the only ones.

The rented Honda's GPS kicked in and told Sean to turn right off the 10 Freeway onto La Brea Avenue.

As he did so, he turned his thoughts as well, from Zeke and Joseph to Dwight "Money" Henderson, the man he was getting ready to meet. Luck had smiled on him two nights ago when Money and his lovely wife had dined at the Ritz. He and Sean had struck up a conversation in the bathroom, Sean had told him he was into real estate, and Money had told him he was looking to get into the game. Years of investigator experience told Sean that Money was someone he should know, and when Money invited him to his home, Sean jumped at the chance. Maybe Money would turn out to be another real estate partner. With a nickname like that, Sean surely hoped he had some.

He didn't have to wait long to find out. Unless Money was house-sitting, he wasn't doing too bad. Sean pressed the intercom and was soon driving through the wrought-iron, gold-tipped gates. A brand-new Jaguar, SUV Escalade, and Porsche Boxster sat proudly displayed in the circular drive that could comfortably accommodate three or four more cars without seeming crowded. Sean thought maybe he should have driven the Mercedes after all.

"Nice place," he said to Money, once the housekeeper had let him in and showed him into the living room. A quick glance told him the furnishings were top of the line.

"We enjoy it," Money replied. "Although Lucia, my wife, wants to move to Bel Air. She's had a penchant for it ever since she found out that's where her idol, Jennifer Lopez, and Marc Anthony live. Lucia's Puerto Rican."

"There are worse places to live than Bel Air."

"True, but I want to be able to see the ocean and am leaning toward Pacific Palisades or Palos Verdes. What can I get you to drink?"

"You have ginger ale?"

"Sure." Money walked over to the bar.

Sean followed. "So you guys are actively looking to move?"

"In about a year or so. Lucia wants to have another child before our little girl gets too much older. She wants them to grow up together. We want to be moved before she gets pregnant, or before she gets too far along."

"The family life seems to agree with you."

Money laughed. "You wouldn't have said that even three years ago. I wasn't a papa but I was most definitely a rolling stone. I went to Puerto Rico on vacation, saw Lucia walking on the beach in a tiger-striped thong, and a brotha was toast. I brought her over two months later and we've been together ever since." Money poured himself a shot of premium vodka and drank it straight down. He looked at Sean and added, "A good woman will make you change your life." He nodded toward the living room where he and Sean sat down.

Sean gave Money the Sam Walters rundown of his life in real estate, and how he'd made his money during South Africa's rebuilding after Nelson Mandela was elected president. Money was duly impressed.

"That's what I want to do, develop a portfolio. Once I buy up several properties here in Southern California, both residential and commercial, I plan to expand the business to Nevada and Arizona and maybe the Midwest, where I'm from."

"It looks like the business you're in is pretty good. What did you say that was?"

"I didn't."

The smile remained on Money's face but Sean

caught the defensiveness he'd tried to keep out of his tone. Most men were happy to boast about their accomplishments, especially in business. As flashy as Money seemed, his reluctance to discuss his professional life seemed incongruent. Sean wondered what Money was hiding.

He tried a direct approach. "Well then . . . what is your business? It is obviously doing well," Sean added as he looked around.

"I make my money through investments."

Direct met with indirect; Sean, or more specifically Sean's instinct, took notice. Especially since he'd just spent a good ten minutes giving his own résumé without compunction. That he'd mixed truth with fiction was beside the point.

"Do you know anything about Zeke Brennan?" Money asked.

Sean's instinct went into high alert. "Of course, everybody in real estate knows who Zeke Brennan is."

"Of course, but I'm speaking on a more personal level. I'm trying to meet him, want to travel in his circle a little bit."

"Nothing like starting at the very top, my brotha!"

"As you can see," Money said, waving his hand across his designer domain, "that's where I'm most comfortable operating."

Sean recognized his opportunity to get Money to open up. The brief background check he'd been able to do revealed a few things: that Dwight "Money" Henderson was a star athlete at the University of Missouri who'd received a small inheritance once his parents, both high-level educators, died. He played two years with the Cleveland Browns before a knee injury effectively ended his professional ball-playing career. He stayed in Cleveland, opened a chain of

nightclubs, and then sold abruptly ten years ago.
That's where the paper trail had ended, at least in the
short amount of time Sean had had to research. That
Money hadn't mentioned his sporting history, Sean
also found strange. His newfound friend was definitely keeping secrets: one couldn't be that tight-
lipped and have nothing to hide.

Sean told Money he'd met Zeke, that in fact, they
were doing some business together. This immediately
piqued Money's interest, so much so that Sean decided to ensure that this liaison with Money continued. "In fact, I'm dating his executive assistant,
Maya Jamison."

Money laughed and slapped hands with Sean.
"My man. Now, that's how you roll. The best way to
get to an executive is through his executive assistant.
I like how you think, man, yeah, I definitely like how
you think."

"Oh, no, man, it's not like that. Maya's a good
woman."

"I don't doubt that. The fact that she works for
Zeke Brennan makes her a great woman! I'm going
to have to have the two of you back over here, have
a nice little dinner. On top of being beautiful, Lucia
loves to cook. And she doesn't have too many women
friends. You'll have to bring your girl over."

Sean nodded, and then finished off the ginger ale.
He wasn't exactly sure of the destination, but he'd
just put the first leg of the journey in place. After another half hour of small talk, Sean's job was done. As
he left he knew two things: one, that he would not be
partnering up with Dwight "Money" Henderson on
his personal buying project and, two, that Money's
intense interest in Zeke Brennan was something he
shouldn't ignore. His intellect didn't know why the

connection was important, but his instinct told him
the information was paramount.

Sean's phone rang as he made his way back to the
Marina. One of his sources had some information,
news he didn't want to share on the phone. Sean
made a U-turn and headed to Culver City and the Fox
Hills Mall where his contact awaited. He'd said it was
urgent. Sean hoped it was the break for which he had
been waiting.

While Sean headed to the mall on L.A.'s southwest
side, Joseph Rosenthal headed toward his newest
property acquisition in Century City. That his firm
now owned three of the four largest office buildings
on the west side should have brought him immense
pleasure. But the acquisition was mere peanuts to
what he really wanted, Angel's Way. There was only
one person standing in his way.

Which brought him to the other reason for his
chagrin, Sean Wynn. Hiring him was turning out to
be like burning money in a bonfire. The man hadn't
provided any information Joseph hadn't already
known, and since he'd made the alliance with Zeke,
under the guise of gaining information for Rosenthal, there'd been even less news. Joseph wasn't
happy with the guy, not happy at all. And he didn't
plan on paying him one red cent outside of the hefty
deposit he'd already spent to secure his services. A
sinister smile crossed Joseph's face as he thought
about the plans that were being put in place to speed
up Rosenthal's guarantee of the Angel's Way bid.
Joseph didn't have time to wait while Sean lolly-
gagged around in search of information. Joseph
always had kept a plan B. Now he wondered if this

investigator should also be included in the plan. Being the astute businessman he was, Joseph knew killing two birds with one stone would be an economical move. And real estate was always about economics.

30

Maya put the finishing touches on dinner while she waited for Sean to come over. It was his first time coming to her home. He's suggested she keep it casual regarding the meal she prepared and she had. But she wanted everything to be perfect. She turned down the oven temperature, placed the spinach salad in the refrigerator and went to take a quick shower before he arrived. Between her meetings with Sean as Sam Walters, his caution to her meeting him at the Ritz lest Zeke be spying on him, and her work at B&A, alone time with Sean had been minimal. They hadn't made love in a week and she had no doubt he'd be more than ready. She hoped he wouldn't be too upset with what she was going to ask of him later.

She was just putting in her earrings when the doorbell rang. Her heart raced a bit as she walked to the door, like a sixteen-year-old going on her first date. Why was she nervous?

She opened the door and found out why. Because of the effects of the chocolate confection standing in front of her. In an instant, she took in his freshly shaven face (thankfully devoid of add-on hair), his striking cleft chin and lips by God. What would have been casual attire on any other man fit Sean like GQ: a collarless, beige and black pin-stripped shirt with the sleeves rolled to mid forearm over a pair of black, silk twill slacks. A bouquet of flowers in one hand and a bottle of wine in the other completed the perfect picture.

"Hey, Sean. Come on in."

The faint scent of Sean's Boss 6 cologne wafted past her nose as he stepped towards her.

"Hello gorgeous," he said, brushing his lips across her cheek. He walked fully into her living room and turned full circle to take in the pastel décor including the deep-cushioned, eight-foot sofa covered in light yellow Chenille, a leather recliner in a rich, vanilla cream, marble and glass tables, copper lamps, and candles strategically placed throughout the room. "Sophisticated chic," he concluded, as he turned back to face her. "It fits you."

"Uh, let me take those." Maya reached for the bouquet of orchids, lilies and roses in varying shades of purple and pink. "Thank you, Sean. They're beautiful. And the wine; you're so much better than I deserve."

"I'm not enough," he countered smoothly. "You deserve the very best."

"That's what I've got."

Their moment was interrupted when Sean suddenly looked down. Maya followed his eyes to see Lucky rubbing up against his leg.

"Oh, I hope you're not allergic. As you can see, I have a cat."

Sean put his head back and laughed loudly.

"What is so funny?"

"I'm just remembering my first impression from

the photo of you in my B&A files: serious pose, hair drawn back, sharp bangs, no smile. I drew my own conclusion of who you were as a person based on that photo. The only thing I got right was thinking you had a cat."

"What did you get wrong?"

"I plead the fifth. But I've never been so glad to be wrong in my life." Sean followed Maya as she walked to the kitchen.

She continued talking, placing the wine in the refrigerator and the flowers in a vase. "Let me guess. You thought I was a workaholic with no sense of humor and basically, no life. If so you would have been right on two out of three. I have a decent sense of humor, except when I'm impersonating maids and trying to spy on investigators and real estate tycoons.

Sean trapped Maya between the counter and his body. "I was just waiting here until your hands were free."

"For what?"

"For this."

He drew Maya into his arms and assaulted her mouth with his skilled tongue. Maya melted into him, her body yearning to get closer than their layer of clothes allowed. Sean planted kisses along her neck, and at both temples.

"I love you, Maya," he murmured.

They were both surprised at that declaration. For Sean, the words seemed to have tumbled out of their own volition. And Maya knew Sean cared deeply for her but to know he loved her just as she did him . . .

"I, I don't know what to say."

"Hum, let's see." Sean held his chin and tapped his finger as he feigned deep concentration. "I love you too would work just fine," he answered.

She laughed. "I do, Sean."

Sean noticed she didn't use the 'L' word but decided not to press her on it.

"Well then feed me some of that delicious food I'm smelling woman, before I ravish you right here on the kitchen floor."

"You said keep it simple," she said as she placed the dish of chicken ala king on the table. "I hope you like it."

Sean leaned over and kissed her lightly on the lips. "Maya, when I'm with you everything is good."

They ate in companionable silence for a moment.

"You know what I realized today?" Maya asked

"What's that?"

"I know very little about you."

"What would you like to know?" he said, mimicking Maya's previous answer from when he'd asked about her.

"Everything. For starters, is Sean Wynn your real name?

That elicited another laugh from Sean. "Normally that would be an unusual question but considering the path our relationship has traveled, a fair one."

He took a sip of wine and continued. "I was born Nathaniel Sean Anderson in New York City. My family moved to Philadelphia when I was nine. That's where I grew up."

"Where did the name Wynn come from?"

"I legally changed my last name to make it harder for anyone to trace my background history. Sometimes adversaries who can't get to the main source go after family members."

"Do you have brothers . . . sisters?

"One younger brother, Randall. He's married with

two daughters who have him wrapped around their finger and one on the way, the son he's always wanted."

"What does he do?"

"He's a police officer, like my dad, and like myself before I became a full-time investigator."

Maya looked at him, surprised. "You were a policeman?"

"That surprises you?"

"On second thought, maybe it shouldn't. You do have that authoritative, 'put your hands up' demeanor."

"Thank you, I think."

Maya laughed. "It was a compliment."

"I joined the force right after graduating college; worked the beat and the streets for four years before being tapped to go undercover for a drug sting. That's when I realized I had a talent for undercover work, and that I loved the challenge. I worked undercover for about five years in Philadelphia before relocating back to New York and starting my own practice."

Maya learned that most of the men in Sean's family had either military or law enforcement backgrounds. His dad was now retired from the force. His mother was a retired school teacher. They'd been married almost forty years.

"They'd love you," he said after telling of his family.

"I'd love to meet them," she replied. And then, "So have you come up with a plan to speed up a resolution to your investigation?"

"Actually, a plan came to me. A man who says he's interested in real estate, but I really think he's interesting in your boss, Zeke."

"Really, who?"

"A guy named Dwight Henderson but friends call him Money. You're going to meet him Saturday night, him and his wife, Lucia. We've been invited over for dinner."

Sean told her how they'd met at the Ritz and about the conversation during his brief visit at Money's home.

"Where does he live?"

"Baldwin Hills."

"This sounds interesting. How did I get invited to the party?"

"I told him you were my woman, of course. I also told him you were Zeke's executive assistant. That's when he really perked up. And that's when my suspicion antenna went up. It makes sense for anyone interested in real estate to know Zeke Brennan's name, but his interest seemed above the norm. As soon as I told him about knowing Zeke and your working for him, he invited us over, started pumping me for information. Said he'd been following the building boom, especially downtown, and wanted to get in the game."

"I'm sure I've never heard of him before. Money is a name I'd remember."

"He has the type of personality that one wouldn't forget, gregarious, charming. Dress to impress. This man loves to flash and by you working for Zeke, he'll expect to see you in nothing but the best."

The talk turned away from business as they finished dinner. Maya put on water for tea and then joined Sean on the sofa in the living room.

"What about the other players you're investigating? Have you turned up anything on Rosenthal?" And then as an afterthought added, "Or Zeke?"

"My findings are not yet concluded but I can tell you that I haven't dug up dirt that's any different from anyone else in his position. No murder or mayhem . . . yet."

"Well, you're probably not going to on Zeke. I'm not saying he's beyond taking extreme measures to get what he wants; but that he's too smart to get caught at it."

"What makes you think Joe Rosenthal is any different? They're both smart men, they're both successful and they both are corrupt to some degree. What makes one better than the other?"

"That one of their names is on my paycheck," Maya said with a straight face. "That and the fact that Zeke has been good to me. Even with what I've learned, I still have a level of respect for him. And I'll always be grateful that he was there for me when Stretch was in trouble. He helped me with no hesitation, Sean, didn't bat an eye." She leaned over and rested her head on his shoulder. "Like somebody else I know."

Sean sensed Maya's vulnerability as she talked about her brother. He wanted to protect her from everything; wanted to wrap her in his arms and love away the fear he saw in her eyes.

"I can understand why you felt so loyal to Zeke," Sean said softly. "And it's clear you love your brother very much."

Maya nodded against his shoulder.

"Come here." He turned her so that they were face to face and pulled her onto his lap. He caressed her face, gently outlining it with his finger before kissing her nose, eyes, cheeks and finally plunging deeply into her mouth. As the kiss intensified so did his longing for her. Maya felt him hardening under her, even as his hand slipped inside the top of her dress and begin massaging her nipple.

The tea whistle sounded. *Perfect timing*, Maya thought.

When she brought back the tray from the kitchen

and set it on the table, she sat a distance away from Sean. "I have something to ask you," she began a bit tentatively. "A favor."

"Anything."

"I want you, us, to slow things down a bit."

Sean put down his teacup. "What do you mean?"

"We were hot and heavy from the moment we met; sleeping together the first night, something I've never done before. I'd like to step back and process what we have, as friends."

Sean prepared to protest.

"Just for a little while," she hurried on. "Until all of this, the investigation, the contract bid, this whole thing is over. There's so much on my mind right now and that's compounded when you're, I mean when we . . ."

"Are you trying to say my loving is blowing your mind so much you can't think straight?"

It was Maya's turn to laugh loudly. "That's exactly what I'm saying."

Sean took a deep breath. "You're asking a lot of me, baby. I want you so much right now I can hardly stand it. But if it will help you get through this process, and feel more comfortable about us, I'll honor your request and try to keep my hands off you."

They finished their tea and the blueberry muffins Maya had served for dessert.

"I have to be up early," she said, when what had started out as a light "thank you for dessert" kiss began to deepen.

Sean sighed heavily. "Okay, okay. But I can already see that keeping my hands off of you is impossible."

When they reached the door, Maya turned, determined to give him a church hug: the one where there was at least two feet of space between the bodies, where the shoulders touched and nothing else. But Sean wasn't having it. He wrapped his arms around her and pressed her against him, nuzzling her ear before giving her a light kiss on the temple. Her kitty was virtually preening now; if the man didn't leave within the next minute, Maya knew she'd go against her own decision to abstain.

She broke the embrace and opened the door in one motion. "See you Saturday, then," she said, while her mind screamed, "please get your fine 'a' out my house before I jump you!" The door closed so fast behind him, she may have clipped his heel.

She leaned against the door and tried to regain her composure. If tonight was any indication, sticking to her decision to not have sex with Sean, while they developed their friendship, was going to be her hardest assignment yet.

31

It had been a long time since Trish had the flu, but obviously some type of bug had bitten her. Either that or something was wrong with the food she'd eaten. She got sick last night and had thrown up again this morning. If it weren't for the fact that the audition she had was for another national ad, this time a major car company, she never would have ventured out of her house. But she had, and she felt the audition had gone well. It better had; judging from the way she felt right now, she'd almost killed herself to make it. Even now she was up in her bedroom, in full pajama mode, at barely six in the evening. Maya had insisted on coming over. She told her when she did to use her key.

"Lord, child, you look like death warmed over," Maya said by way of greeting as she entered Trish's bedroom.

"Fine, and you?" Trish replied sarcastically.

Maya sat down on the side of the bed and placed her hand on Trish's forehead. "Doesn't feel like you have a fever."

"I think it's food poisoning. I think I ate some bad fish."

"Sounds like you better go back to eating chicken."

"Trust me, the meat I eat from now on will walk, not swim."

"Well, I see the illness hasn't dulled your sense of humor. That's good. I brought some chicken noodle soup. Are you hungry?"

"I still don't think I can eat anything"

"What about something carbonated on your stomach. I brought 7up and Perrier."

"Seven-up sounds good."

"Ice?"

"Uh-uh, room temperature."

"Hey, where's Tony?" Maya asked when she returned to the room. She handed Trish the 7up and put a plate of cheese and crackers on the nightstand next to the bed. "Y'all have been practically inseparable these past weeks. So much so, I almost thought you'd forgotten my number."

"No, you didn't go there. Not the sister who went to Palm Springs and I didn't even know about it until you'd already been gone two days. So don't even start."

"Am I ever going to live down not telling you I was going out of town?"

"I don't think so. What if something would have happened to you? Nobody would have known where you were."

"Zeke knew. I stayed at his condo, remember?"

"Oh, right, your *boss* was good enough to know, but your best *friend* . . ."

"Here, you want some crackers? And you know it's bad manners to talk with your mouth full."

"Don't try and shut me up now that I'm speaking truth. I think I will try a cracker, though." Trish took a tentative bite, swallowed, and then another. "I might be able to keep this down."

"It seems like you and Tony are doing good, Trish. I'm happy for you."

"Yeah, I kinda like the roughneck. And lately he's been talking about changing his life, you know, getting out of the game and our moving to the suburbs. I think he means it, Maya. I think he really wants to do something different with his life."

"I'm glad to hear that. I think he's got it in him to do whatever he wants. What do you think that might be?"

"Real estate."

"Really?"

"Yes, he says he's working on a project and afterward will have enough money to buy some houses. He saw a show about turning them fast to make a profit."

"Flipping," Maya interjected.

"Yes, that's it. Anyway, some guy named Money is supposed to be helping him. He's all hush-hush about it."

"Money? Girl, no, that's who Sean and I are having dinner with tomorrow night."

"You and Sean are meeting with someone who knows Tony? Now, I personally consider my man high class but I don't see someone like your Sean and my Tony having the same set of friends."

Maya agreed. She made a mental note to tell Sean about how small the world was first chance she got. And then something else occurred to her.

"When did Tony mention this guy, Money, to you?"

"Earlier today."

"Has he ever mentioned him before?"

"I don't think so. Why?"

"Like you said, Sean and Tony live in different worlds. And if I remember correctly, Sean said he met Money at the Ritz Hotel. So how would somebody who aspires to own primetime office space downtown and dine at the Ritz know Tony, who deals drugs and eats at Taco Bell? That's strange enough and then there's the timing."

Maya frowned, as she pieced together a mental puzzle. She didn't like the picture that was forming.

"What is it, Maya?"

Maya turned to Trish. "Is Tony still active in the gang?"

"You know the answer to that question. Once in, always in. But he knows how important this break is for me, how long I've waited and how hard I've worked. He promised he wouldn't bring anything illegal into my house." Trish paused, remembering that conversation.

"I did get a funny feeling though. We were talking about my favorite movie—"

"*Set It Off*," they said in unison.

"And afterwards I started wondering if his hush-hush plan to get him out of the streets and into the housing market was a bank robbery. Sounds like we're both trippin'."

"I've learned not to ignore those funny feelings so keep your eyes and ears open. You know he and Stretch are joined at the hip these days so you'll be doing us both a favor to pay attention, know what I mean?"

"I hear ya', girl. I'll be looking out."

"Good. You want me to heat up some soup?"

"No, I'm not going to tempt fate. The crackers and soda did settle my stomach though. I think I'll just try and go to sleep. Tony is coming over later."

"You tell Tony to take the couch tonight. You need your sleep."

"Girl, a little 'd' always makes a sista feel better. I thought you knew."

Maya couldn't argue with that. Memories of the recent love matches between she and Sean brought warmth to her cheeks. She looked over and winked at Trish. "I do, my friend . . . I do."

"Hey, baby, you up?" Tony whispered to an obviously sleeping Trish as he came into the room hours later.

"I am now," Trish groggily replied.

"You feeling better, baby?"

"Yeah."

"Good, 'cause I've been thinking about you all day." Tony had already taken his clothes off and slid in naked beside her. He reached for her hand and put it on his rapidly hardening shaft. "Want to know what I've been thinking?"

Trish threw her leg over his and rubbed against his penis with her stomach. "I think you're getting ready to tell me."

"You've got that right."

He had it so right that Trish forgot about everything but the feel of his body inside hers. She forgot she was sick, forgot she was tired, and forgot that she wanted to tell Tony that Maya knew Money.

32

Sean was prompt. At seven o'clock sharp there was a knock at the door. The sight once she opened it almost took her breath away. Sean looked as good as she'd ever seen him; the designer suit wasn't bad either.

Maya had taken special pains with her appearance, knowing that she'd be judged on it. Her freshly cut hair was flipped to perfection, makeup light and perfectly done, and the Armani suit she wore fit so good that she'd gladly pay the eight hundred dollars it had cost all over again. Women weren't stupid; they wouldn't spend a lot of money on an item just because somebody's name was sewn into the collar. No, these clothes fit different, felt different, which in turn made the wearer fit and feel different as well: the fit, good; the feel, like they belonged anywhere they were. At this moment, Maya felt as if she were born for where she was now . . . on Sean's arm.

"Maya, my heart can't take much more of you looking this good," he whispered as they walked to the town car.

She responded with a smile as the driver opened

the door and closed it gently behind her once she was
seated inside. "You look quite debonair yourself," she
said, once Sean had settled in. "You're going all out,
driver and everything."

"Oh, absolutely, darling. We've got to play the roll
of big money."

"*I* have to play the roll. *You've* got big money."

"Touché." He grabbed her hand and kissed it
softly.

"Sean," she whispered.

"Listen, I told Money I was crazy about you,"
Sean teased. "He's going to expect me to be all over
you tonight." He gently nibbled on one of her fingers.
"Think you can handle it?"

"Absolutely," Maya answered. She knew what
Sean was up to: hoping to get her so hot for him that
she'd change her mind about them cooling it sexually
for a minute. She was determined to maintain her
short-term abstinence, but figured that since Sean
planned to be all over her later on, as he'd put it, she'd
better test her resolve now.

She slid over next to him and placed a hand on his
thigh. "I think you've got a little lint, right there," she
said as she picked an imaginary speck off his thin
mustache, letting her finger glide slightly over his
lips before she smoothed an unruffled collar. "There,
that's better."

"Thank you, baby," Sean crooned in a voice that
would melt steel. "I think you've got something on
your mouth too. Here, let me get it off."

Before Maya could react, Sean dipped his head
and covered her mouth with his, gently slaving her
lips with his tongue until they opened of their own
volition. The kiss deepened then, his tongue teasing,

probing, while his thumb massaged sensual circles on the top of her hand, which was still on his thigh.

Maya wanted the kiss to end; she wanted it to go on forever. She felt faint and exhilarated at the same time, the way a person taking a first sky dive might. She reached up and put her arm around Sean's neck and turned her body for better access. She tried to hang on to her faculties, to remember that she was in control of the situation, that it was she toying with Sean and not the other way around. It was a lie that, once again, her va-jay-jay refused to believe.

Sean broke the kiss. "There, I think I got it," he whispered, his thumb still massaging her hand.

Maya simply nodded, not trusting herself to speak. Lord knew she'd need all the time it took to get to their destination just to stop her lips from vibrating . . . both sets.

The rest of the trip was, thankfully, uneventful. Sean conversed as if nothing out of the ordinary had happened between them, and by the time the town car pulled into the gated circular drive, Maya could walk.

"It's a pleasure to meet you," Maya said to Money's wife, Lucia, as he introduced them.

"No, it's mine, really," Lucia said. "I love your Armani. He's got a new, double-breasted one, you know? Have you seen it? Ohmigod, it's to die for."

"Looks like these two are going to hit it off," Money said proudly. "C'mon, Sean, let's get a drink. Wine for you ladies?"

"Sparkling water for me," Maya responded. She didn't need anything making her feel fuzzier than she did already.

"And for me, honey," Lucia added. "Would you like to come with me while I check on the food?" she said to Maya.

Within minutes, Maya felt like she was talking to old friends. She didn't know what she'd expected, but it wasn't this warm, friendly, normal couple. Because he was involved with Tony, Maya had assumed Money was a gangster; that his place would look like a *Cribs* gone bad episode and his woman like Lisa-Raye's Diamond character in *The Players' Club*. But Money looked the quintessential businessman and Lucia could model on any runway. California beauties could play the "b" role in a minute, so her down-to-earth personality was refreshing and her accent charming. Maya was glad once again for the armor of her Armnai, and that she and Sean were playing the role of lovers.

"Baby, look at this picture of Robert Johnson," Sean said as the two ladies joined the men in the living room. "Money just told me it once belonged to B.B. King and that Eric Clapton's got the only other original out there."

Maya had no idea who Robert Johnson was, but the way Money's eyes shone she knew he must be the Jesse Jackson quip, he must be somebody. She walked over to Sean, who placed his arm possessively around her and kissed her on the forehead. "Needless to say it's a collector's item," Sean continued. "Any blues lover would be honored to have that piece."

"It's nice," was all Maya could say. She couldn't stand the blues and the only thing she liked in velvet was clothes. But it would have been rude to say all that, so she let nice suffice.

"Excuse me, Mr. Henderson. You have a call, sir. He said it was urgent."

"Thank you," Money said to the housekeeper, and then to Sean and Maya, "Excuse me."

Maya watched the nicely dressed housekeeper scurry back to whatever part of the house she'd come from. Maya thought of the oversized Goodwill clothes she'd worn to work for Sam Walters and almost laughed out loud. She had looked pit-ti-ful.

"Did I tell you how gorgeous you look tonight," Sean said as he gently led Maya toward an open door that led to the patio and sweeping view of Los Angeles. "More beautiful than this view," he continued as they stepped outside onto the polished tile.

Sean stood behind Maya and wrapped his arms around her. He was almost delirious with happiness; being able to touch Maya freely gave him the greatest pleasure. He intended to take full advantage of tonight's charade. To prove the point, he reached up and lightly tweaked her nipple.

"All right, Sean," Maya hissed. "Don't get beside yourself."

"What?" Sean whispered in mock ignorance. "Can't I love on my baby if I want to?"

Lucia interrupted what would have been Maya's heated response. "Come on, lovebirds," she called out. "Dinner is served."

Their hostess had set an exquisite table and piled the nearby buffet high with dishes native to her homeland: *tostones, ensalada, arroz con gandules, pollo en fricase*, and *besitos de coco* for dessert. When Sean laughingly asked Lucia to "say it in American," she translated the menu: fried plantains, salad, a rice dish made with tomatoes, capers, olives, and peas and a main course of chicken and vegetables. The dessert resembled macaroon cookies, or coconut kisses as Lucia corrected in her smoky accent. The banter was light and the wine flowed as they ate their meal, so much so that by the time the Kahlua was added to their decaf coffee, Maya had almost lost the uncomfortable feeling that arose earlier when she caught Money watching her talk to his wife.

They left the dining room for the large game room, which in addition to lush mahogany wood and pool and poker tables housed the '80s video games *Pac-Man* and *Space Invaders*, an Xbox console, and a deluxe Wii Nintendo set.

Maya turned to Lucia. "I didn't realize you had children."

"We have a daughter, Izabella. But she's just sixteen months old. The biggest kid is the one over there." She cocked her head toward Money, who was showing Sean an extensive, mounted collection of knives and swords. "And I have several nieces and nephews who practically live in this room when they come over."

The two men walked over to join the ladies as they sat at the poker table. "So, I understand you're executive assistant to the Donald Trump of the West Coast," Money said. "What's it like to be in Zeke Brennan's world on the regular?"

"Probably as you imagine, never dull," Maya replied.

"I'm surprised you're not getting in the game yourself. You've got access to insider information, helping out a mogul make his millions. He should be mentoring you."

"Actually, you're right, and I am doing that. I just scored my first sell this year, a building in Santa Monica."

"Is that right?" he said, rubbing his chin slowly.

Maya watched her stature rise in Money's eyes as she went from Sean's woman to businesswoman in two seconds flat. She also caught that predatory look again, the one that made her uncomfortable earlier when she was talking to Lucia. Money seemed an affable enough gentleman, but every now and then a flash of something else, something sinister showed in his eyes.

"How would a brotha like me get to meet a man like Zeke Brennan?" he asked.

"It wouldn't be easy. Not only is Zeke incredibly busy but he's also quite selective when it comes to his personal space. Most of his associates have been in his life for years. His hiring Sean so quickly was an exception to the rule."

"You didn't tell me you worked with Zeke. Holding out on me with the details, I see." Money laughed as he directed the comment to Sean, but his eyes told a different story.

Maya started to feel uneasy. Something just didn't seem right here. But just as quickly, she shook off the emotion. Except for these out-of-place seconds of discomfort, the evening had been lovely and she truly thought Lucia could become a friend. She decided to focus on the positive.

"Come on, now," Money continued. "There's got to be a way to get on the inside. Country clubs, golf, where does he hang out?"

"Well, here's something. His wife holds a charity event every year for her foundation, Americans for Afghanis. It's a thousand dollars a ticket, and higher donations are encouraged. That's coming up next weekend. I could see if there are still tickets available. I assume you'd want two?"

"Yeah, yeah, that would work. And actually . . . see if you can get me four tickets."

Three sets of eyes looked in his direction. "Four?" Lucia asked.

"Yeah, I have a couple buddies who are looking to break into the real estate market with me. This would be a good way to get them some exposure."

Maya immediately thought of Tony, and Trish's comment about him getting involved in real estate. But something prevented her from asking Money if he was one of the buddies he had in mind. And if it was Tony, was the fourth guy someone she knew as well?

She was pleasantly buzzed, but Maya still had her wits about her. After leaving Money's estate, she stayed well on her side of the town car as they journeyed through the streets of Los Angeles. Sean was surprisingly quiet as well, and to both her relief and disappointment, didn't try to make any moves on her. She picked up her purse and placed it in her lap when still two blocks away from her house. She wanted to make a quick, clean getaway as soon as the tires stopped turning.

Sean had other plans. "May I come in for a moment?"

"That is not a good idea, baby. I don't know if I could keep myself from doing to you what my body is wanting to do."

"That's what I'm counting on," he said. "This is business. I want to discuss your invitation to Money and his wife to attend the charity. It's a conversation I need to have in private."

"Can't we do it tomorrow?"

"We could."

"Okay, you can come in. But only if you promise to be on your best behavior."

"Baby, I don't make promises I might not be able to keep."

Maya hit him playfully as she placed her foot out

the door the driver had opened. The two weeks or so until the Angel's Way bid was announced couldn't come soon enough. One would think it had been months instead of days since she'd had sex. Sean had turned her into a nymphomaniac and she wanted nothing more than to have wild, crazy sex with the man of her dreams.

Sean spoke briefly to the driver and followed Maya up the walk. He stayed a step behind her to admire her juicy backside. Maya could feel his eyes on her and warned him without turning around. "Behave," she whispered.

After offering Sean a seat and asking his preference of coffee or tea (leaving out the proverbial me), Maya went into her room and changed into the oversized T-shirt she'd almost worn to dinner the other night, a matching pair of lounge pants, and fluffy house shoes. Satisfied that she'd left sexy in the bedroom, she walked into the kitchen and started water to boil. She placed a bag of peppermint spice tea into each cup, added a dollop of honey, waited for the whistle, filled each cup to the brim with hot liquid, and walked into the living room. She placed Sean's teacup in front of his seat on the couch, then walked over and sat in the chair opposite him.

"What do you need to discuss?"

"I'm not sure how comfortable I am with your inviting Money to meet Zeke. As far as backgrounds go, his basically checks out. I'd just feel more comfortable with more time to research him before you bring him into our circle."

Maya resisted commenting on the "our" term he was starting to use more frequently. "I think it's perfect timing," she said instead. "And I have my reasons for wanting to find out more about Money Henderson."

She hesitated a moment before divulging, "I think I know one of the buddies he's planning to bring to the party."

"You do?"

"Yes, my best friend's boyfriend. He's had a challenging past, including time in prison, but wants to turn his life around. I think he's partnering with Money."

"I know a bit of Money's history. He was a college football star, spent two years playing pro ball, and then opened up a string of nightclubs. Don't you find it interesting that with all the possible connections he could use to break into the world of real estate, he'd partner up with an ex-felon? I can't put my finger on it, but something is out of sync here."

"I feel it too. When we were at his home, there were a couple times he looked a certain way and made me uncomfortable. Like you, I can't explain it, and the possible connection to Tony is rather interesting. . . ."

"Do you know if Tony is involved in gangs?"

Maya nodded yes.

"Something's been brewing in the hood for a couple weeks, something that may involve a high-level figure in the world of real estate. I have somebody working for me on the inside, a Crip. I sure hope this Tony isn't involved in an ill-planned, ill-advised plot."

Maya thought of her brother and hoped he wasn't involved either. But he and Tony had been hanging together since their time in jail. It was time for her to have another talk with her brother. "More tea?"

"No, thank you. I know you'd probably like to turn in, so . . . I guess I'll be going."

Maya stood and gathered the teacups. She walked into the kitchen, placed them in the sink, and was once again startled by Sean's close proximity. "Stop sneaking up on me! I didn't hear you—"

The rest of Maya's words were swallowed up by Sean's lips on hers, his tongue action shooting fire straight to her belly. He ran his hands up and down the soft T-shirt fabric, cupping Maya's round buttocks and grinding his hardness into her. They began to converse, between kisses.

"Sean, I really don't think we should."

"I don't either."

"You know I want to just be friends for the next couple weeks."

"I know."

"I'm not sure I can trust you to stop if you stay."

"Right, can anyone ever be totally trusted?"

"Probably not."

"So you want me to leave?"

Maya looked deep into Sean's hopeful eyes, a hope and desire that were mirrored in her own. "No," was her whispered response.

It was all Sean needed to hear. He swooped her up and headed out of the kitchen. "Where?"

"Upstairs."

Sean carried Maya upstairs and laid her on the bed. He quickly stripped off his clothes. Maya adored him with her eyes. He knelt down beside her. "I didn't bring condoms," he whispered.

"I have some," she replied. She pulled his head toward her and kissed him passionately. Without breaking their bond, Sean climbed on top of her. Only then did he allow his lips to leave her mouth to trail elsewhere: temples, eyelids, tip of her nose. He nibbled her ear before gliding his tongue down the length of her cheek, placing butterfly kisses along her throat. The oversized T-shirt worked to Sean's advantage; it came off with one quick pull over her head. The draw-string pants were equally respondent to his desires to have her naked. Once this was accomplished, he continued his oral assault, spending considerable time at each nipple, along her navel, a spot he knew was sensitive, and along the inner sides of her thighs. He purposely ignored her paradise, wanting to save the best for last, and continued the journey down to her toes, lavishly sucking each member, while simultaneously adding the pleasures of a foot massage.

Maya squirmed and tossed, her kitty crying for attention. She placed her hands on Sean's head, encouraging it upward from the underside of her knee, where again he'd found a sensitive spot and tongued the crevice expertly.

After what seemed an eternity, he rose and slowly parted her legs. Maya moaned in expectation. Sean kissed her feminine flower, and then blew gently. Her nub hardened in response. He kissed her again, deeper, longer this time. Maya's thrashing became more pronounced, her moans louder. Sean continued, alternating between fast and slow licks, long and short. He continued until Maya thought she would die from ecstasy. Just when she reached the pinnacle, and was cascading in the waves of her first orgasm in weeks, he plunged deeply, fully into her, not waiting to set up an intense pace. He withdrew almost completely out of her and then plunged in again, and again, turning her on her side and continuing the dance. Maya matched his rhythm, equaled his intensity. Sean couldn't go deep enough inside her; for Maya, she could not kiss him hard enough. Theirs was a thirst that could not be quenched, but still they kept trying. Into various positions, in different rooms, until night became morning, they tried. Finally, as the dawn said its good morning, they fell back on Maya's bed, totally exhausted, totally sated. Maya rolled over and curled up in Sean's arms. He relished the feel of her head on his shoulder, his leg thrown protectively over hers. Maya tried to be angry at herself for breaking her own promise, but she couldn't. Sean had put a smile on her face that guilt could not wipe off.

33

Sean tweaked Maya's butt playfully as they walked into the Ritz. After sleeping in late, Sean talked Maya into joining him for brunch. They both felt light and carefree, the intense lovemaking providing the stress relief they both needed.

"We should have played," Maya pleaded. "I know I would have beaten you if we'd played one game, even half a game. My brother is the king of pool players. I learned from the best."

"The best of what was available to you," Sean countered. "But when the best of the best plays the best, you'll see that there are varying levels of greatness."

Maya pushed Sean in mock disgust. "Oh, please, spare me." They both laughed as they entered the restaurant, so engrossed with each other that they almost ran directly into Joseph Rosenthal and an associate Maya didn't know, coming from the opposite direction.

"Sean!" Joseph said, extending his hand toward Sean while never taking his eyes off Maya. "This is a surprise."

"It is indeed," Sean countered, shaking Joseph's

hand. Noticing his blatant stare, Sean added, "Joseph, Maya Jamison. Maya, Joseph Rosenthal with the Rosenthal Group."

"It's a pleasure to see you again, Mr. Rosenthal. You may not remember but we met about a year ago. I'm Zeke Brennan's assistant."

"I thought you looked familiar. But something's different. That's it, you've changed your hair."

"Very keen observation, Mr. Rosenthal. You're right, chopped it right off."

"It's a very flattering cut," Joseph said, although his eyes had already left her face to travel the length of her body and back. Only then did he seem to remember he wasn't alone. He introduced the man next to him as an associate before asking Sean and Maya to join them for brunch.

"Certainly," Sean answered for both of them. He gave Maya's hand a little squeeze as the waitress showed them to a table with an ocean view.

The four engaged in small talk until the orders had been taken. Then, not to Sean's surprise, Joseph began a campaign to get Maya on his team.

"I could use a savvy assistant like you," Joseph said, "smart, beautiful, ambitious. But I'd do more than give you a salary. I'd give you a percentage of everything I made."

Maya's expression said she was duly impressed.

"A small percentage to be sure, but I believe in sharing my wealth with those who are loyal to me."

Joseph was probably hoping Sean would miss the near sneer he tossed in his direction, but Sean caught it. He didn't miss much.

"I am loyal," Maya said. "But I also know that one has to go where the opportunity is."

"That's it exactly." He turned to Mark. "Smart girl, huh?"

"Well, I tell you what," Joseph continued. "I've got it on good authority that the Angel's Way project is as good as mine. We'll be increasing our workforce when that happens. I'd like to talk to you about working with me, Maya. I think I could make excellent use of your . . . assets . . . and in the process, make you a very rich woman."

Sean wanted to punch Joseph in the face. Instead he placed a possessive arm around Maya. "Did you hear that, sweetness? He thinks he can make better use of your assets than Zeke Brennan."

Maya followed the subtle taunt. "Actually," she said as she cupped Sean's cheek and kissed him lightly on the mouth, "you've been making pretty good use of my assets yourself." She turned to Joseph. "I'd be very open to talking about a position at your company, where I could put my business administration and sales education and experience to work." She grinned suggestively, almost laughing out loud at the way Joseph ogled her. Nothing made a woman more attractive than for a man to know she was already taken. Feeling the animosity Joseph had for Sean, and knowing how he felt about Zeke, made Maya's desire to yank his chain a bit irresistible. "If B&A gets it, however, I'd have to keep being a Brennan babe."

"Speaking of your boss, I hear his wife is having her annual benefit on Saturday, the one for the orphans and other poor children in Afghanistan. A good cause, supported by a good lady."

"Will you by any chance be gracing us with your presence, Mr. Rosenthal?"

"No, but Mark here, he'll be there."

Maya discreetly touched her knee to Sean's. They both felt the same thing. Something was up.

"Just keep your cool," Sean told Maya as they walked to the elevator. "We're probably thinking the same thing. Just like right now Joseph is probably straining his eye sockets to see if we get into the elevator together. Let's not disappoint him."

"Sean, really, I probably should go home. Next week is going to be crazy busy and—"

"You don't have to stay." Sean gave her a kiss on the tip of her nose. "Just go up with me to get Joseph going. I'll change my clothes and take you home."

Maya knew that once Sean took off his clothes, hers would follow. But what was a woman to do? She'd tried to get him to take her home. Sometimes it was best to just go with the flow. Kitty readily agreed.

They were all over each other as soon as the elevator doors closed. Maya wondered how she could ever have thought to give his luscious lips up and Sean wondered how he'd survived without regular grips of Maya's behind. They were hot and ready for round two as Sean swiped his card in the hotel's key slot.

"After you, my queen," he whispered in his British Sam Walters voice.

"Yessuh," Maya replied softly, Martha in an instant.

Kisses silenced them as they entered the suite. They hugged and turned the corner arm in arm: to find a beautiful, naked woman sitting cross-legged in Sean's bed.

Maya jumped back, shocked beyond words.

Sean raced forward. "What the hell?"

Tangier grabbed the comforter and hurried to cover her nakedness. She recovered first. "Darling, didn't you get my message that I was returning this morning?"

Maya raced toward the door.

"Maya, wait."

She ran faster, almost made it to the elevator before Sean caught her. "Maya, I swear on my life, I don't know how that woman got into my room."

"You want to protect me, keep me safe? You told me you loved me. And all this time she's been here. Save it, Sean."

"Maya, don't let her do this. It's what she wants. I don't know how she got in my room, but I'm going to find out. Come with me."

"Why?"

"Because I want you to hear the truth. That bitch is going to pay for breaking into my room!" Sean knew this might be the last time Maya listened, so he continued to talk. "No, she left, went back to London. When she wouldn't stop calling me, I told her about you. And that it was over between me and her. I'm sure she's hoping to come between us, separate us, just as she almost did the other time she came. But you're stronger than she is, Maya; you're not the type to run away. Stand with me baby, and I guarantee she'll never bother us again."

Maya's breath was shallow and rapid. She gave Sean a curt nod and followed him back to the suite.

This time he made a noise when he came through the door.

"Oh, thank God. The little tramp is gone and you've come to your senses. I ordered up some—" Tangier stopped short at the sight of Maya, standing all of her five feet five inches next to Sean.

"Maya, dial hotel security."

Tangier's eyes dripped venom in Maya's direction. "Are the women in Los Angeles so desperate? He's practically my husband, you know." Tangier wrapped the silk kimono robe around her body a little tighter, but not before exposing a generous left boob.

Maya turned and walked to the phone. She requested the head of security in a voice that brooked no argument from the person on the other end of the line, and one that surprised Tangier. She'd never considered having a worthy opponent.

"Fine, I see you're going to be difficult," she said, deciding a change of tactic was in order.

"I'm tired of putting up with all these women," she said to Sean, even as she quickly slipped out of the kimono and pulled on a vibrant blue sheath dress. She reached for the card to her room, on the nightstand beside her. It was the only thing she'd brought with her as she'd meticulously planned a way to finagle her way past the weekend maid with arrogant claims of being his wife and threats of having her fired for questioning her right to be in the room.

Tangier gathered herself to her full five feet nine inches and prepared to sweep past Sean in a dramatic exit.

He grabbed her arm forcefully. "You're not going anywhere."

"Let go of my arm, Sean."

Sean did so, even as he positioned himself in front of the door. "Maya, this is Tangier, my friend with benefits for the past two years, until I met you. She came to the States unannounced and I told her in no uncertain terms that I did not want her here. I reiterated that in a phone conversation a couple weeks ago, one in which I told her our relationship, such as it was, was over. The behavior you're seeing exhibited right now is one of the reasons why."

Tangier turned to Maya. "You can't possibly believe such bullshit. We're practically married. He pulls this stunt every time he has an assignment out of town. Who was it in South Africa, Sean? Helena? What about San Francisco? I think her name was Maven."

Tangier saw Maya's resolve waver and pressed on. "I'm the only woman for Sean, always have been, always will be. I'm the yin to his yang, the pea to his pod, the up to his down. Women like you come and go, but I'm always the one left standing."

Her speech was punctuated by a knock on the door. "Security."

Sean's smile was lethal as he turned to answer the door. "We'll see who's left standing in just a few minutes."

"Mr. Wynn, sir, how may we help you?"

"You may help me by explaining how someone not on record, nor guest list, nor anything else was let into my room. This woman is trespassing and may have committed robbery. Not only do I want the police called, but I am going to hold your establishment accountable for anything missing."

The blond-haired officer's face turned beet red. "Why, Mr. Wynn," he sputtered, looking from Sean to Maya to Tangier. "I—I—we'll get to the bottom of this. This woman is not supposed to be here?" he asked, pointing to Tangier.

"She is trespassing, in my room illegally, and someone from your hotel allowed that to happen. I want to know how!" Sean allowed his voice to rise for affect, before walking over to Maya. Tangier started toward the door. "She is not to leave this room," he said to the guard, who promptly stepped in front of the door, effectively blocking Tangier's getaway. "My fiancée and I were returning from a wonderful night together, only to walk in and find my ex sprawled buck naked in my bed. Is that the way you treat your special guests, Mr. . . ."

"Mr. McVee, sir, and no, no, I can assure you . . . one moment." The security guard barked a series of orders into his cell phone.

"I want the police called," Sean continued calmly. "Once you verify that what I'm saying is true, I intend to file charges."

"You can't be serious," Tangier exclaimed, realizing that her plan to one-up Sean's new woman was going horribly awry. "Look, it's obvious you intend to keep lying, to not acknowledge what we have. Fine, just let me go."

"I tried to do that but you refused," Sean answered. "This time, I'm calling for backup."

Forty-five minutes and a police statement later, a tearful Tangier was led away in handcuffs. The charges were unlawful entry of an establishment and attempted robbery. Sean knew he would drop the charges in exchange for a restraining order and Tangier's one-way ticket back to London, under police escort if necessary. Having her arrested might have seemed harsh, but jail for the twenty-four hours it would take to have his attorney draw up release papers would show her better than he could tell her: Leave—me—the—fuck—*alone*.

34

Maya tried to keep her composure as chaos ensued around her. After Tangier had been carted off to jail, Sean had been upgraded to a larger suite, thirteen hundred square feet of pure luxury, free to him for the remainder of his stay. They'd said the free and up-graded accommodations were because of how much they valued him as a customer. Maya figured it was more that he didn't sue the hotel and create a scandal. Whatever the reason, she and Sean had taken full advantage of the new abode, especially the king-sized, rope-embossed, four-poster bed. Maya figured she was over Tangier's rude interruption somewhere between the third or fourth orgasm. Even so, Sean was still trying to convince her she was the only one. She believed him, but renewed her vow to not have sex with him. Not until she knew him better, and was felt absolutely confident of her place in his life.

From the Ritz, Maya had come home to a cell phone she'd unwittingly left behind. Trish had left a message: The case of whatever virus she had had again reared its ugly head. Tony was there, but Maya called and threatened bodily harm if Trish didn't go see a doctor. She promised to do so after the car commercial shoot.

Maya arrived to work Monday morning tired and on edge. She hadn't been able to reach Stretch all weekend, which was unusual. He knew that she worried about him and normally returned her calls promptly.

Now, to top it off, Ester just buzzed to let her know Vicki Brennan was on her way to Maya's office. Maya was beginning to wonder if one hour outside of sleep could pass without her dealing in madness. She'd completed the work for Mrs. Brennan's charity event; had dropped off the programs herself. Mrs. Brennan rarely came to B&A. Their one previous meeting, to discuss design options, had taken place at a nearby restaurant. Why in the "h" was Mrs. B coming to see her?

"Hello, Maya." Vicki stepped inside, preceded and proceeded by a profusion of floral fragrance. Her dress was immaculate and not a hair in her upswept do was out of place. She closed the door and approached Maya's desk with an outstretched, French-tip-manicured hand. "Good to see you again, dear. I wanted to thank you so much for inviting your friends to the event. And just in time as we've totally sold out. You were delightful last time. So glad you're coming again."

Delightful doing what? Maya had barely said two words to Mrs. Brennan at last year's gala. She'd picked at her salad, passed on the steak, made small talk with a table of shallow socialites, and taken an early cab home. But none of these thoughts accompanied her: "Thank you, Mrs. Brennan. Good to see you too." An awkward moment passed as the two women stared at each other while absorbed in their own thoughts. Maya looked at the computer screen and the PowerPoint presentation that needed to be done like yesterday. The timing wasn't exactly perfect for social calls.

"I'm sure you're busy but there is something else I'd like to ask you."

Maya resisted the desire to roll her eyes. There weren't enough hours in the day to do what had been requested of her already. She tried not to show her chagrin.

"I'll get right to the point. How well do you know Jade Laremy?"

Maya stopped in midclick. She would have been less shocked if Vicki had asked how well she knew Osama Bin Laden. "Not well," she managed to eke out of compressed lungs.

"Do you have any idea how well she knows my husband?" Vicki queried as she calmly checked and rechecked her manicure.

"I'm sorry, Mrs. Brennan, but don't you think that's a question for your husband?"

"Do you think Zeke would come straight out and tell me he was having an affair?"

"I guess not."

A kind smile accompanied Vicki's harsh words. "All men are liars and all women are lie detectors. The longer we're with a man the more astute our detectors become. I've been with Zeke for almost thirty years. I intend to be with him thirty more, unless death separates us. But that's the only thing that will. I don't think Jade is worth half Zeke's fortune . . . do you?"

Maya looked at her pointedly. "I don't think she's worth a dime, Mrs. Brennan."

A peal of laughter rang out from Mrs. Brennan. "You're adorable, Maya. Zeke speaks highly of you too. Are you sure you don't know anything of how well Zeke and she . . . work together?"

Maya fixed Vicki with the same pointed stare. "I don't think there's anything I know . . . that you don't."

"Hmm, well said. I have a feeling not much gets past you, Maya." Vicki Brennan rose and once again stretched out her hand. "I'll see you on Saturday, then."

Maya couldn't resist, especially since it was normal, expected even, that all of Zeke's employees who could afford it, attend the benefit. "And Jade?"

"Oh, she's more than welcome to come too. I've met more than one of Zeke's temporary twats in our three decades together. It would do her good to attend such an upscale affair, if only to glimpse the lifestyle she'll never live. Her days at B&A are numbered. Thanks for your time, Maya. We'll see you Saturday."

Vicki waltzed out but her floral garden remained. Maya opened her door to try and diffuse the pungent odor. Her phone rang as soon as she sat back down.

"Why was she here? Was she asking about Jade?" Ester's excitement seeped through even her hushed tone.

"What's going on?" Maya asked. "Hold on a minute." She walked over and closed the door. "What did I miss last week?"

"You know Mr. Brennan went out of town, right?"

"Okay."

"Everybody thinks that Jade went with him."

"Whoa. How does everybody know?"

"Because one of Mrs. Brennan's friends supposedly saw them together in New York! Well, she saw somebody, and the person she described sounds like Jade."

"But how does the whole office know?"

"Yes, I will be sure he gets the message. Have a nice day."

Somebody had walked up to Ester's station. Maya didn't even care that the conversation had been interrupted. From the looks of things, it wasn't the only thing that would end abruptly. So would Jade's career at B&A.

Rusty stuck his head in the door. "Will you have a minute later on today, Maya? Zeke wants us to talk about closing the other Santa Monica property you submitted."

"Is this the same Zeke that has been frantically finishing the PowerPoint presentation for his trip to China next week? Sorry, Rusty. This is top priority, and I'm still playing catch-up with my regular work today."

"Maybe we can make it a dinner meeting, then?"

Maya's phone rang. "I can't even think right now, Rusty. Can I check the schedule and call you later?" Without waiting for an answer, she picked up the phone. "Yes, Zeke, um, Mr. Brennan. Sure, be right there."

"You call Mr. Brennan by his first name?" Rusty inquired.

"Only by accident," Maya lied as she brushed past him. The office rumor mill was already running rampant with talk of Jade's familiarity with the CEO. Maya didn't want to get her name added to the mix.

"What was Vicki doing in your office?" Zeke barely gave Maya time to get in his office and close the door.

"She, um, asked if I was attending the charity event this Saturday."

"That's all?"

Maya didn't know how to answer. So she said nothing.

"Maya, did Vicki ask you about Jade?"

"Look, Zeke, I don't want to get in the middle of this."

"Vicki's stopping by your office put you in the middle. Now, answer my question."

Maya's mind was too filled with lies to handle another. "Yes, she asked about Jade."

"What did you tell her?"

"That I didn't know any more than she did."

"That's all you said?"

"That's all she asked."

Zeke visibly relaxed and offered Maya an apologetic smile. "Thank you, Maya. I'm sure you've heard the rumors."

If you only knew. Maya blocked the visual memory of her firsthand knowledge of said rumor: Jade's mouth on Zeke's "d." She was glad when Zeke changed the subject.

"How's the presentation coming?"

"Slow, with all the interruptions."

"If you think you'd work better from home, you have my permission to take off and finish it there."

"That would be great, Zeke."

"No worries. My team looks out for my best interests and I look out for my team."

Maya almost sprinted back to her desk, so ready was she to get out of the tension-filled office. Was this the same office she'd wanted so desperately to return to . . . the same job? It was the same building, with the same people, and the same projects. But it, like almost everything else in her life, had changed.

Maya entered her office and stopped short. Jade

Laremy was staring out the window, her back to
the door.

"Excuse me?"

"Oh, hi, Maya."

"What are you doing in here?"

Jade slowly walked around Maya's desk; Maya
knew she'd been snooping. "I'm finished with my reports and came to see if you could use some help."

"You could have called."

"I just happened by your office."

"No, you just happened *into* my office, and I don't
appreciate it. Let's not even try and act like there's a
spirit of camaraderie here. If you have something to
ask, ask it, something to say, spit it out. If not, I've got
work to do, work I have *well* under control." Maya sat
at her desk and began rifling through papers, employ-
ing Zeke's dismissal code.

"I like your office, Maya."

Had this fool lost her mind? "Jade, I'm busy."

"I think I'll be getting a promotion soon. Then
we'll be equals."

Maya's exasperation showed on her face. "Jade,
you and I will never be equals in this lifetime."

"I guess you're right, some people, people like
you, will always have that underling quality."

"People like me?" Maya half rose out of her chair
before she knew it, and Jade had no idea the extent
of the danger. If Maya became violent, Jade would
get a beat-down meant for at least three people. She
did not want to go there.

"I'm leaving," Jade said flippantly. "But I came here
hoping we could be friends, hoping we could work together. Mr. Brennan wants to give me more responsi-
bility, help you lighten your workload. Things will go

much easier if you don't fight the natural progression of things."

"Girl, if you don't get out of my office there will be a fight all right. And progress won't have nothing to do with it."

Maya gathered the things she needed to finish her work, locked her office door, and went home. She stayed home the next day as well, but making sure she was in the office loop, asked Ester go through her in-box, separate her correspondence, and relay any time-sensitive or pertinent information she uncovered. She checked her e-mails from home and rescheduled the lunch appointment she'd set with Rusty.

She'd just finished the PowerPoint presentation when her phone rang. She hoped it was Malcolm. It was Sean.

"Hey, Sean."

"How's it going, baby? You sound stressed."

"I am a bit, lots of work. What's up?"

"I was hoping we could meet later, at the house in Playa. Zeke called me, well, he called Sam, and asked how you were doing as my assistant. I told him fine, and that we had a meeting later. You might want to mention that we talked, but I do want to meet you to go over a few things."

Maya hung up from him and called Zeke.

"Zeke, I just remembered. I'm supposed to be working with Sam Walters this afternoon. Is it okay if I email this presentation to your Blackberry account later on, and make any recommended changes first thing in the morning?"

"That sounds fine, Maya. I take it you haven't learned anything of significance about Sean Wynn. I'm sure you would have shared anything you found out."

"No, and I'm not sure there's anything Sam can tell me that your investigation hasn't uncovered."

"Then there's no need to continue this assignment. Go ahead and meet with him today but after this, I'll tell him I need you back in the office. If he still needs someone to help him, I'll refer him to my friend's temp agency."

Maya raised her eyebrow at Zeke's comment and couldn't help but smile. If someone wanted to take her place, and give to Sean, as Sam, what she was providing, they'd better come to his home with more than a computer. They'd better come with unconditional trust, a healthy sexual appetite . . . and love.

35

Maya tried again to reach Stretch and again got voice mail. She tried not to panic anymore than she already was, or let her imagination run wild with grim scenarios of why her brother hadn't called. Still, she wanted to make sure Stretch knew the extent of her anger and did so in the message she left on his answering service, which began with: "Malcolm, it's Maya." As was the case in the past, when she called him by his given name instead of Stretch, he'd know she meant business and hopefully return her call immediately.

Moments later she arrived at the home in Playa del Rey and used the key Sean had given her to go inside. After greeting Maya with a quick kiss and asking if she wanted anything to drink, which she declined, Sean got straight to the point.

"My contact in the hood told me to be careful at the charity event coming up this Saturday. Says something might go down there and people could get hurt. I don't want to believe it, but I think somebody might actually try and take Zeke Brennan out."

"Take him ou—you mean kill him?"

"Or incapacitate him to the point where B&A suffers."

Maya was shocked. This was corporate America, the epitome of class and culture. People didn't kill at this level . . . did they? "Do you think it's Joseph Rosenthal?"

"I don't know who or what, and neither did my contact. But he was sure enough to tell me about it, and this man doesn't pass on information without being sure of his facts."

An idea suddenly dawned on Maya. "Do you think this has anything to do with Money?" *And Tony*, Maya thought but didn't voice aloud. *And Stretch*, but Maya refused the thought.

"I thought of that. Again, I don't know. And it's too close to the event to find out much. We just have to do what we can to protect your boss. He's meeting me later tonight."

"I thought I left this kind of stuff behind in south central," Maya said to herself.

"At the end of the day, people are people no matter how high you climb. This is a turf war, baby. Instead of colors, it's buildings, cash, and lots of it. Some might think that offing an executive is a small price to pay for a billion-dollar reward."

"I've got to go."

"You sure you don't want to stay while I talk to Zeke?"

"No, I need to talk to someone myself."

Sean stopped Maya with a firm hand on her arm. "Don't tell anyone what I've told you."

Maya left the room without answering. That way, she didn't have to lie.

As soon as she got in her car, she reached for her cell phone. Stretch answered on the second ring.

"I was just getting ready to call you, My-My. I met a baby girl who whisked me away to Las Vegas—"

"You need to meet me at my house, Malcolm," she said without greeting.

"I don't know if I can do that, sis."

"Did that sound like a question? I'll be home in thirty minutes."

She made it there in twenty. Malcolm was sitting in a brand-new Mustang, his loud hip-hop music entertaining half her quiet neighborhood, whether they wanted to "ride or die" or not.

He shut off the music and followed Maya's car into the garage. "What it be, big sis?" he asked when she got out. "And why are you trying to act like we're still twelve and you can tell me what to do?" He bopped her upside the head playfully, like he used to do when they were twelve.

"Stop it, boy, I'm not in the mood for playing." Still, she pushed him back in a playful manner and headed into the house. Malcolm always did that, brought out her playful side. Even when the message was clear: Life was not a game.

"My, you've been tripping for about a month now. What, your boy ain't handling his business?"

"Boy, what boy?" Maya hadn't told Malcolm about Sean.

"You know you can't do nothing I don't find out about. I know you and some dude had dinner with Money."

Maya's eyes narrowed. "How do you know that?"

"I hears thangs."

"Let me guess, from Tony?" It was the only person in common with whom Money could have shared their evening.

"Ah, girl, I can't reveal my sources. But you need

to watch out. Just because a person lives in a fancy
house don't mean they're all on the up-and-up."

"Just what do you know about him, Malcolm?"

"I know enough to say he's not the type for you to
get involved with. And who's this dude you're with?"

"His name is Sean, he's a business associate interested in L.A. real estate. And we're dating. Now,
what do you know about Money Henderson?"

"Why did you ask, no, demand that I come over?
Let's talk about that."

"We are talking about it." Maya sighed, all out of
lies and charades. This was her brother and she was
not going to hide anything from him. She told him
about Sean's concerns for Zeke's safety and that
someone from the neighborhood might have been
hired to harm her boss.

"Malcolm, if you have anything to do with this, get
out now. Sean and Zeke are meeting as we speak,
putting a plan together for Zeke's safety on Saturday.
If I know them, they'll have undercover cops swarm-
ing the place, and hidden cameras capturing everything and everyone who goes in or out of the the
Beverly Hilton that night."

Malcolm turned from his sister, placed his hands
on his hips, and looked out the window.

"Money is attending the event and asked for two
extra tickets. Are they for you and Tony? Is Tony involved in this too?" Maya walked around so she could
see her brother's face. "Malcolm, I want you to swear
on the memory of our mother that you will not come to
the hotel that night and that you'll talk to Tony and get
him to back out too. I don't care what Money or whoever told you, or how much they offered, it's not worth
the price you'll pay for the murder of someone like
Zeke Brennan. His lawyers will put you guys under the

jail. You'll get life without parole at best. If something really bad happens, it might be the death penalty."

"Girl, you always were dramatic—"

"Malcolm, I'm serious. *Please* promise me you won't go off and do something stupid. I don't know what I'd do if anything happened . . ." Maya's voice broke.

Malcolm walked quickly to the door. "I gotta go." He'd stepped outside before she could stop him.

"Think about Mama, Malcolm," Maya yelled after him. "And tell Tony!"

She shut the door, too exhausted to cry. Rarely had she played the Mama card, but desperate times called for desperate measures. She unconsciously fingered the locket around her neck. "Please, Mama," she whispered even as she walked purposefully back to her computer. As much as she wanted to, this was no time to break down. Zeke's downtown renovation presentation was due tomorrow, and he was leaving for China the day after his wife's benefit. Maya decided to go over every detail one last time. That way, she'd stay too busy to worry.

"Like I said, I'm not sure all this is necessary, but I'll go along with it." Zeke glanced at his watch, ready to go meet Jade, who was waiting for him in a room upstairs.

"I appreciate it," Sean said. "I'll go over all this with your bodyguard when we meet tomorrow. Hopefully you're right, and we're all just overreacting. But better safe than sorry, right?"

"Better to know who's behind this. It sure smells like Joe." Zeke stood and laid a twenty on the table to cover their drinks. "He's not beyond a strong-arm tactic or two."

Sean stood as well and smiled. "He said the same thing about you."

"Baby, why can't you come with me? This is the first big-time industry party I've attended, and the first time I've asked you to come with me." Trish knew she was whining but she didn't care.

"I told you, Trish. I've got something to do Saturday night."

"What's so important that you can't break it for a date with your woman? C'mon, Tony. This is the first time in two weeks I haven't been sick. All that time cooped up in the house and I'm almost stir-crazy." She walked over to where Tony combed his hair in the mirror, and slid her body suggestively behind his. "Don't you want to get your groove on with me, get our party on?"

"After Saturday night, we'll throw a big party, baby, we'll throw a dozen parties if you want to."

Tony had been talking like this all week, like he'd been to a psychic and knew he had the winning lotto ticket. Trish hadn't forgotten about her bank robbery worries. Didn't these types of crime usually happen on Saturday night?

"I tell you what. Why don't I go with you to wherever you have to be, and then we can go to my party?"

"No."

"Why not?"

"Look, Trish, stop sweating me on this. I said no!" Tony felt his temper rising and worked to calm down. He turned from the mirror and held Trish in his arms. "I can't take you with me, baby, it's a business meeting, confidential. But I tell you what. If it's over early enough, I'll call you, you can get dressed and we'll go hobnob with Will and Jada."

"It's not that type of industry party, Tony," Trish said. "We might see the woman from the Pinesol commercial, maybe a few D- or C-listers, but it's highly unlikely we'll bump into the A-list crowd."

Tony kissed Trish tenderly. "The minute you walk into the room, the A-list crowd will be there."

A rush of love for Tony surged through Trish's heart. She kissed him, even as she reached for his belt buckle. She knew he was on his way to Money's, and there was no time for a full lovemaking session. Still, she wanted to prolong the time before he left her. She bent on her knees and took in his manhood, trying to lavish a lifetime of passion on him in a matter of moments. His sustained shudder a short time later told her he'd felt the love.

Tony didn't even try to rein in his temper. He knew all along he should have rolled solo. "Why you springing this on me now, dog? Everything's set. This is no time to back out!"

"Look, man, they're onto the game. You know Maya, man. She wouldn't have come to me if she didn't know something."

"What could she know that affects what we're doing? And who is they?"

Malcolm told Tony about Sean and what his contacts thought they knew.

"That's bullshit, man." Even as he discounted it verbally, Tony knew what Malcolm said could be legit. Who could have talked? Nobody knew about this but him, Money, and Stretch.

He looked at Maya's brother. "Who'd you tell, man?"

"Man, I didn't tell anybody. Who'd you tell?"

Tony didn't answer, but remembered a conversation he'd had with his cousin in Long Beach, a conversation about where was the best place to stash two hundred g's. He was too close to back out now. Their plan was foolproof. Two minutes tops and his whole life would change. He'd be able to have the life he always dreamed of, and give Trish everything she wanted. "Look, Stretch. Are you in or out?"

He stood, barely breathing, waiting for the answer.

36

A parade of limos and town cars lined the streets around the Beverly Hilton. Designer fashion and diamonds in platinum seemed to be the required attire. The men, tucked and tuxedoed to perfection, added a masculine glamour. The music, an upbeat blend of world beat rhythms liberally sprinkled with instruments popular in the Middle East, placed a touch of the exotic on the upscale affair. The liberal flow of wine and champagne had the entire crowd happy. Vicki Brennan stood in the middle of it all, splendid in a shimmering gold LaVascati, held court as if she were royalty, and greeted her guests as if they were as well.

Maya sat at a table near the middle of the room with Ester and her date. Buying her ticket had been a small price to pay to have someone else besides Sean that she trusted in the room. Sean had rarely sat down, moving back and forth between the table and the front entrance, the men's room and the bar. She didn't know what or who he was looking for, and had finally decided it was better not to know.

"Where's Mr. Brennan?" Ester asked. "Shouldn't he be by his wife's side, greeting the guests?"

"This is her baby," Maya absently responded. "Her night to have the spotlight. I know he leaves for China first thing in the morning. He'll probably be here shortly." Maya tried to enjoy the music as she continued looking around, hoping against hope that Malcolm had taken her advice and would stay away from the event.

When she turned back toward the entrance, it was to see Sean coming toward her. Money and Lucia, looking like Hollywood, walked next to him.

"Who's that?" Ester whispered? "She's beautiful. I hate her."

Maya laughed. "You'll love her, she's cool people. Her name is Lucia." Maya stopped talking as the trio approached the table. "Hello, Money, Hey, Lucia."

Money walked around the table to shake Maya's hand. "It's Dwight tonight," he said with a smile in his voice. "We've gone uptown."

"Dwight it is," Maya replied. She introduced them to Ester and Ester's date. And then, "Lucia, girl, you are wearing that dress."

"Thank you," Lucia replied. She sat down next to Maya. "I won't be able to eat, drink, or breathe tonight, but no pain, no gain, right?"

"Right."

Maya kept one ear toward Sean and Money even as she chatted with the ladies at the table. She heard Money inquire as to Zeke's whereabouts. She didn't hear Sean's answer. The two continued talking as they headed to the bar. Vicki came over to the table and greeted everyone. She seemed especially interested in Lucia; asked where she was from, who she'd come with. But she was cordial to everyone and after a minute or so of small talk, moved on to greet other guests.

Sean and Dwight returned to the table just as the salad was being served. Somewhere between the appetizer and the entrée, Maya began to relax. Zeke's arrival was uneventful, as was his meeting Dwight. In fact the men seemed to hit it off; turned out Zeke was a big college football fan and knew of Dwight's achievements. Dwight was obviously pleased when he sat back down at the table, though "cool dude" was all he said about his and Zeke's brief conversation.

While Sean was still on high alert, he took some time to focus on Maya, who he'd never seen look lovelier. "Baby, you look good enough to eat. I sure hope you don't intend to make me sleep alone tonight." He nuzzled her shoulder. "You look beautiful, Maya Jamison."

"And you're the most handsomest man in the room, Sean Wynn."

As the waiters came to the table to remove their dinner dishes, the music changed to a haunting rendition of Carlos Santana's "Europa."

"Let's make room for dessert. Dance with me?"

Maya turned to see a sprinkling of couples on the dance floor. What a great excuse to spend a few minutes in Sean's arms. "Of course."

As soon as they reached the dance floor, Sean enveloped Maya in his arms. His hands roamed her body of their own volition; he worked to keep the movements limited to her back and arms. "Ooh, you feel so good."

Pulling her head back slightly, she kissed him on the cheek. He turned his head and connected his lips to hers. "Don't even start, baby, or we'll have to leave the floor and get a room. I'm about to burst just holding you like this."

"A room, huh? Well, I won't tell if you won't." She

took her body and covertly rubbed it against Sean's thigh. His moan was her answer that the seduction was working.

"Let's go see how soft the Hilton's beds are."

"But, baby. What about dessert?"

"We'll have the chocolate cake delivered. And then I'll eat if off you."

Maya laughed as Sean turned her toward the door. He'd like nothing more than to do just what she'd suggested, and forget all about the potential danger the night held. But he couldn't, not yet. Not until the evening was over and everyone was safe. Instead of walking out of the room, he pulled her behind a large, potted plant so he could kiss her senseless.

That's when the shooting started. There were four or five in quick succession, followed by screams and a surge of people running from the ballroom's entrance.

Sean placed his body in front of Maya and reached behind him into his waistband.

"Sean, you have a gun!"

"Stay here, Maya!"

"Sean!"

Sean raced toward the commotion near the ball-room entrance.

Maya half sat, half stood, paralyzed as people ran around her. The band stopped playing in midnote and darted off the stage. She tried to get her mind around the fact that the very thing she'd feared, and Sean suspected, was happening. Someone had come for Zeke. Had they shot him? Was he dead? And then she thought about who could have done the shooting.

"Malcolm!" As she raced toward the entrance she wasn't aware that the voice screaming her brother's name over and over was her own.

Maya pushed her way through the crowd, tossing and tussling until she got to the front. At the sight that greeted her, she almost fainted. There were two bodies lying on the floor. One of them was Zeke Brennan. Against her will she turned her head to look at the other one. Her hand flew to her mouth. "Oh my God," she said, trying to get past the policeman holding her back with his arm. "No! No! No!"

37

"Are you sure you're going to be all right, Trish? Maybe it would be better if you joined us." It had been a little over a month since Tony was killed by Zeke's bodyguard. She'd rarely left Trish by herself since then.

"You two go ahead," Trish said, trying valiantly to put a smile on her face. "It's enough that you forced me to come with you two to Hawaii. You don't have to hover over me every waking minute." Trish's mood turned somber. "Actually, I could use the time alone. I think I'll take a nap."

"At least promise me you'll eat something. You need to keep your strength up, Trish. For you . . . and the baby."

"I will."

Maya didn't believe her and walked over to the desk. "Here, let me order for you. What do you want?"

"I want you to leave!" Trish said. She tried to soften it with a laugh. "I mean it, Maya. I know it's because you care about me but I'm fine, really. You two go on and enjoy your dinner. I'll be fine."

Maya told her she believed her, but still ordered a salad, dessert, and a large glass of milk from room service. "We won't be gone long, maybe an hour. And then we'll be right next door, Trish. I'll call you a little later, so please answer the phone, okay?"

Trish looked at Sean. "Why do best friends have to get on your nerves?"

"Oh, didn't you know?" Sean asked with a serious expression. "It's part of their job."

An hour and a half later, Scan and Maya returned to their room. As promised, she called Trish, who answered with a groggy voice, obviously asleep. Maya made plans to meet her for breakfast and then hung up, satisfied her friend was okay for the night.

Sean walked up behind Maya and kneaded her shoulders. "You're still so tight, baby. Take your clothes off. I'm going to loosen you up."

Maya, exhausted, didn't argue. After all that had happened in the past couple of weeks, she was happy to turn the reins of control over to someone else. She stripped out of her clothes and lay on the bed. To her surprise, Sean's touch was methodical, his ministrations focused. She'd thought it was a prelude for seduction, but Sean was actually giving her what felt like a professional massage.

As he kneaded more than a month of mayhem out of her shoulders, Maya reflected on what all had taken place in a few short days. Zeke had made a full recovery, the bulletproof vest he wore having absorbed most of the bullet. His near brush with death must have restored his sanity because four days after Mrs. B's gala, Jade was history—from Zeke's private room and B&A. Money, whose name Tony had whispered to police before he died, was taken in for questioning but later released because of insufficient evidence to charge him with anything. Joseph Rosenthal, who it was believed but not provable was involved in the murder attempt, feigned genuine interest and sent a huge bouquet of flowers to Zeke's office. And as if all that craziness wasn't enough: The Angel's Way project bid went to neither B&A nor the Rosenthal Group, but to a China-based company with L.A. partners: Phillip Campbell's company, Real Developers, and Sean Wynn's company, S.W.I.

Amazing that good could come from tragedy but it had. One of the positive developments was Maya's revelation and, finally, acknowledgment of just how much she loved Sean Wynn. Seeing Tony snatched away from Trish, in the span of a moment, made Maya realize how short and tenuous life was, and how precious love was if one could find it. She'd gone to Sean after the funeral and spilled her heart to him, professed her love. It had been a transforming day for both of them.

"Turn over, love," Sean commanded.

Maya did so, drinking in the sight of Sean's bare chest and strong, barely covered thighs.

"I still can't believe it," she said, trying to keep her mind off the tremors that were a result of Sean's touch on her feet. "You really are the president of S.W.I.? That's the only thing about the information we got on you that was legit, that this was your company. But we were so busy trying to find out what we didn't know that that distracted us from seriously considering your real motive for being here, to get in on the bid."

"That wasn't my plan initially, but once I met Phillip, it all started coming together. S.W.I. was already in place, so it made it easy for me to come in as the third partner they were looking for." Sean eased a forefinger along the side of Maya's thigh. "And I wasn't without distractions myself."

"But how did you do it? We all knew who was bidding on this job, or so we thought. It's crazy that you're really . . ." Maya didn't finish the thought, that he was a billionaire investor with properties on seven continents.

"That I'm really who I said I am for once?"

"Something like that."

"Come on, baby, let's get you in the shower and wash this oil off."

Sean led Maya as if she were a baby into the marble-tiled bath. He stepped out of his shorts, his member bobbing and weaving in search of its Mayan treasure. But Sean was a patient man. He wanted to love Maya fully, completely, but only after she was totally relaxed.

Sean turned on the water and when the temperature was just right, he and Maya stepped into the shower. He soaped up a sponge and gently rubbed it all over her body. She tried to return the favor, but Sean wouldn't allow it. "This is all for you," he said.

He washed her thoroughly and then wrapped her in a soft bath towel. Next, he led Maya to the bench in the bathroom, reached for a bottle of lotion, and massaged it into every inch of her skin. When he knelt down to attend to her legs, he couldn't resist a brief, tender kiss in her paradise. Maya's legs spread in readiness, but Sean didn't prolong the moment. He handed her a satin robe that lay across the vanity and helped her into it. That it wouldn't remain there long was beside the point; he had a few more things to give before he could receive.

He led her through the living room of their ocean-front suite and out to the patio. A sea of orchid petals led from the door to the patio's edge. On the table was an ice bucket with a bottle of champagne and two crystal flutes. Obviously this had been done while she and Sean were in the shower. It seemed as though Sean was good at planning more than large development deals.

"This is beautiful, Sean," she whispered as she kissed him softly on the lips. "Thank you."

"You're welcome," he said. He stepped away just long enough to pour them both a glass of bubbly. "To the woman of my dreams, the stealer of my heart. I love you, Maya Jamison. Thank you for making me one proud, happy man."

"And I love you, Sean. Thanks for being patient with me, for waiting until I came to my senses. Letting you leave my life would have been the craziest thing I ever could have done."

They sipped their drinks slowly, watching the sun set. "More?" Sean asked.

Maya declined. She wanted to show her appreciation for all Sean had done for her and didn't want to get sleepy behind too much alcohol.

"Then, let's go in," he suggested.

The tranquil mood was interrupted by a knock on the door.

"That must be Trish," Maya said, as she went to answer it.

Instead of her best friend, a resort employee stood on the other side of the door with a package in hand. Maya frowned when she saw the familiar B&A address in the return portion of the airbill. She tipped the messenger and hurried to open the medium-sized cardboard box.

"What's that?" Sean asked as he came inside.

"I don't know."

Maya's frown deepened as she immediately recognized some of her personal affects from her office:

a picture of her and Stretch she kept on her desk, a paperweight, her business cards, makeup she kept in her desk drawer.

"What the 'h'?"

Her movements became more frantic as she scanned the boxes' contents, finally dumping them out on the bed.

She turned to Sean. "I don't understand. This is my stuff, my personal stuff from my office."

She reached for the box and looked at the airbill. Ester's name was in the sender portion. That was the only part that made sense, as she'd left her information with her in case there was a work emergency.

"Why would she do this? Why would she empty out my office? And why would she send it to me instead of waiting until I got back." Then it hit her. *Jade.* She went to the phone.

"What are you doing?"

"I'm calling Ester so I can find out what's going on."

"Put the phone down, Maya," Sean said calmly.

He'd said it too calmly. Maya slowly turned around.

"What is it, Sean?"

"Ester must have misunderstood when I told her to mail your things. I meant for her to mail them to your condo, not here."

"You? What are you talking about?"

"I was going to tell you later, it's my surprise. I told Zeke you're not going to work for him anymore; you're never going back to B&A."

"You *what*?"

"I told you that after this was over, we were going to be together. I'm not going to have any woman of mine working for someone I don't trust. And I don't trust Zeke Brennan. So I called him right before we left to come here and told him you wouldn't be back."

Maya was livid, so much so she forgot all about abbreviated curse words. "How dare you! I worked my ass off to get where I was in that company. Who do you think you are to decide where I work, and when I quit?"

"I thought I was your man."

"Oh, and this is how you treat your woman? Like you're a Neanderathal, about to drag me back to your cave by my hair?"

"I thought you'd be happy, Maya."

"Happy! I'm pissed, Sean. It should have been my decision when and how to leave B&A. Zeke can ruin me and my chances in L.A. You know what. I can't talk to you right now. I don't even want to look at you." She began throwing the contents back in the box.

"Where are you going?"

"To Trish's room. I can't—" Maya's sentence was interrupted when she saw a black velvet box previously hidden under the file folders that were at the bottom of the box. The only jewelry she kept at the office was several pairs of earrings for in case she ever forgot to wear them. But they were in a larger jewelry box, with several storage squares, not one like this.

She reached a tentative hand for the box and opened it. Inside was a seven-carat yellow diamond set in a platinum band. Inscribed across the inside of the lid were the words: *Maya, will you marry me? Sean.*

She turned wide eyes toward him. He was smiling like a Cheshire cat.

"Sean, what's this?"

"Isn't it obvious?"

"It's an engagement ring."

"I knew you were smart."

"But how did it get in here, with stuff from my office and all of this . . ."

Sean's smile widened.

Maya's eyes narrowed. "You liar."

Sean laughed. "What?"

"Did you really tell Zeke I resigned?"

Sean could no longer keep a straight face. "No, baby. I bribed Ester into mailing some personal items from your office, then put the ring inside once the box arrived."

"When did you have time to be so devious?"

"I set it up with Ester before we left and then placed the ring in the box when you went to check on Trish."

"You are so bad."

"Isn't that what you love about me?"

She walked toward him as reality dawned. Sean had just asked her to be his wife! She threw her arms around him. Tears ran down her cheeks as she continued to kiss him.

"I didn't think I could be happier than you've already made me," she whispered.

"Will you make me happy too?" he asked.

"I'll do anything."

"Just say yes."

"Yes, yes! I love you, Sean Wynn."

Sean's eyes bored into Maya's as he eased his body on top of her. He spent the next several moments kissing her mouth tenderly yet passionately, the way he'd done every other part of her body. Maya's hands roamed Sean's hard body, not able to get enough of the feel of him, the flow of him. She reached down and cupped his hard buttocks, spreading her legs as a sign of welcome. "Please, Sean."

Sean kissed her on the mouth once more, then rose

and placed his manhood at the tip of Maya's paradise. "This time, it's forever," he said as he slowly glided himself inside her, then began to love his woman with long, passionate strokes.

"Yes, forever," Maya whispered, her hips rocking fervently even as she gripped him tight inside her. She didn't ever want to let him go, and Sean had no plans on leaving. They both knew that the ecstasy they felt was more than physical; it was the soul mate kind of connection that only happened once in a lifetime. Maya and Sean were overjoyed that it had happened to them.

38

Six months later

"How are we going to get all this stuff home?"
Trish asked, rubbing her rounded stomach as she
looked around the disarrayed living room of Sean
and Maya's Santa Barbara mansion.

"One of Sean's drivers will drop it off," Maya said.
"Or we'll have a company deliver it."

Trish prepared to rise. "Here, let me help you. Aw!
Stop it, Anthony," she said to her stomach. "He's just
like his father was," she continued, walking over to
help Maya place the extensive amount of baby
shower gifts into boxes. "Impatient, stubborn, it's like
he's trying to kick his way out of here."

"You tell that boy you've got three weeks to go and
that he can't come until we get his nursery set up."

"You tell him, Aunt Maya," Trish said. "And I told
you it doesn't matter if the house isn't perfect before we
move in. I'm not trying to rush out of our suite at the
Marriott. I still can't believe people live like this . . . and
now I'm one of those people!"

Maya smiled her understanding. It was hard to

believe how much both their lives had changed in six months. Maya had resigned her position at B&A and told Ester that she'd soon be joining her as Maya's assistant at S.W.I.'s newly opened Southern California branch office. She'd wanted to start right away on her plans of fitting into Sean's conglomerate of businesses, but after all that had happened, Sean had insisted she take a three-month break. They had gotten married two months ago on the island of Lanai in Hawaii. There were only a handful of guests at the elegant, sunset ceremony: Sean, Maya, Malcolm, Trish, Ester, Sean's friend, Neil, who thought Ester the most beautiful woman he'd ever met, and the minister. It was the most perfect day of Maya's life.

Trish's life had done a one-eighty as well. She was about to have her first child, Tony's son. As a gift to her and the baby, Sean had purchased her a three-bedroom, two-bath home in Woodland Hills. Malcolm was working with Sean during the day, and taking computer classes at night. He'd asked everyone to start calling him Malcolm; the name Stretch belonged to his old gangster lifestyle, a life he'd vowed to leave behind. Trish's commercials were big hits with the target market and Trish was now a minicelebrity. And not only had the Champion advertising team embraced her pregnancy, but they'd capitalized on it by filming a new set of commercials. In this one, a noticeably pregnant Trish took a bite of chicken and rubbed her stomach. "Me and my baby? We're *both* champions!"

The sound of male voices told Maya and Trish the men were back.

"You were right, Malcolm," Sean said as he walked into the room. "Half of Babies 'R' Us is in our house!"

"I told you," Malcolm said. He walked over and gave Trish a kiss. "But that's okay, because me and my babies . . . we're all champions!"

Everyone laughed as Trish swatted at Malcolm. "You nut!" she said, beaming at the love that had come to her out of the blue. What had started out as late nights reminiscing with Malcolm about Tony had turned into late nights of Trish and Malcolm realizing theirs had become more than sisterly/brotherly love. Malcolm vowed he'd be a father to little Anthony, and Trish promised to give him a child of his own. In hindsight their being together seemed obvious; but with twenty-twenty, it always is.

"Come on, roly poly," Malcolm said, helping Trish up. "Maya, can we get this stuff later? Mami's tired. She needs to get her rest."

"No worries," Maya said.

"We'll have it delivered," Sean added.

"Thanks, girl." Trish gave Maya a hug. "The shower was awesome. You did your thing for a sista."

Maya hugged her brother as she continued talking to Trish. "Anything for two of my favorite people."

Sean and Maya stood in the door as they watched Trish waddle out to the car, Malcolm mocking her as he swayed his tall, lean frame from side to side. Their laughter traveled with the wind, settling its warmth around Sean and Maya as they closed the door.

"You know what I think?" Sean asked, pulling Maya toward him. "I think you'd look cute with a little waddle like that."

"I am not going to waddle," Maya protested. "I'm going to be cute pregnant, with all my extra weight going into the perfect little ball in front of me. Then I'll have the baby and drop those pounds in time to head up my part of the Angel's Way project."

"Oh no, we're not having any working mothers here. You're going to stay home with our child."

"*You* might stay home with it, I'm going to be out conquering Los Angeles."

Sean silenced Maya's protest with a kiss that took her breath away. He decided it was better to get to work on the baby project and argue about the consequences later. He had no doubt that Maya could conquer anything she put her mind to. Because he wasn't an easy man to tame and she'd conquered his heart. And that, he thought as he led them to the bedroom, was the truth.